# Surgeon at Arms

Books by

Richard Gordon

*Doctor in the House*
*Doctor at Sea*
*The Captain's Table*
*Doctor at Large*
*Doctor in Love*
*Doctor and Son*
*Doctor in Clover*
*Doctor on Toast*
*Doctor in the Swim*
*Nuts in May*
*The Summer of Sir Lancelot*
*Love and Sir Lancelot*
*The Facemaker*
*Surgeon at Arms*

by

Mary and Richard Gordon

*A Baby in the House*
A Guide to Practical Parenthood

# SURGEON AT ARMS

## Richard Gordon

HEINEMANN : LONDON

William Heinemann Ltd

LONDON MELBOURNE TORONTO

CAPE TOWN AUCKLAND


First published 1968

© Gordon Ostlere 1968
434 30235 X

Printed in Great Britain by
Western Printing Services Ltd, Bristol

—for he made me mad
To see him shine so brisk, and smell so sweet
And talk so like a waiting-gentlewoman
Of guns, and drums, and wounds,—God save the mark!—

*King Henry IV, Part I*

### HE COULDN'T BELIEVE IT.

It was outrageous, ridiculous, but frightening, like finding the Houses of Parliament in the middle of Salisbury Plain, stumbling into St Peter's Square round a corner in Wimbledon, or coming across the Taj Mahal amid the alleys of the City. The front was magnificent. The portico presented a decorated frieze, four stout pale columns of Portland stone, and all the exuberant self-confidence of a Victorian London railway terminus. Behind rose a flattish dome, topped by four minarets, two of them emitting smoke. Then the building seriously got down to business. Its slate-roofed, double-storied, mean-windowed blocks spread in a fan, sticking their ugly fingers into an empty countryside wearing the ragged robes of autumn. All round ran an eight-foot-high wall, topped with unfriendly-looking broken glass. Everything was in yellow brick, which in the pale afternoon sunshine gave the place the look of being constructed from a million bars of Sunlight soap.

But the grounds were magnificent. Lawns, shrubberies, orchards, flowerbeds, and kitchen gardens were laid out neatly on each side of the long winding driveway, all tended with care befitting a palace. He supposed they must have had an embarrassing surplus of labour. There was a Gothic chapel, with a magnificent clock which had scattered unnecessary hours for a century. There were more modern outbuildings with larger windows, and even more modern corrugated iron Nissen huts with no windows at all. There were signs everywhere. One directed CASUALTIES to some more workmanlike entrance in the rear, another SHELTER directly into the earth, a smart new blue-and-gold board where he parked his car announced MINISTRY OF HEALTH—EMERGENCY MEDICAL SERVICE—SMITHERS BOTHAM SECTOR HOSPITAL.

It still struck him as a most peculiar name.

The entrance hall beyond the portico was a disappointment, dark and poky, painted in official spinach green and mustard yellow. Behind a small counter sat an old man with a blue uniform and sadly drooping moustaches, to whom he announced himself, 'I'm Mr Graham Trevose. I'd like to see Captain Pile, please.'

The old man looked at Graham Trevose wearily. For ten years he had sat behind that counter, hardly molested from morning to night, contemplating his pension. But now there were changes everywhere, he'd hardly time to get through his *Daily Mirror*. 'From Blackfriars Hospital, sir?' he asked.

Graham nodded.

'Have you an appointment?'

'For two o'clock.'

As the doorman turned to a small switchboard beside him Graham unbuttoned his fawn overcoat, felt for his gold case, and lit a cigarette. He noticed the hall led to a dim, narrow concrete corridor, stretching apparently to infinity. His eye fell on two doors with big brass keyholes and bolts but no handles. A terrible place to find yourself in, mad or sane. He shuddered.

Smithers Botham was a mental hospital, 'The Asylum' to the villagers, despite the term having been tactfully dropped about the time alienists mysteriously turned themselves into psychiatrists. It sprawled across the sunward slopes of the Downs south of London, which in that autumn of 1939 had lost to the safety of the countryside everything the nation held most precious—the schoolchildren, the expectant mothers, the contents of the National Gallery, the B.B.C., and the Admiralty.

The moment which had dominated British politics for five years—the arrival of the German Air Force to bomb the capital —seemed most regrettably at last about to occur. The Government confidently expected half a million air-raid casualties in the first week of the war, and something had to be done about patching them up. So the great London hospitals, too, rose stiffly from sites they had occupied for centuries, and shifted to the Home Counties in fleets of converted Green Line buses, doctors, nurses, students, instruments, beds, bed-pans, and all. Blackfriars Hospital, which had tended the sick beside the Thames since the Great Plague, was displaced to Smithers Botham, the others found secure homes in similar nineteenth-century mental institutions scattered so conveniently round the metropolis. The Government could never have kept Londoners healthy through the blitz without these vast and ugly buildings. The bread cast on the broad waters of Victorian compassion was washed ashore in the nick of time.

The Smithers Botham mental doctors, themselves dispatched with the rightful inmates to Scotland, had watched the war approach more bitterly than even Mr Chamberlain. The upper reaches of prewar medicine had many agreeable backwaters, none pleasanter than a job in such a place. They enjoyed free houses in the grounds, free vegetables piled daily on their kitchen tables, even free laundry—which was always beautifully turned out, laundrywork being thought a useful occupation for madwomen. Their main vexations were their own colleagues, who could be difficult, many doctors of unreliable personality choosing to escape from the harsh world behind the same walls as their patients. But their duties were delightfully light, the treatment of mental illness at the time being as passive as the treatment of criminals, consisting mainly in keeping both classes locked well away from public view.

Now the Smithers Botham gymnasium was partitioned into a row of operating theatres, where long-established cats snoozed in the warmth of the sterilizers or disported themselves among the beams above. New laboratories were fashioned from damp little outhouses, where sometimes toads came hopping round the test-tubes. The long bleak wards, re-equipped and refilled with rows of empty beds, after ten weeks of war still yawned hungrily for the half-million casualties, while bats flicked up and down the corridors at dusk, scaring the night nurses. The evacuated Blackfriars staff fitted in as best they could, the matron numbering among the first horrors of war her charges having to sleep without their usual collective chastity belt of spiked railings. But there were unlooked-for rural compensations—fresh air, a croquet lawn, tennis courts, even a cricket pitch, where the more athletic housemen took their exercise in the mornings and the more amorous ones took their girl-friends at night. And everyone agreed the flap would be over by Christmas, in spring they'd be home again in London.

Graham Trevose looked at his wristwatch. Ten past two. 'I suppose Captain Pile knows I'm waiting?'

'He's very busy just now, sir.'

'My own time's not exactly valueless, you know,' Graham told him, not as unkindly as he might.

The old man looked wearier than ever. 'There's a war on, sir.'

Graham winced. He always did at the expression which had come to excuse any incompetence or incivility. Instead of replying he sat resignedly on a short wooden bench, eyeing a red-and-white poster telling him his cheerfulness, his courage, and his resolution would give them victory. In a spot like Smithers Botham, he felt he was going to need all three.

GRAHAM TREVOSE was odd man out, as usual.

The Second World War found the British Government prepared to take a more tolerant view of many things than during the First. Conscientious objectors were allowed to fight fires in preference to the enemy, soldiers' mistresses (if reasonably permanent) were given an allowance, and where the cure for hysteria in British soldiers at Ypres was a British bullet, by Dunkirk 'psychological exhaustion' had become entirely respectable. The Government had a particular new enthusiasm for plastic surgery. Men with faces smashed on the Somme were, if lucky, returned home looking grotesque, and if unlucky, either died or recovered so splendidly they were sent back to present another target. Then Harold Gillies created with the basic elements of surgery and the penetrating eye of an artist his brandnew science of facial repair, though until the Armistice his notion of returning casualties to the world looking roughly like human beings attracted derision from many senior officers, to whom it was a matter of supreme indifference if a man got his face shot off or his backside.

But the Government's enthusiasm outran its supply of trained plastic surgeons, who were as scarce as trained pilots. Apart from Graham Trevose, there were only four, installed in special new units round London. Gillies, being the senior man, insisted on first choice and went to Basingstoke in Hampshire (it was convenient for his fly-fishing). An unknown surgeon called Archie McIndoe descended on the charming little local hospital at East Grinstead in Sussex. But Graham went nowhere. He had been overlooked, he assumed deliberately.

Graham was a realist. He knew he was dismissed by his profession as a 'beauty doctor', a trivial practitioner, a refurbisher of distraught débutantes who had inherited daddy's nose along with his money. He had admittedly specialized in offering hope to young actresses who saw their names one day in lights, or to old actresses for whom the lights were starting to dim. He had erased the scars of hunting accidents from the cheeks as neatly as those of dissipation from below the eyes, and the 'Trevose nose' was famous in London society—a little too famous: women were starting to recognize its distinctive handiwork across crowded cocktail parties. Perhaps he had made and spent too much money, lived too fashionably. Perhaps his private life unfitted him for employment by His Majesty. He had recently had a close shave from the General Medical Council over the famous 'infamous conduct'. Or perhaps, he told himself wearily, some stupid clerk in the Ministry had simply mislaid his file.

When the war was a month old, before he had set eyes on Smithers Botham, Graham was surprised by a telephone call inviting him to meet Brigadier Haileybury at his club the following evening. Before the war, Haileybury, too, had been a civilian plastic surgeon, and the pair had for twenty years lived in mutual dislike. It was a dignified but deadly feud, and like all feuds afforded the onlookers much innocent amusement. But Graham accepted the invitation. He had nothing else to do. And it would be the first time that he could remember Haileybury buying him a drink.

The newly created brigadier was already waiting. Of all the man's virtues, Graham found his strict punctuality the most regularly irritating.

'Well, Trevose, you're looking fit.'

'That's very kind. So are you.'

'I'm finding it difficult to get enough exercise, sitting all day behind a desk.' Haileybury held an administrative job in the Army medical services. He had a flair for organizing people. 'Shall we find a quiet corner in the morning room?'

6

Haileybury ordered sherry. He was a tall, thin, bald, graceless man with large red hands more fitting a stevedore than a surgeon, wearing an immaculate uniform with red tabs. 'I've just seen Tom Raleigh,' he stated.

'Oh, Tom.' Tom Raleigh was a young plastic surgeon, Graham's partner until the arrangement was disrupted through the Trevose temperament, which was almost as famous in London as the nose.

'You know he's been called up for the R.A.M.C.? I could have had him left in civvy street had you wanted his services. But you'll remember, when I enquired, you turned the idea down very flatly indeed.'

Graham did remember. He'd learned Tom had supplied evidence leading to that close shave with the General Medical Council. A stroke of treachery he was disinclined to overlook. But he said only, '*His* services? No one seems to find any use for my own.'

'I assure you that you're misinformed, Trevose,' Haileybury said hastily. 'I admit there was some hesitation. . . .' He stopped. Under the circumstances, it seemed best not to recall the past. 'Anyway, you'll shortly have your chance to join the civilian Emergency Medical Service. I thought that something really should be done about you.'

The condescension grated on Graham, but he said nothing. He was adjusting himself to being a nonentity, while Haileybury was now one of the nation's élite, as you could tell from a glance at his clothes.

'But I have something better to offer.'

Graham looked up.

'I have never made a secret of my disagreement with you on many things, Trevose, personal and professional.'

'No, you haven't,' Graham concurred.

Haileybury had passed his civilian years between the wars with a modesty indistinguishable from drabness, his bachelor home in Richmond as plain as his sister's cooking, his few amusements harmless to the point of boredom. Where Graham saw plastic surgery as an exciting art in the most rewarding medium

7

of all, human flesh and blood, to Haileybury it was a science, the calculated repair of injuries and defects rather than interference with the endowments of Nature. He would have been almost as reluctant to reshape an actress's nose as to perform her abortion.

'Neither have I made a secret of my admiration for your workmanship,' Haileybury went on. 'Your surgery on burns at Blackfriars called for far wider recognition.'

'I found it a very interesting branch of plastics.'

'I supposed you didn't publish it because you found the surgery of pretty women even more interesting.'

'That's unfair. It was simply because I hadn't the time.'

'Forgive me. Perhaps it's not the first occasion I've misconstrued your motives.'

'Misconstrued?' Graham smiled. 'Are you being honest with yourself?'

'I think that my next remarks will prove that. I am going to offer you a responsibility which, to be frank, I would offer no-one else.' The brigadier leaned back impressively. 'The responsibility for all facial and related wounds in the Army. Let your mind dwell on it a moment. I can promise you a perfectly free hand. Within the usual limits you will be your own master. I can promise you first-class accommodation and equipment. You can pick your own team. You can organize your own training programme and choose whom you want to train. No one will interfere. I give you my guarantee. Come! Just think. Isn't it a splendid chance to make a second reputation?'

Graham said nothing. His quick mind had fallen on the suggestion like a terrier, worrying the different elements from it.

'Of course, you're already famous,' Haileybury conceded. 'Far more than myself. Everyone in London knows Graham Trevose.'

'By "everyone in London",' Graham suggested, 'I presume you mean the few despised for regularly getting their names in the papers by the many who wish they could?'

Haileybury shrugged his shoulders. 'I'm trying to say this would bring a different sort of fame. It's a chance to get yourself

8

remembered as Gillies was in the last war. Surely that would be reward enough?'

The idea appealed to Graham. He would be making himself known to men who had, at the most, only seen his name in the gossip columns. It suited his exhibitionism, which had saddened his friends in the profession as much as it had enraged his enemies. He would be running his own show, pushing his own ideas, moulding his own assistants. Haileybury would be as good as his word—that was another of his infuriating virtues. Anyway, it would be better than doing nothing.

A thought struck him. 'You mean I'd have to join the Army?'

Haileybury looked surprised. 'That would be inescapable.'

'What rank?'

'Lieutenant-colonel.'

'Is that the best you can do?' Graham asked crossly.

'That's a very high rank.' Haileybury was shocked. 'Quite a number of senior men are coming in as majors.'

'Then it's out of the question.'

Why, he would be subordinate to Haileybury! Even if he, too, became in time a brigadier, the fellow would by then be a general, or some such. He would have to call the bloody man 'Sir'! A grisly thought.

'Totally out of the question,' Graham repeated. 'I was a civilian in the last war and I'd best stay a civilian in this one. I'm not the military type.'

Haileybury sipped his sherry with a pained look. 'Neither are most young men in the country, but they are finding themselves obliged to be.'

'I hope you're not suggesting I lack a sense of duty?'

'I am suggesting nothing of the kind,' said Haileybury patiently. 'If anything, I am suggesting you lack a sense of perspective. I made my offer because I thought, firstly, it was in the best interests of the Army, and secondly, it was in the best interests of yourself. You turned it down with hardly a second thought.'

Graham sat looking surly. Haileybury saw the delicately built-up reconciliation was about to come down with a crash.

9

'Perhaps I am pressing you too severely,' he retreated. 'I cannot expect you to decide on such a far-reaching matter in a couple of minutes. Please excuse my unreasonableness,' he apologized with unexpected good grace. 'Perhaps you will accept it as evidence of my enthusiasm for your services? Telephone me in a day or two, when you've mulled it over. Here is the number of my extension.'

Haileybury spent the rest of the meeting talking about the disastrous effect of the war on county cricket, a topic Graham found painfully boring.

# 3

'TREVOSE?' asked Captain Cuthbert Pile of the Royal Army Medical Corps, sitting in his office at Smithers Botham. 'Trevose? Never heard of him. What's he want, Corporal?'

'He's from Blackfriars, sir,' said Corporal Honeyman.

Captain Pile groaned. 'Not another? He doesn't need accommodation, I hope? I'm doing miracles as it is. The Ministry can't expect me to squeeze anyone else into the place. What's his line?'

'He seems to be a plastic surgeon, sir.'

Captain Pile looked horrified. The war had forced acquaintance with fellow-doctors in many outlandish specialities, but the company of professional face-lifters he felt outside the line of duty. '*I* don't want to see him.'

'You made an appointment, sir. For two this afternoon.'

'Oh? Did I?'

'You'll remember the Ministry telephoned, sir. The gentleman has just joined the Emergency Medical Service.'

Captain Pile rummaged busily through the papers covering his broad desk, which commanded a fine view of the sweeping front drive. There was a fire flickering in the oversized marble grate and an overall glow of mahogany-and-leather Victorian comfort. It had been the office of the Smithers Botham medical superintendent, then a consultant psychiatrist in the Army, where he was, in time, to have greater influence and invoke more widespread exasperation than a good many generals.

'Where is this Trevose? In the hall?'

'Yes, sir. He would have come to see Annex D, sir.'

'Annex D,' observed Captain Pile sombrely. 'Very well, Corporal, I'd better have a word with him. You go back to your work.'

Corporal Honeyman withdrew to a small adjacent office to continue reading *Lilliput,* which he kept in a desk drawer with his bars of chocolate. He was a willowy young man with thinning, dandruff-laden hair, glasses in circular steel frames, and a battledress which chafed his long neck. He was a sight which depressed Captain Pile deeply. Corporal Honeyman had been a clerk in an estate agent's before joining the Army through love of his country and dislike of living with his mother. The Army found he could use a typewriter, and sent him to Smithers Botham. He felt he would have been tolerably happy there, had it not been for Captain Pile, whom he was coming to care for even less than his mother.

Captain Pile sat reading through some documents, feeling a little wait would put his visitor in his place. His own civilian career had been sadly frustrating. An intolerance of sick humans had led him into various medical administrative jobs, an intolerance of even healthy ones had made all of them short. But in the Army he felt he was fulfilling himself, having command of all Service patients finding themselves in Smithers Botham and charge of the general running of the place. He rose, and inspected himself carefully in the gilt-framed mirror over the mantelpiece. Red-cheeked, dark-moustached, well built, if inclined to be stoutish for the late thirties, he felt he filled his new uniform stylishly. He placed his cap on his well-brilliantined head, took his gloves, leather-bound stick, and greatcoat, and opened the door on the hall.

'Mr Trevose?' He found the caller slight, pale, and fortyish, with large eyes in a large head, wearing under his overcoat a double-breasted chalk-striped grey flannel suit cut with smartness—flashiness, the captain might have said. 'I know nothing whatever about plastic surgery,' he told Graham proudly. 'And frankly I'm too busy to start learning such subjects now. I suppose you make women new noses and that sort of thing?'

'That sort of thing,' said Graham.

'Must be very profitable.'

They went on to the broad front steps, Captain Pile giving a quick glance up and down. There might be a soldier or two about to award him a salute. But there were no soldiers, only a schizophrenic cutting the grass. 'Annex D has been empty for a while,' he explained. 'It's not one of the best wards, but your other people from Blackfriars have bagged those already. I'm afraid you've rather missed the bus.'

They started across the lawn.

Captain Pile unlocked a heavy teak door in another yellow-brick wall with more broken glass on top. Graham's spirits, already sinking under the weight of Smithers Botham's massive ugliness, plunged further. The annex was ghastly. It looked older and bleaker than the rest of the hospital. It was as narrow as a ship, two stories high, a hundred yards long. Slates were missing from the roof, a good many windows were broken, and all of them were backed with stout iron bars. A jumble of small buildings sprouting iron stove-pipes were tacked on one end as an afterthought. The garden had for some seasons clearly been left to its own devices. Even Captain Pile looked faintly apologetic.

Inside was dark, damp, and empty. On the bare floor were sheets of newspaper, streaming toilet rolls, a pile of black-chipped enamel mugs, and other wreckage beyond Graham's powers of identification. Something scampered in the corner. The smell was strange, but predominantly faecal.

'Do you mean human beings actually lived here?' Graham exclaimed. 'And not so very long ago?'

'It's a bit musty,' Captain Pile agreed. 'I gather they used to keep their senile dementias in the place. You can't expect those sort of cases to take much notice of their surroundings.'

Graham eyed a wooden partition dividing the long room, its door swinging ajar. 'What's through there?'

'The night ward. This would be the day room.'

Graham picked his way gloomily through the rubbish to the far end of the annex. Of the tacked-on buildings, one revealed itself as the kitchen, with a stone floor and a black iron range. The second contained some cracked washbasins and three large bath-tubs raised proudly on pedestals in the middle. In the third, Graham found himself facing what appeared to be a row of horse-boxes. He discovered the half-doors opened inwards, to disclose lavatories with no seats and the chains encased in lengths of pipe running from cistern to handle.

'The patients have hanged themselves on the chains,' Captain Pile told him informatively.

Graham stuck his hands in his pockets. After turning down Haileybury's offer he had signed a contract with the Emergency Medical Service, and was committed to install and run a plastic surgery unit at Smithers Botham. Though he was always able to see a new face in the battered and bleeding remains of an accident, as a sculptor can in a lump of stone, it was beyond him to depict the rotting building as a busy, complex, cheerful, sterile centre for healing the wounded.

'That day room would have to be my operating theatre,' he suggested glumly. 'The place must be ripped apart, replumbed, fitted with sinks, sterilizers, electric points. We'll have one ward in the night room and another upstairs. God knows how we'll shift anaesthetized patients up there—fireman's lift, I suppose. I'll want partitions for the anaesthetic room, the surgeons' room, the nurses' room . . . and where am I supposed to fit the photographer's studio, X-ray, somewhere for the dentists? I'll need extractor fans, heating, reinforced ceilings for the lights, doors widening, new windows made. Those horrible iron bars must come off for a start. I want the whole place painted a bright pastel shade. Duck-egg blue, something like that. I'll have gay curtains, white bedside lockers, flowers everywhere, comfortable chairs, radios, the prettiest nurses in the hospital. My patients get depressed enough with themselves, without any encouragement from their surroundings.'

'Duck-egg blue, did you say?' murmured Captain Pile, mystified.

'I want those two far tubs in the awful wash-house partitioned off. They'll have to do for the saline bath unit. The

14

kitchen we'll have to equip again from scratch. We'll put locks on the lavatories. I'm far more likely to hang myself on the chain than the patients are. No, no, it's all impossible,' he decided abruptly. 'No one could turn this place into anything but a pigsty. They can burn it to the ground, as far as I'm concerned. They'll have to send me somewhere else.'

Captain Pile grunted. 'Where else had you in mind?'

Graham lit another cigarette. The dreadful man was right, of course. Hospital accommodation was as precious as anti-aircraft guns. It was Smithers Botham or nowhere.

'We'll have to make the most of it, I suppose,' he said resignedly. 'Baron Larrey did wonders for Napoleon's wounded in cowsheds.'

'Well, it's not my pigeon.' The captain was becoming impatient. 'You'll have to take up rebuilding problems direct with the Ministry. Have you seen enough? I've got to get back to the grindstone.'

Graham stopped half-way along the ward. He noticed a door with a cracked glass panel leading to a veranda under a rusty green-painted roof. It reminded him of a similar one in the sanatorium where he had been sent to die as a young man, a war ago. He wondered if that verandah were still there, and who was lying in his place to count the rivets of the roof in the feverish boredom of tuberculosis. As he turned away, another door with a small glass peephole caught his eye. He swung it open. A tiny high barred window disclosed a cubicle lined entirely with black padded leather, even the floor. A padded cell. Graham couldn't recall seeing one before.

'I expect you'll find a use for it,' Captain Pile suggested helpfully.

Graham walked back across the lawn in silence. It was all horribly depressing. But, he reminded himself, it was better than having to say 'Sir' to Haileybury.

# 4

BY THE FIRST CHRISTMAS the war was still a novelty, something to expose the nation's pettiness rather than its greatness. Olympia housed not Bertram Mills' circus but Germans, Nazis interned with anti-Nazis in scrupulous British fairness. Débutantes put their hands enthusiastically to driving ambulances, and showgirls theirs slightly less so to the udders of cows. Royal Academicians were painting trees to disguise factories, and keepers at the London Zoo were armed, in case bombs sprung the cages, to organize big-game hunting in Regent's Park. In Bloomsbury, the Ministry of Information was emitting propaganda of praiseworthy gentility and over Westphalia the R.A.F. were dropping leaflets in impeccable good taste. Citizens were advised to walk in the blackout with white shirt-tails exposed behind, lighting cigarettes in the street after dark attracted abuse and sometimes prosecution, and for protection against motorists with two dim half-moons for headlights, the ponies of the New Forest were striped with white paint like zebras. The weather was more irksome than the war, the countryside for most of the winter being covered thickly with snow, a fact unmentionable in the papers lest it reach the attention of the enemy.

At Smithers Botham there was a wonderful house-party atmosphere, with snowballing, skating on the pond, and amateur theatricals, like Dingley Dell. The fighting in Finland stimulated the students to inaugurate a sauna bath, rushing naked from their steaming wash-house to roll with wild shouts in the snow in full view of any female who might be passing in the blackout (an extraordinary number always were). The vast wards stayed half-empty, most civilians on the Blackfriars waiting-list being required to hold on a little longer to their hernias and varicosities in contribution to the war-effort. Space must be kept for the half-million casualties, enjoying a stay of execution. Trained hands remained idle. The nurses occupied themselves making and remaking beds, and the housemen occupied themselves making and remaking the nurses.

Five miles away, in the Kentish market town of Maiden Cross, the local hospital was overwhelmed with cases of meningitis, of which there was an epidemic that winter, with a befitting outbreak of German measles. On Christmas Eve an old man was hit by a lorry in Smithers Botham village, and rushed by ambulance to the splendid portico. Captain Pile hastily redirected it to Maiden Cross, admission of such cases to Smithers Botham being against the regulations. The ambulance driver protested, but set off along twisting and slippery roads, and if the old man died on the way the coroner pronounced afterwards he would most likely have done so anyway.

Something more horrifying happened on Boxing Day. A lady visiting her sister hospitalized with a goitre was caught short by her pregnancy, and enthusiastically delivered by an orthopaedic surgeon occupying the operating theatre at the time. But Smithers Botham was not classified by the Ministry for midwifery. No one had the slightest right to be born there. Captain Pile confessed himself greatly distressed by the irregularity. The versatile orthopaedic surgeon apologized, but found himself caught in a baffled correspondence with Whitehall, which continued on and off for the duration of the war.

New Year's Eve fell on a Sunday, and Graham had spent the day as usual at Smithers Botham. There was so much to do. He was astounded how the squad of builders were performing a workmanlike miracle in the annex. Huts were thrown up in the neglected garden, pipes and wires sprouted everywhere, they were even starting to apply the duck-egg blue, and if this turned out nearer royal purple the place was at least beginning

17

to take something of its shape in his mind. He began to gather staff. Tudor Beverley, a young plastic surgeon from Canada whom Graham had met on a lecture-tour, unexpectedly appeared on the Smithers Botham portico and was promptly press-ganged as his first assistant. He even had a few patients, whom he was obliged to operate upon in the main theatres. His first case was the removal of a soldier's tattoo, a splendid emblazonment on his arm dedicated to Florence, who had apparently become unworthy of the honour. Graham pickled it in a jar of spirit, and kept it on the desk of his hut office until the end of the war. He treated a sailor with a jaw fractured while fighting, regrettably not the enemy but another sailor in a pub off Piccadilly. There were a number of smashed-up dispatch riders, the motor-bike at the time striking Graham as the most dangerous weapon in the British Army.

Feeling he should prepare himself as well as the annex, Graham read as many textbooks and papers about wound surgery as he could lay hands on. He listened to Archie McIndoe at the Royal Society of Medicine, and to Sir Harold Gillies more intimately at Basingstoke—and more exhaustingly, Gillies being a forceful and sometimes eccentric exponent of his genius. Graham had resigned himself to the annex being something of a sideshow. The other four plastic units were better housed, better equipped, and better staffed, destined to take most of the work, if the war didn't fizzle out. He even half-regretted not submitting himself to Haileybury. He would at least have had a uniform. He had come to avoid his club in St James's because he felt the members looked askance on his lack of it. Most seemed to possess one, though whatever their martial duties these did not prevent their spending a good deal of time in its comfortable leather armchairs. But he had made his decision, and if it were the wrong one it unhappily wouldn't be his first.

On that New Year's Eve he left his Bentley in a mews garage off Curzon Street and walked the few yards to his house in fashionable Queen Street by the light of his pocket torch (screened by law with two thicknesses of tissue-paper). As he approached his front door he saw a girl standing on the step, her identity solved by an invitation flashed at him by a torch through her mackintosh pocket.

'Do you want to come home with me, darling?' she enquired.

'I'm afraid this is my home, here,' Graham told her politely.

'Oh, sorry. I hope you don't mind?'

He noticed she was young, and very plain. The regulations which forbade the lighting of shop windows threw a kindly shade on goods more immediately for sale, and the West End of London was as alive with seductive murmurs as Prospero's Isle. Graham supposed the girls hadn't enjoyed such a busy time of it since the lightless days of Boswell. He entered the empty house, reflecting sombrely that the difference between many women he knew of easy-going morals and these seedy and undoubtedly infected creatures was exactly the same as between Haileybury and himself. Even Haileybury had done the occasional beautifying job for guineas. But Graham had for the best part of fifteen years sold his services without question to all comers. And what was left? He had been dreadfully extravagant. His contract at Smithers Botham had exchanged an income of thousands for one of hundreds and debarred him from private practice—if he could have found any, plastic surgery suddenly being fashionable no longer, perhaps because the possibility of having one's head blown off ousted any dissatisfaction with the look of it. He was terribly in debt. And the income-tax inspector, as always, clanked across his life like Marley's ghost.

He fixed the blackout in the upstairs drawing-room, switched on the light, and poured a whisky at the corner cocktail cabinet. Usually he drank only to relieve the tedium of other people's company, now he was drinking twice as much to relieve the tedium of his own. His servants had left, a genteel middle-aged woman came in daily from Finchley to clear up his mess, which she referred to as her 'war work'. His son Desmond was in his first year at Cambridge, reading medicine. Unlike the First World War, which emptied the medical schools into the ranks

19

of Kitchener's army, the Second barred medical students from joining the colours as firmly as miners or middle-aged ploughmen. For safety's sake, Graham had sent Desmond to spend Christmas with his cousin Alec, also destined for medicine, Alec's mother Edith then running a guest house for the better class of evacuee in Devon. Graham swirled the whisky round his glass. Edith Trevose had been successively his own fiancée, his sister-in-law, his brother's widow, and his mistress, but despite these disturbing changes in status still his friend. He wondered whether to ring her up, but decided against it. It might start new complications. And anyway, the long-distance telephones were becoming dreadfully unreliable.

He reflected again that he should give up his Queen Street home, store the furniture, and take a room at The Oak inn on the village green at Smithers Botham. He would exchange the Bentley for a Morris, and be patriotic over petrol. It was all an excuse to save money, to live a simpler life, until the fuss was over—as everyone knew from the newspapers, the Germans were already short of everything from shells to shoeleather. He poured himself another drink. Here was Graham Trevose, he thought sadly, the fashionable plastic surgeon, the favourite guest of a thousand smart parties, and nobody even wanted to talk to him. He had always far keener pity for himself than for his patients. He felt loneliness like pain, to exist without a woman's company struck him as hard as solitary confinement. Without the compensation of a caress he became as wretched as a stray dog, to wake at night alone he felt a foretaste of the grave. He'd enjoyed affairs enough before the war, but what was their lasting satisfaction? he asked himself bitterly. As little as a handshake. Now everyone he knew seemed to have disappeared, and if the Germans did arrive that night to blow him to pieces there was hardly anyone to care.

He had a wife, of course, but she was in a home in Sussex, mad for fifteen years.

# 5

THE HURRICANE had two self-sealing petrol tanks in the wings and another in the fuselage, directly in front of the pilot. On the August Sunday morning when a Messerschmitt 109 caught him over Dungeness he calculated, after a panicky moment wondering if he were alive at all, that he still had a fair chance of eating his dinner that night. As he jettisoned the cockpit hood a stench of petrol struck him. In a second his world was alight. He never remembered how he fell clear. His next recollection was the petrol replaced by a smell even more pungent. It reminded him of something. It was the stink of burning wool, which stuck in your nose when they cleared up after the clip back home.

He didn't remember getting clear of his parachute harness, but he must have managed it somehow because he was free when they reached him. His only worry was whether a Mae West could really keep a man afloat. The sea was dead calm, he felt no pain, no unusual sensation at all. Like everyone else, he'd been flying without goggles and gloves. It made it easier to see the enemy and to handle the controls. He watched with detached interest bits of skin and flesh come away from his hands and forearms, like fragments of roast chicken, and float in the water. A civilian lifeboat picked him up. As two men in black oilskins got him aboard he noticed their faces, and wondered what the hell they were staring at.

It was the same expression on the face of the girl looking down at him. She was in a white apron, a nurse he supposed.

21

Pain, shock, and morphine had by then turned him from a human being to a collection of organs struggling to function together as best they could. He asked where he was, but she didn't seem to understand. He wondered suddenly if he were in France, put in the bag by the Germans. Then she said, 'You're all right. You're in hospital. In Kent, not far from Tunbridge Wells.'

He'd heard of Tunbridge Wells. It struck him as an odd sort of place to find himself in.

He floated on a cloud of euphoria as they were obliged continually to increase his dose of morphine. He didn't know if he'd been lying there for a couple of days or a week, though it was in fact more than a month. Gradually his body seemed to grow some sort of skin against the painful world. A variety of doctors in white coats came to see him, and generally dug about with forceps and probes, most painfully. As he began to notice things again, he saw when they changed his dressings his hands were black, clawed, and wizened. They reminded him of the hands he'd once seen on the body of an aboriginal, brought into the sheep station after lying for months shrivelling in the sun of the outback. He asked for a mirror, but was told the hospital hadn't any to spare. They had been broken by a freak of blast in the bombing, they explained, and glass was in short supply.

His room was small, white-painted, and sunny, looking on to a small garden. He wondered what sort of hospital it was, and if there were any other patients. He certainly saw no sign of them. Over the next few weeks the pain began to ease and the needles became less frequent. One afternoon he noticed there was a mirror right in the room. It was over the washbasin, though they'd covered it with flowered curtain material fixed by strips of sticking-plaster. He crawled out of bed, staggered, and fell. He managed to struggle across the floor, and to tug the flowered covering aside with the point of his elbow. He wondered who he was looking at. The face in the glass was swollen, black, and running with pus. There was no nose, and the eyes stared through a pair of encrusted lids. The door

22

opened and the young nurse came in, scolding him like a naughty child for getting out of bed.

A few mornings later the blue-uniformed sister, a stout and kindly woman, appeared at his bedside with a stranger. He was a civilian, thin, pale, weedy-looking, with a large head and eyes showing too much white.

'Bluey Jardine, isn't it?' began the visitor affably. 'The Australian? I've heard a lot about you. Sorry to make your acquaintance in these particular circumstances.'

The patient looked suspicious. Whenever anyone new appeared in the room, it seemed to mean something unpleasant was going to happen.

'My name's Trevose,' the civilian went on. 'I'm a surgeon who specializes in your sort of trouble. I suppose you know well enough you were pretty badly burnt?'

'Am I going to live?'

'Yes, of course you are. But it'll take a good deal of treatment getting you into shape. We're going to see rather a lot of each other in the immediate future, I'm afraid.' Graham took a bundle of case-notes from the sister. 'You weren't wearing goggles and gloves?'

'I don't reckon so.'

'A sadly common omission,' murmured Graham. With sterile forceps and a kidney-bowl he began picking away the dressings. Another case of 'airman's burn'. If only these chaps would keep their gloves and goggles on, he thought, they'd have at least some sort of protection in the cockpit. The first-aid station had smeared tannic acid jelly all over the raw surfaces, of course. Damnable stuff! Why couldn't the muttonheads at the top issue orders banning it? It would take weeks for him to pick the dried tannic acid crust away, before he could even think about skin-grafting. The hands were terrible. The face was a pretty bad mess too, but that didn't matter so much. A face was a decoration, but you needed hands to live.

'Right, Sister,' Graham decided. 'I'll have this one.' He turned to the man in bed. 'Would you like a change of scene? This hospital, however excellent otherwise, hasn't the facilities

23

for the sort of surgery you need. I run a little show nearer London where we can look after you properly.'

Bluey hesitated and said, 'I reckon I'm in the hands of you quacks now, aren't I?'

'Good. I'll send a car for you tomorrow morning. Do you like ice-cream?'

'I don't mind it.'

'Vanilla or strawberry? I'm afraid there's no chocolate.'

'Vanilla will do me.' Bluey was mystified. Bits of him were burnt to cinders, and they talked about ice-cream. This doctor, whoever he was, seemed an odd bloke.

'We'll be feeding you it till you're sick,' Graham told him cheerfully. 'See you later.'

In the corridor the sister chided Graham with more severity than usual, 'But Mr Trevose! You *did* say you wouldn't kidnap any more patients.'

'This officer will be my last—honestly.'

'It does make life so difficult for us, you know.'

'Of course I do. But leaving Bluey here will make life very much more difficult for *him*. Should the powers that be object—'

'But they *will* object, Mr Trevose.'

Graham grinned. 'Just say I behaved in such an overbearing and arrogant manner you had no alternative but to give in. Say I threatened physical violence if you like. With my reputation they'll believe you.' He patted her amiably on the arm. 'Don't worry, Sister, I'll see there's no trouble. I'll take full responsibility. It's really quite easy. I'm one of the few people at the moment who don't have to give a twopenny damn for the grandest air-marshals, generals, admirals, or anyone.'

She hesitated. She had quite taken to Graham, who had set himself to be resolutely charming towards her. 'You do behave badly sometimes, you know,' she told him gently.

'I behave badly frequently. But it's a change doing so on someone else's behalf instead of my own.'

The following morning Bluey Jardine arrived at Smithers Botham in Graham's second-hand Morris, driven by a green-uniformed W.V.S. worker, with most of him hidden by a

24

tartan rug. It was then October 1940, and the population had found more to worry about than whether to wear their shirt-tails outside their trousers at night. But it had been a lovely summer. The cherry trees had flowered charmingly over the little Gothic mortuary, the patients were kept awake by owls serenading to the crickets' violins, the tomatoes ripened wonderfully along the sunny walls of the main operating theatres (nourished by the unused offerings of patriotic blood-donors). It was difficult at Smithers Botham to believe the Germans might leap from the seas or the skies any moment. The litter of old iron gathered from surrounding fields to make room for growing food was put back again to frustrate enemy gliders. At the portico, the words 'Smithers Botham' were painted from the blue-and-gold notice to baffle Nazi para-chutists dropping on the lawn, doubtless dressed as nuns. The chapel clock was hushed, chimes being classified with sirens, whistles, and football-rattles as the portents of varying sorts of doom. The L.D.V. crawled enthusiastically on their stomachs everywhere, carrying shotguns and threatening with much ferocity anyone moving after dark they disliked the look or sound of.

The vast main wards of Smithers Botham remained almost empty. People heard so often on the B.B.C. of 'hospitals and churches' being hit by bombing all over southern England that these seemed highly dangerous places to find yourself in (whether there was a comparable decline in churchgoing no one bothered to find out). The reluctance of these civilians to present them-selves for long-awaited treatment Graham found a godsend. After Dunkirk, the annex had been alarmingly overcrowded. If he wanted to throw up more huts, he was told they were 'unavailable'—an infuriatingly handy expression of rebuff. If he wanted more beds, he knew where to look. With the amiable connivance of Mr O'Rory, the Blackfriars gynaecologist work-ing at Smithers Botham, Graham sent Tudor Beverley and his houseman to shift some unoccupied ones from O'Rory's wards. When the traffic was interrupted angrily by Captain Pile in the middle of the lawn, Graham drove to Maiden Cross and bought camp beds in the sports' shop. Captain Pile appeared in the annex to object wrathfully, but even he could hardly evict the sleeping patients.

'It's most irregular, Mr. Trevose. You can't just increase the number of beds in the hospital like that.'

'But the men would be terribly uncomfortable on the floor,' Graham pointed out mildly.

Captain Pile went redder than ever. He was having a bad war. His command was admittedly complete over the military patients at Smithers Botham, who on his approach were expected, with the difficulty of saluting smartly from the pillow, to stiffen themselves under the sheets as though they were corpses already. But the civilian doctors from Blackfriars took no notice of him at all. It was most frustrating. The senior ones made clear that the possessors of Fellowships from the grand Royal Colleges could hardly be bossed by a mere Licentiate of the less exacting Society of Apothecaries. The younger ones defaced his signed notices, often quite obscenely, predictably named him 'The Haemorrhoid', and made up rude songs about him which they sang outside his office window. And Trevose he found more maddening than the rest put together.

'If I may say so, your wards give me a great deal of unnecessary trouble,' he continued warmly to Graham. 'You make absolutely no attempt to maintain proper discipline in this annex. Why, you're actually mixing officers with other ranks!'

'Surely this is hardly the moment to insist on the niceties of military etiquette, Captain Pile?'

'But it is *against regulations*! What have you done with those board partitions? I had them sent specially to divide up the wards, officers one side, men the other.'

'I'm keeping them handy. They'll be essential if we get anyone from the women's Services. Though I suppose it would be all right bedding them down among the men, as long as the ladies weren't officers?'

Captain Pile decided to ignore the question. You could never be quite sure with a man like Trevose if he were being serious. 'And what about all this ice-cream? I gather you're getting it from some merchant in Maiden Cross. I must insist the practice stops forthwith. You must know it's quite out of order for anyone except the catering officer to have foodstuffs sent to the hospital?'

Burned men lose protein from the raw surface of their bodies, and Graham had discovered sadly with his own palate that the Smithers Botham diet was miserably mean in such a costly essential. The dishes consisted mostly of porridge, stew, and rice pudding, which, being boiled in the same vats, had interchangeable tastes. Though like an old-fashioned Christmas pudding they occasionally offered keepsakes, a dirty bandage, a broken tooth, once even a well-worn rubber heel. Graham supposed that none of the original inmates was expected to notice what he ate, anyway. During the hot summer he had hit on the idea of ice-cream, telling the manufacturer to cram in as many protein-rich eggs as he could find. But all this seemed too complicated to explain to Captain Pile.

'I eat it all myself,' he said. 'Incidentally, I pay for it from my own pocket.'

'But you buy churns of the stuff!'

'I happen to be particularly fond of ice-cream.'

Captain Pile looked baffled. Trevose was an eccentric, quite off his head. 'Furthermore,' Pile recalled, 'you sent six shirts to the hospital laundry last week. The maximum permitted number is three.'

'Good God,' muttered Graham.

When Bluey arrived at the annex he had no idea what might be in store for him. He had no imagination at all. It was an essential ingredient of his limitless courage. The Ministry of Information, hungry for heroes, had trumpeted him as the Australian 'ace', printing his photograph and his number of enemy kills in the newspapers. He was a rewarding subject, tall, good-looking with dark wavy hair, unmarried, a sportsman splendid at cricket, swimming, and tennis. But a hero has no more likelihood of being pleasant than lesser men. Bluey was pushful, overbearing, and vain, as malicious behind the backs of his superiors as into the faces of anyone unlucky enough to be set below him. Since puberty he had seduced as many girls as he could lay hands on, regarding them all as the fortunate recipients of his passing favour. In the air, he would risk his neck for anyone. On the ground he would lift a finger only for himself. No one in the squadron had much time for Bluey.

'Good morning, Flight-Lieutenant Jardine.' A young nurse with a mature air, holding a board with a clip of notes, approached as he stood at the ward door trying to take it all in. 'We've put you in the far end bed. That's a bit of an honour, you know. It's supposed to be quieter.'

Bluey looked round anxiously. It was certainly a change from the last hospital. The long narrow lower ward of the annex was crammed with beds, though the patients were mostly dressed and lounging about, smoking, laughing, or chatting noisily. They struck him as an odd bunch. The majority were bandaged heavily about the head, some wore slings and plaster casts, others had their hands in bulky dressings like boxing-gloves. The ward radio was at full blast. It always was at Smithers Botham, from early tea to lights out, right through the war. Graham often idly wondered how many people died to the strains of Geraldo.

'Do you want me to turn in?' Bluey asked.

'Not unless you're tired. In the annex we like to keep everyone up and about. Dr Bickley thinks it stops you getting bad chests.'

'Who's Dr Bickley?' asked Bluey warily. You never knew how many of these medical jokers were waiting to have a go at you. 'I'm under Dr Trevose.'

'Dr Bickley's the Gasman. The anaesthetist. You'll meet him later. You can smoke whenever you like, there aren't any rules. Have you got enough cigarettes? The boys'll help you light them.'

'I'm all right.' He wasn't going to feel gratitude towards anybody.

'Is there anything special you like to eat? We'll try to get it, but we can't guarantee results.'

'I'm not particular.'

28

'Here's Peter.' The nurse smiled. 'He'll look after you. He's the oldest inhabitant.'

The nurse left Bluey with another man in flight lieutenant's uniform, his tunic hanging from his shoulders and his sleeves pinned to the pockets. Bluey inspected him with fascination. His face was mostly hidden in crêpe bandages, but a strange yellowish-pink sausage sprouted from the middle of it. This was fixed to his left wrist, held against his cheek by a plaster cast. His hands were bandaged, but his thumb was free enough to grasp a cigarette in a long holder.

'I'm Peter Thomas,' announced the apparition amiably. 'Welcome to the mausoleum. You're the Australian, aren't you? I remember seeing you in the *Daily Mirror*. If I recollect aright, you were sharing the page with Jane.'

'What do they do to you in this place?'

'Make you look like an advert for Brylcreem.'

Bluey stared round. 'How long before they let you out?'

'Well, it's inclined to be a long job, as possibly you can see for yourself. The Wizz doesn't believe in rushing things.'

'The Wizz?'

'The Wizard. Trevose. He made this elephant's trunk affair. It's a wrist pedicle. It started life as a slice of skin from my belly. The Wizz kept my wrist attached to my navel for weeks, before raising it to higher things. It's all a matter of re-establishing the blood supply before making the next move. You'll soon pick up the lingo. We become very professional here, you know. The pedicle's going to be part of my nose, incidentally.'

The two officers started walking along the line of beds.

'It's noisy,' observed Bluey. 'The place I came from, they shut me up alone in a room.'

'Life is very informal in annex D. Everyone mucks in together, all Services, all ranks. It's the Wizz's idea. Good for morale, he says. Though I rather think he does it to annoy the brass-hats. We had an admiral in here last week. He fell on his face down a ladder. Drunk, doubtless. I don't think he cared for the atmosphere much. The only gentleman enjoying privacy at the moment is a German bastard shut in the padded cell.'

29

As Bluey stopped short his companion gave a laugh. 'Didn't you know? This used to be a nuthouse. The change isn't always apparent. Which part of Australia do you come from?'

'Outside of Melbourne. My people own a sheep-station. I came over to join up before the war.' His near-lidless eyes stared round. 'Maybe all this means I'm on my way back again?'

'They'll notice a change in you,' said Peter Thomas crisply.

It was a remark in the spirit of annex D. The men had grown a shell of arrogance towards the world which had brought them to such straits. To be pitied was so unbearable, any eye sensed to be softening with compassion fired only an explosion of rudeness. The nurses got used to it—if they didn't, Graham had them shifted to more conventional wards. The elderly hospital padre found his attempts to 'cheer up the poor boys' so unwelcome, his Christian fortitude collapsed beneath him and he avoided the place. Even well-meaning ladies with baskets of gifts saw them accepted without a flicker of gratitude. After all, the patients felt the country owed them more for their pains than a few bars of chocolate.

'I suppose I've caught it pretty badly?' Bluey hazarded.

'Oh, I've seen worse,' Peter Thomas told him with an air of authority.

'When did they get you?'

'I was one of the earliest. I've been in here so long I'm practically one of the staff.'

'What's happening outside? Nobody's told me any news.'

'The Germans seem to be crying off. In daylight, at any rate.'

'That's funny. I thought we'd go on like that. Flying every day till the end of the war.' They stopped at Bluey's bed, the last before the partition dividing off the operating theatre. 'I was just starting to believe in my luck.'

'If you like, I'll see if I can find a newspaper,' Peter Thomas offered helpfully. 'Though the selection isn't very uplifting. There'll probably be a *Daily Press*, which is good for at least one laugh.'

'Thanks. I reckon I've a lot to catch up.'

Bluey sat on his bed and inspected his surroundings. There

was no need for mirrors in annex D. He could see himself in the monstrosities all round him. He suddenly realized he was an outcast, a frightening object, something to make any man wince and any woman run away in horror. For the first time the bitterness of his humiliation swept over him. He wanted to cry in self-pity. But his lachrymal glands were burnt, and even to weep was impossible.

# 6

BRIGADIER HAILEYBURY was a fair-minded man. He knew Trevose was a prima donna, unwilling or temperamentally unable to fit into any co-ordinated effort, even to win a war. And of course Pile didn't help. The fellow was unbelievably stupid. But the line must be drawn somewhere. Authority must be established. On the morning following Bluey's arrival he appeared at Smithers Botham to make his first inspection of the annex.

He could readily believe Pile's account of indiscipline among Graham's patients. He needed only to recall the notorious laxity of Graham's own life before the war. It would have to be checked, even if it meant a row. Haileybury was aware that he and Graham had quarrelled every second time they met, and recalled uneasily that he himself generally got the worst of it. Trevose had a quick tongue, and a slick way of putting things. But now Haileybury told himself he was dressed in authority— which was neither little, nor, in view of the summer's military disasters, likely to be brief.

He marched across the lawn with Captain Pile, admiring the flower-beds. As the operating theatre now blocked one end of the annex, entrance was between the horse-box lavatories and the kitchen, where twice daily the nurses portioned out food dispatched from the central Smithers Botham kitchens in re-putedly heatproof trolleys. As the pair entered, the door of the washroom opened and Graham himself appeared. He was

32

wearing a surgeon's green gown with a gauze mask dangling below his chin, and seemed busy.

'Haileybury, I was delighted to learn of your impending visit,' he began affably. 'I'd been hoping you'd look us up all summer.'

'I'm glad to find you so cheerful, Trevose. No one knows better than myself the difficulties under which you've been obliged to work.'

'I agree, we haven't sufficient equipment, sufficient room, sufficient staff, or a sufficient number of hours in the day, but we manage. I'd like you to see our star turn,' he invited. 'Nurse, give these two gentlemen masks and gowns. Step inside. It's the saline bath unit.'

In a partitioned corner of the wash-house one of the bath-tubs was in use. Sitting up to his waist in water was a man—or so it was to be assumed, the creature being without hair, eyebrows, or nose, the skin of his face and even his eyelids burnt away. There were two nurses working on him in white gowns and rubber gloves. One was moistening the man's head with a trickle of clear solution running from a glass vessel suspended near the ceiling. The other was manipulating a pair of forceps in the stream, picking away plaques of hard black material embedded in the pus and raw tissue. Captain Pile, whose eyes had become used to inspecting official rather than human material, felt his stomach turn over.

'Very interesting,' said Haileybury.

'Somewhat Heath Robinson, but it works,' Graham explained. 'It's got plenty of snags. For one thing, the saline solution in the carboy up there cools too quickly. It's a nuisance for the nurses to keep replacing it.'

'Doubtless,' said Haileybury.

They watched the operation in silence. After a few minutes Graham led them out. 'Why do you do it to them, Haileybury?' he demanded.

Haileybury untied the tapes of his surgeon's gown. 'Do what?'

'Plaster those burns with tannic acid jelly. Do you know what I feel when I look round my wards? No hatred of the

33

Germans. Their fellows are getting even worse treatment, I know that well enough, I lectured there before the war. No, I simply writhe with indignation over the stupidity of my own countrymen.'

'So you think tannic acid is stupid, do you?' Haileybury asked drily.

'I think it's criminal.'

'But you must know perfectly well, Trevose, it happens to be the regulation treatment. And what else would you suggest? That the dressing-stations do nothing in the way of first-aid at all?'

'That's exactly what I do suggest. I'm charitably assuming you treat burns with the equivalent of grannie's cold tea because, one, you can't think of anything better, and two, you want the casualties to feel something's being done for them. Well, something's being done, all right. Medieval mutilation.'

'I really don't think I need comment on that,' said Haileybury wearily. 'Ever since I've known you, you've ruined your advocacy of any cause, worthy or not, with the extravagance of your language.'

Graham suddenly felt angry. 'This situation doesn't need any language at all.' He pointed to the closed door of the wash-house. 'Haven't you eyes to see for yourself? That patient's a pilot officer, observer in a Blenheim, which failed to take off properly for some reason or other. The pilot was burnt to a cinder. By the time that poor devil turned up here his head and neck had skin like an elephant's. You know what it was, don't you? Congealed tannic acid. His hands were worse where he'd tried to pull his blazing clothes off. The fingers were drawn into the palms, webbed together, one black horrible mess. That's his real tragedy. With time and luck I can give him a face which will pass without too much comment in a crowd. But he'll probably never feed or wash himself again, even light his own cigarette. He'll be dependent on someone for the rest of his life. An awful prospect for both parties.'

Haileybury decided to be firm but patient. If the argument was to end in his favour, Trevose needed even more thoughtful

34

handling than usual. 'I can appreciate how you feel involved with these men, Trevose. But you must try and see our arrangements as a whole. The application of tannic acid as a first-aid measure to burns isn't some shot in the dark. It's been most carefully thought out. It is the official procedure. It is *regulation treatment*,' he emphasized.

'Then it's got to be changed. Do you know the first cases I had in here? A pair of naval ratings, picked up after an hour in the sea at Dunkirk. Both were badly burnt in the arms and legs. Both did splendidly. No tannic acid. Just salt solution like I'm using here, Nature's own.'

'Now you're being fanciful.' Haileybury started to sound irritated. 'I'm certainly not going to let you rush all of us into something entirely new.'

'Am I? Send me a lot more burns and make up your mind in six months. I'd like you to pull a few strings for me, by the way,' Graham invited airily. 'The unit's got to be expanded. I shall have to squeeze a second operating table into the theatre somehow. Tudor Beverley can run that himself. He's good enough. I'll need more assistants. And we want more huts desperately. It's like a slum in here.'

'You might reduce your difficulties if you ceased scouring the countryside for extra patients,' Haileybury told him bleakly.

Graham gave a grin. 'You heard about that, did you? It's the Services' own fault. It's weeks before I see some of the cases. They go on a ghastly traipse all over the shop, rotting for weeks in hospitals in Scotland or Wales, miles away. Faulty organization, that's the trouble. I'd like you to do something about that, too, please, and quickly.'

Haileybury became angry despite himself. 'Have you thought of making life easier for yourself and everyone else with some attempt to understand how Service administration works?'

'The only administration I understand is the one which gets me my own way.'

'No one's yet signed for the extra beds shifted here, sir,' interrupted Captain Pile, who was feeling out of it.

'Oh, do be quiet, Captain!' snapped Haileybury. 'Listen,

35

Trevose, I know you're an enthusiast. Often enough, I'll admit, in a perfectly good cause. But you can't expect the Services to make fundamental changes according to your whim of the moment. Please get that into your mind for a start.'

'Do you imagine I haven't thought about these problems just as carefully as you or anyone else? You must issue instructions banning tannic acid.'

'Are you giving *me* orders?'

'Yes.'

Haileybury drew a breath. 'You might have the courtesy to recognize my position, even if you don't respect it.'

'Why should I? It's I who have to handle the patients. Anyway, I know far more about burns than you do.'

'You would seem to have lost nothing of your high opinion of yourself.'

'It's a justifiable opinion,' Graham told him off-handedly.

'As far as I could make out before the war,' Haileybury exclaimed, 'your best skill was concentrated in your cock.' He stopped, looking confused. He could not remember using the expression before. Trevose always seemed to bring out vulgarity in him.

'Then do as you please,' Graham said casually. 'I'll get the tannic acid banned by the R.A.F., at least. You know a Member of Parliament called Fergusson?'

'I've heard of him,' Haileybury admitted surlily.

'He's just collared a job in the Air Ministry. Have you met his wife Sally? Wonderful pair of tits. Guaranteed to stop the conversation at a party. Well, I made them. The couple are pathetically grateful.'

'You mean, you intend to go behind my back?'

'I've no inhibitions about going behind anyone's back if I think it's in a good cause.' Haileybury said nothing. It was all most frustrating. 'You know, I've made so many bad decisions in my life,' Graham told him with returning cheerfulness, 'it's good to find once in a while I've hit on the right one. I mean staying out of uniform.'

'I would offer no view on the rightness or wrongness of that.'

36

Haileybury looked at him sourly. It seemed he had lost the argument, as usual. He vaguely wondered why. 'As I am here, perhaps you would invite me to look round your wards?' he added as sarcastically as possible.

'Of course.' Graham smiled. 'You know that I am always ready to oblige an old acquaintance in any professional matter whatever.'

Graham opened the door of the ward. It was a terrible thought, he told himself, but he was really quite enjoying the war.

## 7

'BUT WHY DON'T YOU divorce her, Graham?' asked Denise
Bickley. 'I can't understand why you don't divorce her.'

It was a subject which Graham chose to skip away from as
quickly as possible. 'I hate having truck with lawyers, I suppose,'
he told her. 'They give me the creeps. With their undertakers'
clothes and their undertakers' faces, burying all your hopes
under a mound of stony possibilities.'

'But unfortunately not at undertakers' rates,' smiled John
Bickley, the anaesthetist, across the log fire.

It was a Sunday afternoon in the first week of 1941, when the
*Luftwaffe* was bombing the country nightly, the onion had
become a fragrant memory, whisky and bananas had vanished
with the other flavours of peace, and the war was starting
to change from a perilous adventure to a wearisome way of
life.

'But you *can* divorce her, you know.' John's wife Denise was
chillingly well informed about everything to do with the married
state. 'You can these days. The law's been changed.'

Why does the woman continually go paddling in the muddy
waters of my soul? Graham asked himself. 'So I understand,' he
agreed. 'A. P. Herbert's Act altered everything. Maria's been
mad for over five years, so I'm legally at liberty to rid myself of
the encumbrance whenever I feel like it. Of course, it was
different when I first had her locked up.'

Graham had hoped that putting the situation so starkly
might shame Denise into changing the subject, but she per-

38

sisted, 'I'd have thought it worth taking the trouble, if only to get things straight.'

'But how could it make the slightest difference to my life?'

'Supposing you wanted to get married again?' Denise exclaimed.

Graham laughed.

'Well, you never know.'

'I'm forty-six. Hardly the romantic age. Anyway, who's to be the bride?'

'How old must Maria be now?' asked Denise.

'Let me see—she's nine years older than me. Which makes her fifty-five.'

'How's she bearing up? Physically, I mean,' asked John. It was an attempt to turn the conversation. He knew Graham's sensitivities far better than his wife did.

'Her body's extremely well. I went down with Desmond to see her over Christmas. She's put on a lot of weight—they generally do, I gather. But her vital organs are functioning perfectly, though admittedly her blood-pressure's a bit up. Her mind's quite unbalanced, of course. She doesn't know me, sometimes she doesn't know her own nurses. On good days she washes herself. On bad days she wets the bed.'

Denise lit a cigarette and said, 'It must be dreadfully upsetting, seeing her like that.'

'Not particularly. I can hardly be expected to correlate her with the person I married. She was what they called a "society beauty", you know. The only daughter of our popular tub-thumping millionaire, Lord Cazalay.' A lot of things have happened since then, Graham reflected sombrely. Lord Cazalay's gone bust, for a start.

'Graham, may I ask you one thing?' Denise puffed earnestly. 'I'm only trying to help, you do understand that, don't you?'

'Ask anything you like,' said Graham resignedly.

'Do you still love her?'

'I never did.'

'But surely you must have done once?'

'I don't know. I don't know if I've ever been in love with

39

anybody. I fancy I have some sort of inborn immunity to the condition, like some people have for tuberculosis. Or perhaps I just expect too much.'

'But that's a tragedy, Graham! A life without love.'

'Is it? Aren't people over-obsessed with such attitudes? It's all the fault of the pictures and the wireless. Anyway, I've enough satisfaction for one lifetime in my work.'

'That tannic acid row was fun,' laughed John.

Graham's face lit up. He developed an almost schoolboy eagerness when anyone started talking about the annex. 'It was amusing, wasn't it? I told you, if McIndoe and myself made enough fuss in the right places they'd ban it. Fergusson grasped the point at once, luckily. Haileybury was so delightfully furious. He suffers a terrible spasticity of ideas, that man, his mind's as rigid as a plank. In peacetime I never had much use for the bigwigs who impose their authority on the profession, you know that, John. I never realized how gratifying it would be to extend my range in the war.' He looked at his wrist-watch. 'It was a wonderful lunch, Denise, but I must go.'

She looked disappointed and asked, 'Won't you stay for another cup of coffee?' She always did, every Sunday.

'I promised to see Peter Thomas this afternoon. A vital consultation—he's bursting to go on leave. Then I've someone to interview for a job. I'd like an early start in the theatre tomorrow, John,' he added. 'An awful list of oddments has piled up. Tim O'Rory's sending us a newborn baby with a hare lip. It ought to be done as soon as possible, I think, to give the poor little thing a chance to have a go at mother's milk.'

'I'll have the case on the table at eight.'

'I'd be much obliged,' said Graham.

When he had gone, Denise started clearing the dishes and declared, 'I really can't understand about Graham and Maria.'

Her husband, tall, bony, wearing an old jacket and chalk-striped flannels, stretched himself in front of the fire. 'Perhaps he doesn't think a divorce would be in Maria's own interests.'

'I couldn't believe that for a moment,' she said impatiently.

40

'Graham's one of the most selfish men I know. He's totally self-centred about everything, even the war.'

John started refilling his pipe. 'I imagined our Graham had undergone something of a sea change this last year.'

'*I* certainly hadn't noticed it.'

He stuck a spill of newspaper into the fire. Matches were becoming almost as precious as razor-blades. 'Do you think he really is so selfish? The plastic surgery racket was pretty tough in London before the war, you know. If a man didn't push himself, nobody else would take the trouble. Now that it doesn't matter a damn to Graham if he operates on three cases a week or thirty, perhaps he can afford the luxury of indulging his better nature.'

'He hasn't been showing much of it to you lately, has he? In the annex, I mean.'

John shrugged. Never an easy-going colleague, Graham was becoming worse-tempered in the theatre than ever. 'With the amount of work we're getting through, some tension between surgeon and anaesthetist is inevitable.'

Denise picked up the tray. 'If he *did* divorce the woman, it would all be perfectly respectable. He wouldn't have to take a girl for a week-end to Brighton, or anything like that.'

'I rather think you need a permit these days to pass a week-end in Brighton,' John observed mildly.

'Oh, you never take anything seriously,' she complained, disappearing into the kitchen.

Graham usually walked from the Bickleys' cottage back to Smithers Botham, on the double assumption that it did him good and he ought to save his official petrol. He started along the bare country lane wondering how he could get out of these Sunday lunches. Denise's insensitivity was deadly.

She had come into his life on the shoulders of John, a friend of twenty years' standing. John Bickley had given the anaesthetics since Graham was a young house-surgeon making a false start on throat work, in the days when children were submitted to the rape of their tonsils under the oblivion of asphyxia more than anaesthesia. Perhaps Denise was jealous, Graham

41

wondered. The relationship of surgeon and anaesthetist had something in common with marriage. He and John had half a lifetime of shared experience, together having faced the triumphs, failures, and excitements concentrated in the few square feet round an operating table. As Graham had become a fashionable plastic surgeon so John Bickley had become a fashionable 'doper' or 'stuffist', hurrying with his rubber tubes and cylinders from nursing-home to nursing-home on a time-table more complicated than Bradshaw's. The surgeons allowed him ten per cent of the operating fee, so he had to keep in with a good many to keep going. The year before the war he had married Denise, whom he had met at a suburban golf-club. She was tall, slim, blonde, and athletic, and had money. It struck Graham that ever afterwards John occupied himself by keeping in with her.

Graham hadn't liked Denise from the start. She had taken him over, as she had taken over everything else connected with her husband, even his Saturday's golf. It was becoming a complication to their work in the theatre, and Graham wouldn't countenance any complication likely to affect his patients. The Bickleys had found a cottage near Smithers Botham—very luckily, the arrival of Blackfriars having shifted most of the white elephants squatting on local estate agents' books. Having neither children nor evacuees, Denise had first invited Graham to live with them, confessing her astonishment at his tolerating the pub. But he was never a man to lack excuses. She insisted he at least called for Sunday lunch. She had a pressing sense of social duty, devoting much energy to organizing the wives of Blackfriars consultants scattered round the countryside into cosy if meatless dinner parties, into fours of bridge or sets of tennis, and into the knitting of large quantities of Balaclava helmets.

She loved quizzing him about Maria. It seemed to be her Sunday treat. Graham could anyway hardly explain his motives for not divorcing his wife when he didn't know them himself. Perhaps he had no more than a vague reluctance to put down some decrepit animal which once strode vigorously in the sun-

42

shine of admiration. Or perhaps, he thought more darkly, his wife was a mother-substitute, his feelings towards her loaded with guilt—but one mustn't take too much notice of the psychiatrists, they told a lot of fairy-tales. Somehow he must see less of Denise, particularly now it looked as though they'd be living in each other's pockets at Smithers Botham for life. Only General Wavell in the Western Desert was providing any encouraging sweeping black arrows on the front-page maps of Lord Arlott's *Daily Press*. Graham wondered glumly if the ebullient Australian newspaper proprietor, whom he had known well enough in peacetime, had foreseen that his task of chirpingly maintaining civilian morale every morning would have reached its present bleak severity.

Reaching his office in the hut outside the annex, Graham changed his shoes, pulled on a white coat, and sent a nurse for Peter Thomas.

'I hope I'm a specimen worthy of display to the outer world,' Peter began cheerfully.

The patient's flesh sausage was by then detached from his wrist, and starting to turn into something like a nose. The rest of his face was a patchwork of skin, too yellow and too shiny, Graham thought, cut from various bits of his body. Graham removed a dressing and saw with satisfaction that some sepsis in the corner of his last graft had healed. 'The sulphanilamide powder seems to have done the trick,' he announced. 'It's saved me the necessity of having to use you as a guinea-pig for penicillin.'

'Penny what?'

'Oh, it's some stuff they invented at Mary's. Their Prof. Fleming found a mould which kept killing off the bugs he was trying to grow in his lab. It must have been very irritating, until he put two and two together. Our medical unit are working on it. It's supposed to be secret, though God knows why. The stuff's as rare as hens' teeth.'

'What's it look like?' asked Peter, with interest.

'Very yellow and sticky, and personally I don't think it's going to be the slightest use.'

43

Graham took the man's hands. Not much movement yet. Annoying.

'Is that physiotherapy girl bullying you to use your hands, Peter?'

'Quite delightfully so.'

'I think we can risk doing without your company for a couple of months,' Graham decided. He turned to the folder of notes on his desk. 'Then I'm afraid it's back for the next stage.'

'How long, O Wizz, how long?'

'Altogether? The next step shouldn't be too bad. I'll make you some eyebrows from the hair on the nape of your neck. But I've never made a secret that we'll be very old friends by the time we finally part. You're a major construction job.'

'That's an interesting way of putting it.'

'I'm sorry. It must make me sound dreadfully heartless.'

'But that's the secret of your success, Wizz! You've got a ward full of monsters, and you look on us as so many construction jobs. Exactly the right attitude. Surely you know how sickening it is to be pitied?'

Graham nodded. 'Yes, of course I do. But I'm not putting on an act, you know. I've always looked on my patients as construction jobs. I could never have run the sort of practice I had before the war otherwise.'

'You must find us lot rather a come-down after remodelling film stars.'

'Quite the opposite,' said Graham warmly. 'When I came out here I knew I'd have to remodel my operative technique— after all, a land mine makes rather more mess than even the worst car smash. What I didn't know was the extent to which I'd have to remodel myself. What did I do before the war? I lifted a face or reshaped a nose, took out the stitches, collected the fee, and that was that. But I live with you fellows, day and night. You've always got some interesting problem for me to solve, psychological if it isn't surgical.'

Peter laughed. 'You make us sound like a bunch of damn nuisances.'

'On the contrary, you've presented me with an object in life.

44

You didn't seek out my service, like my patients in peacetime. You'd no choice, the war washed you up on my doorstep. I feel I owe you something.' He laughed, too. 'It's terribly stimulating. And terribly gratifying. This "Wizz" stuff, it's stupid really, I'm only doing my job. But it means more to me than the most gushing praise I ever got for hanging a new pair of tits on an actress. You boys are highly selective in your appreciation of anything.'

'We're exposed to an awful lot of well-meaning hypocrites. We soon learn to pick out the genuine ones.'

'Or perhaps it's just a form of selfishness on my part?' Graham philosophized. 'I like to think of you as worthwhile memorials to my surgery. I've reached a depressing age. I'm beginning to realize I'm at the whim of any passing disease. "Death hath ten thousand several doors for men to take their exits"—a sobering reminder from Webster. But what am I complaining for?' he apologized. 'You've been near enough to getting yourself killed.'

'Yes, and I was terrified. I've vomited in the cockpit. Once, though I kept pretty quiet about it, I accomplished what you would refer to as "defaecation".'

'You'd no hopes of the life hereafter?'

'I preferred to wait and see.'

'I expect you're right. I had a brother once, a medical missionary. He at least departed this life in a spirit of glowing optimism. Do you want some cigarettes?' Graham felt suddenly the conversation was becoming too self-revealing. But now he never had a chance to reveal anything of himself to anybody. 'They're called Sweet Caporals—Canadian, it seems.' He had given up smoking, mainly through the tediousness of queueing, but scrounged what he could for his patients. 'Do you want another book?' He tossed a paperback on his desk, alongside the unfamiliar white packet. In peacetime, he hardly got through a book a year. Now he spent most evenings in his room at The Oak reading. There was nothing like a world war to simplify your life. 'It's *Decline and Fall*, by Evelyn Waugh. Very funny. How's Bluey getting on?' he added.

'Somewhat restless.'

Graham lit the cigarette in Peter's holder. That was bad news. Bluey had to stand at least another dozen operations, and needed all the patience he could muster.

'Though his morale has improved considerably,' Peter added, 'since getting his hands on a supply of rum. God knows where from. He keeps it in his locker, which I presume is strictly against regulations.'

'The annex houses enough trouble without regulations,' Graham said briefly. He looked at his watch. 'Very well, Peter, off you go on leave. Now there should be a female waiting for me. I don't know what she's like—young, old, fat, thin, as ugly as sin or a goddess. She wants to take over as ward sister, God help her.'

Peter looked surprised. 'The Dragon's going?'

'Yes, Sister James has decided to join the Q.A.s and nurse the Army. You can hardly blame her. After the annex she'll find even a pitched battle a rest cure. As the Blackfriars matron has broken off diplomatic relations with me through the disgraceful behaviour of my patients,' he told Peter with a grin, 'I am obliged to find most of my own staff. This one's been recommended by a surgeon I know in a children's hospital. Just about the right background for handling you lot, I'd imagine. Send her in, will you?'

The prospective sister struck Graham as resembling a Botticelli virgin with disastrous dress-sense. She was slight, fair, and transparent-looking, wearing lisle stockings, stout laced black shoes, and a suit of green and very hairy tweed. She had no hat, her hair was in the usual page-boy bob. Big eyes, Graham noticed, a pretty mouth, if rather over-large. No trace of make-up, but a good skin. He decided she didn't look nearly tough enough.

'It's Miss Mills, isn't it?' he asked, as she sat with hands crossed demurely in her lap. 'I'm afraid all I know about you is confined to a telephone conversation with Mr Cavill, and the line was terrible.'

'Yes. Clare Mills. I'm Mr Cavill's staff nurse.'

46

She had a soft voice, speaking with great deliberation. Graham noticed she had a trick of emphasizing her last syllables. Probably nervousness, he suspected.

'How old are you?'

'Twenty-three.'

How the nursing profession thrusts responsibility on its daughters! Graham reflected. Before the war, they had to be twenty-one and of unspotted character before being allowed to handle the Blackfriars sick at all. But perhaps women were built for it. After all, there was no responsibility like motherhood, and that was liable to catch a girl unawares anytime.

'I'd better make plain from the start that the work here isn't hard, Miss Mills. It's exhausting. I'm an impossible taskmaster. I'm demanding, boorish, and usually most ungrateful. I don't expect loyalty. I expect devotion. I tolerate incompetence badly, and fools not at all. It's a mystery how I manage to keep any assistants in the place. And the patients are much worse than I am. Life can be hell for nursing staff in the annex. Though, to be fair, most of them seem to find it an enjoyable hell.' Graham smiled at her. 'Would you like to end our interview here and now?'

'I should very much like the post, Mr Trevose.'

'Why?'

She hesitated. 'I've always wanted to work on a plastic surgery unit.'

'A strange ambition.'

She paused again, and went on shyly, 'You once operated on a friend of mine, Mr Trevose. She was a girl—seventeen at the time. She had a deformed lip. Her name was Susan Wright.'

Graham tried to remember. It was impossible. He had operated on so many girls. 'I can only hope the operation was a success?'

'Oh, yes!' She suddenly became animated. 'It made an enormous difference to her. Not only physically, I mean, but mentally. She told me all about you, Mr Trevose—how understanding you were, how skilful. Perhaps it gave me the ambition of one day working for you.'

47

Graham folded his arms. She was terribly young, but old Cavill had praised her warmly enough. She'd be pretty to have about the annex. Perhaps the boys would take pity on her delicate looks, though he doubted it. And she had a neat hand with flattery. A sensible girl. It was a talent which had taken him a long way at the beginning of his career.

'Can you start on Wednesday?' he asked her.

# 8

BLUEY JARDINE bared the upper half of his left arm with an air of resignation. He knew exactly what was coming to him. It was a Friday morning, following the Sunday when Graham had sent Peter Thomas on leave, which gave Bluey the dubious honour of being the ward's oldest inhabitant. He had then been in the annex four months, and into the theatre eight times. Like everyone else, he had developed a keen interest in the science which was bedevilling him.

The routine of an operation had become as familiar to him as the routine of flying. The injection about to enter his arm was his 'premedication', and he even knew the names of the drugs. There was one hundred-and-fiftieth of a grain of scopolamine, which dried up your mouth and lungs and stopped you bubbling and drowning yourself once you were under. There was a third of a grain of omnopon, which was just another name for morphia, and gave you guts. He twitched as the staff nurse punctured his skin with the syringe. The more needles they stuck into you, the more you came to hate them.

He lay back in bed, wearing long white knitted socks and a short over-laundered cotton nightshirt which fastened with rubber buttons at the back. He didn't seem to be growing as drowsy as usual. Perhaps the injection was losing effect. Only to be expected, he told himself. Once he could get drunk on a bottle of beer, now it needed a couple of crates. He wondered how many more operations the Wizz had in store for him. It never occurred to Bluey that he might ask Graham to stop, to leave him with a half-patched face and makeshift hands, but in peace. He accepted his treatment as something which went on until it reached its natural end, like the war.

As they wheeled him the few yards from the ward to the operating theatre on a trolley he searched the ceiling for a peculiar star-shaped crack, as he always touched the dried kangaroo paw in his tunic pocket before flying. Sometimes when they trundled you out you were dead scared, others you didn't give a damn. He supposed it depended how rough they were on your last visit. Anyway, the operation today was kid's stuff. He'd soon get over it. With luck, he'd be out on the grog again on Saturday night, as usual.

The anaesthetic room, improvised out of flimsy partitions, was hardly big enough to hold the patient, the ward nurse accompanying him, the tall frame of John Bickley, and the anaesthetic trolley gleaming with dials, bottles, piping, and coloured cylinders. Bluey raised his head from the pillow. The Gasman, his long green gown pushed up to his elbows, was holding a large syringe.

'Not another bloody needle?'

'You're a favoured customer, Bluey. No gas this time. I'm sending you off with an injection.'

'Go on?' This was an interesting departure, something to tell the ward afterwards. The anaesthetist rubbed a swab of cold antiseptic on the crook of Bluey's left arm. 'What's the stuff called?'

'Evipan.' John drew back the plunger of his syringe, a swirl of blood telling him the needle lay safely inside the vein. If the injection went by error into the skin of Bluey's elbow there would be an abscess, and a terrible row with Graham. 'There, you didn't even feel the needle, did you? Now count, out loud. . . .'

Bluey reached fifteen, yawned deeply, and fell asleep. John plucked out the syringe, simultaneously freeing Bluey's breathing by holding up his chin. 'This stuff was invented by our friends the Germans,' he told the nurse. 'I ought to use it as a routine. The boys get pretty browned off, being suffocated

50

every time with gas. That can't be much fun when you have to face a dozen operations on the trot.'

Like all specialist anaesthetists, John Bickley brought to his work the artistic touch of an experienced chef. First he held a triangular padded mask tight to Bluey's patchwork face, and concocted a delicately proportioned mixture of oxygen and nitrous oxide gas. Then he moved a lever on a bottle of blue liquid to add a trace of trichlorethylene vapour—a more powerful anaesthetic to deepen Bluey's unconsciousness. John edged across the lever on another bottle to admit the pungent vapour of ether, the main ingredient of the dish. Bluey coughed fiercely. He always did, John reflected. He should insist that Graham stop his patients smoking for at least a week before their operations. But Graham objected that would be bad for morale, and they'd smoke in the lavatories, anyway. Graham objected to almost everything he suggested, it struck John wearily, ever since he had started calling for Sunday lunch.

Two coloured bobbins already danced up thin vertical glass tubes on John's anaesthetic trolley, indicating the volume of oxygen and nitrous oxide flowing to his patient. When he judged the anaesthesia deep enough, he sent a third bobbin spinning by adding carbon dioxide to the mixture. This stimulated Bluey's breathing, until he was heaving away as though finishing some desperate race in his sleep. With economical movements, John laid aside the face-mask, reached for a narrow, stiff, greased, red-rubber tube, and inserted it into the remains of Bluey's right nostril. He edged it inwards gently—an unsuspected nasal polyp would bring blood all over the shop and an even worse row with Graham—listening to the breath-sounds as it slipped behind Bluey's flaccid tongue, then finally through his widely open larynx into his windpipe. It was a technique invented by Harold Gillies' own anaesthetist, Ivan Magill, to deliver the anaesthetic directly into the patient's lungs while leaving his face and mouth as a sterile unoccupied battlefield for the plastic surgeon.

'That looked pretty easy, I must say,' observed the nurse, who like all nurses had long ago ceased to be impressed by her medical overlords. But her remark pleased John. The trick was rather like playing darts in the dark, not easy at all. Only the experience of twenty years made it seem so.

As Bluey himself knew, the operation was to be a simple affair. Graham cut a thin graft of skin from Bluey's thigh with a Thiersch knife like an oversized razor, then stitched it along his chin where a former one had failed to take. Bluey was back in bed within the half hour, struggling to consciousness through dreams about flying, which were always unpleasant but soon forgotten. He woke up deciding he didn't feel as bad as usual. The Gasman's injection was a winner. The next night he'd be fit enough to finish the bottle of rum in his locker, then slip out with half a dozen others to The Oak.

Knowing the habits of his patients, Graham made a point on Saturday nights of taking a bus to the pictures in Maiden Cross. That Saturday he queued to see an American film about the war, in which all the Germans conversed in villainous guttural undertones, all the British officers had Oxford accents, and all their men talked like Sam Weller. The star was Stella Garrod, the woman Graham had made a fool of himself with before the war. He wondered wryly if she ever bothered to think of him. In fact, she spoke fondly and often of her affair with the little London surgeon, immorality with Englishmen having, after Dunkirk, considerable kudos in Hollywood.

When Graham reached home on the last bus the pub was already closed, but Bluey and his companions had been disinclined to finish the evening. They had staggered down the Smithers Botham drive singing *Cats on the Rooftops*, and the night being moonlit someone noticed a collection of builders' materials stacked outside Captain Pile's office under the gleaming portico. Bluey gave a whoop as he found a tin of paint and a brush. A porter appeared through the complicated blackout screening the front door to investigate, but identifying denizens of the annex retreated instantly. Bluey painted across the portico a single word in large letters, one on each of the four columns. Then they went singing and laughing back to the annex and bed. The night nurses were used to it.

Early the next morning Mrs Sedgewick-Smith came down the hospital drive, hurrying to a long-standing appointment with the elderly padre. Mrs Sedgewick-Smith was the wife of a stockbroker who commanded the local Home Guard, and before the war had filled the vacuum of her life by fussing over the mental patients at Smithers Botham, or as many of them as remained socially presentable. She had organized whist drives, jumble sales, demure dances, and extremely amateur theatricals, invited the inmates for tea or for outings in her Rolls, all of which she bracketed as 'giving the poor things a nice little break'. The war presented even more poor things as targets for her deadly solicitude. She had installed herself as unofficial welfare officer at Smithers Botham, and was beginning to hope the war would go on long enough for somebody to give her a medal for it.

She saw the word.

She was horribly shocked. It was not a word which could possibly appear in print, but she had of course overheard it, from workmen, soldiers, lunatics, and the like. She had always imagined it spelt with a 'ph', like 'phutt'. To see it splashed in black paint across the portico was absolutely outrageous. And on a Sunday morning, too. She would have to find Captain Pile.

Captain Pile occupied a comfortable villa in the grounds, where he managed to live in unmilitary domesticity with his wife and two children. He was in his braces, enjoying his breakfast. He put on his tunic and inspected the word officially. Though he used it frequently himself, he had to affect an air of disgust as pained as his informant's. Mrs Sedgewick-Smith must be humoured at all costs. She was a powerful lady at Smithers Botham, the dispenser of valuable grace and favours, mostly unobtainable off the ration.

When Graham arrived at the annex at nine for an informal Sunday ward-round with his new sister, his spirits fell as he noticed Miss Mills in close conversation at the ward door with Captain Pile. He caught sight of Mrs Sedgewick-Smith, and they dropped further. He had often noticed her fluttering in and out of the Tudor house across the village green, but hearing she was a professional busybody had taken pains to avoid her. Besides, she was thick with Denise Bickley, and probably knew far more about his personal affairs than she deserved.

'Good morning,' Graham greeted the visitors politely. 'Anything I can do for you?'

'I'm afraid a most serious matter has arisen, Mr Trevose,' Captain Pile told him solemnly.

Oh God, this is going to be a bore, Graham thought.

'I expect you've seen the main entrance this morning?' the Captain added.

'No, I came here direct, through the orchard.'

'A word—a most offensive word—has been written across it in paint. Mrs Sedgewick-Smith was most disturbed to see it.'

'I'm sorry about that. But—I know the annex has a bad name —why hold my patients responsible?'

'For the simple reason they were seen by the night-porter. Flight Lieutenant Jardine and some others.'

Graham nodded slowly. That's encouraging, he thought, Bluey's getting enough function in his hands to wield a paint brush. 'Then I can only apologize most sincerely to both you and Mrs Sedgewick-Smith.'

'You realize they'd been drinking?'

'Had they? I don't mind that. I even encourage it,' Graham explained mildly. 'It's a matter of pride to my anaesthetist if they feel capable of taking a few drinks after his attentions.' Seeing the captain's irritated expression he continued, 'You see, I want these men to live a normal life. Or as normal as they can manage. I want them to think of an operation as something as casual as a visit to the dentist, not the upheaval of a lifetime.'

'That's all very well,' the captain told him testily, 'but you have to maintain discipline—'

'I'll talk to them,' said Graham firmly. 'I promise. Isn't that enough? It won't happen again.'

'No, that is *not* enough, Mr Trevose. You cannot simply take the affair into your own hands. It is my duty to see that appropriate action is taken.'

54

'Listen, Captain,' said Graham briskly, 'I alone am responsible for these patients. Neither you nor the Army nor anyone else has the first idea how to cope with them. Will you kindly understand that?'

His patience suddenly broke and he felt angry. In peacetime he had been a somebody, the friend of rich and influential men, a doctor with a name almost as familiar to the general public as Lord Horder's. Now he was being lectured by some hack in a uniform which passed as a substitute for intelligence.

'Can't you see? These men aren't invalids.' Graham's outstretched arm indicated the ward, where the patients were lying in bed reading the Sunday papers, trying hard to give the impression they weren't listening. Bluey himself was asleep at the end, snoring loudly. 'Underneath their wounds and scars they're full of life, fit and lusty. They were youngsters with charm and sex-appeal, and what happened? In a few seconds they were turned into objects of horror. Then they were locked up in this converted madhouse. And that's not to be their fate for a week, or a month, or even a year. When the war's over and everyone's back in their comfortable little slots these patients of mine will still be coming up for another graft, another pedicle, another operation of some sort. How are they going to face that miserable prospect if they can't run wild now and then?'

Captain Pile tried to say something, but Graham went on, 'Do you know what happened in the last war? When I first heard of plastic surgery I was a patient myself in a sanatorium. There was a plastic unit billeted in half the wards. Every afternoon, under King's Regulations, the men had to be marched by an N.C.O. round the countryside for exercise. You can imagine the effect. People weren't so well educated then, were more superstitious. You'd have thought an army of ghouls was advancing on them. They locked their doors, covered their windows, and hid their children. So the Army confined the poor fellows to hospital, with nothing to look at but each other—an inspired piece of morale-building. I don't want any of that nonsense in this war. There's one thing my patients ask from

55

the world, and only one. To be treated as normal individuals. Oh, I know it's difficult, they're freaks. But the effort isn't much to ask.'

'I think Mr Trevose is perfectly right,' announced Mrs Sedgewick-Smith.

Captain Pile spun round. The unexpected desertion of his ally appalled him. Trevose was a difficult customer at the best of times, and that morning he needed all the support he could muster. She stood tugging the hem of her tweed jacket and staring at Graham with large grey eyes. She must have been quite a good-looking girl, Graham thought. Even now, I could do her face a power of good.

'After all,' continued Mrs Sedgewick-Smith crisply, 'there are no children roaming the hospital. And the rest of us surely know that expression exists.'

'Exactly,' said Graham.

Mrs Sedgewick-Smith had undergone a change of heart. She had been dying to meet Graham for eighteen months. He was *the* Graham Trevose, the man you once saw in the *Tatler*, the surgeon one or two of her friends could talk about, quite breathlessly. Now she saw him at close quarters she realized he had a distinction, a dignity, an authority, an air about him which Captain Pile despite his uniform so sadly lacked. In short, Graham Trevose was a *gentleman*. And, war or no war, the ladies and gentlemen of England had to stand shoulder to shoulder together.

'We mustn't wallow in our indignation,' she continued calmly, 'and I'm sure the paint can very easily be cleaned off. Mr Trevose, I appreciate every word that you have said. Isn't there anything I can do for your patients? To give them a nice little break?'

'There most certainly is. And it isn't very much. Just ask them to tea, invite along some girls, and talk about the weather.'

'This is nothing to do with a breach of discipline,' Captain Pile broke in furiously.

'Surely, Captain, if Nelson could turn a blind eye you can?' asked Mrs Sedgewick-Smith tartly. 'There are so many regu-

56

lations these days, none of us can avoid breaking one or two, can we?'

Captain Pile fell silent. He had been rather afraid of this turn in the conversation. Regularly every Friday Mrs Sedgewick-Smith brought him half a dozen eggs from her hens, in a cardboard box labelled as Red Cross library books. A side of bacon had once been smuggled into his house, wrapped in a sheet to resemble the laundry. There had been pots of gooseberry jam, pounds of sugar, even a few ounces of butter. It would be sad if the flow ceased. Captain Pile was extremely fond of egg and bacon for his breakfast. It was a testing decision. Should he pawn his military honour for a handful of eggs?

'I suppose if you don't feel inclined to press the matter, Mrs Sedgewick-Smith, I—'

'Extremely sensible of you,' she said quickly. She turned to Graham with a smile. 'Mr Trevose, I do hope you can drop in for a little drink some evening? I'm sure my husband can find something in the cupboard.'

Graham promised. The bargain struck him as cheap at the price.

When Graham finally started his ward-round, he said to Sister Mills, 'I'm sorry about that. It doesn't happen every Sunday morning.'

'Oh, what a pity.' She smiled. 'I thought you were terribly impressive, Mr Trevose. Though I can't for the life of me see what all the fuss was about.'

'Neither can I,' said Graham. It suddenly occurred to him he didn't even know what the word was.

THE HOSTESS opened her own front door. In peacetime, as she was half-tempted to explain, there would have been a maid in a lace apron. 'I'm so glad you could come,' Mrs Sedgewick-Smith greeted them brightly.

Bluey and the half-dozen others who had courted disgrace on the Saturday night found themselves standing on Mrs Sedgewick-Smith's doorstep the following Monday afternoon. Graham had conscripted them as a punishment. The outing had not struck them as at all attractive. Tea didn't promise much fun, and an invitation from the local grand lady had an intolerable air of condescension about it. But if the Wizz told them to go, go they must. Even Bluey agreed a bloke would do anything to please the Wizz.

'Hello, Missus,' announced Bluey. 'Here's the Home for the Sick and Crippled. Frankenstein's monsters' annual outing.'

Mrs Sedgewick-Smith gave an uncertain smile. But years of intense social struggle with the wives of other stockbrokers had tempered her conviviality like steel. She hesitated only a second before continuing, 'But *do* come in. Quite a charming afternoon for the time of year, isn't it?'

Bluey led his companions into the hall. He stared round. Graham had warned him to be on his best behaviour, but he was determined to keep the social balance tilted in his favour.

'Old place you've got here, Missus.'

'Oh, yes! Parts of it go back to Henry the Eighth.'

Bluey sniffed. 'Smells like it.'

There was an awkward silence as the patients stood grinning at their hostess, like mischievous children with Hallowe'en masks. I must treat them as normal people, she reminded herself, as perfectly normal people. Like the charming young men who used to call before the war for tennis. And surely if they were officers they must also be gentlemen? Even the one with sergeant's stripes on his sleeve was aircrew, and as things went at the time socially acceptable. Her loss for something to say was relieved by the oak door of the sitting-room opening, to emit a slight girl in a yellow-and-white flowered dress, with rigidly outstretched hand and a rigidly fixed smile.

'My youngest daughter Stephanie,' said Mrs Sedgewick-Smith, on a note of enthusiasm.

'Spiffing to meet you,' said Stephanie, hand still outstretched.

Stephanie was at an age which should have changed her from a grub in boarding-school uniform to flutter gaily amid the dances and parties of the 'season'. As it was, she was trying to decide whether to start as a probationer nurse at Smithers Botham or to make Sten guns in the shadow factory at Maiden Cross. But Graham had prescribed girls, and girls being like everything else in short supply, Mrs Sedgewick-Smith had patriotically concluded that Stephanie must do.

'You should have warned us, Missus, you'd a houseful of beautiful women,' said Bluey sarcastically.

'You mustn't say things like that,' smiled her mother. 'You'll turn her head.'

Stephanie went pink. 'Oh, *Mummy!*'

'You must forgive my daughter for being a little shy,' Mrs Sedgewick-Smith apologized uneasily. 'You see, she doesn't have much chance to meet young men these days. The war has quite ruined our social life.'

'It's ruined a lot of things,' said Bluey.

They went into the timbered drawing-room. There was a small fire, an eggless cake, and meat-paste sandwiches spread with margarine—Mrs Sedgewick-Smith considered raiding the butter-ration as carrying compassion too far. She fiddled anxiously amid the teacups, aware that her guests were going to

59

be terribly difficult to entertain. Of course, one couldn't—or at least mustn't—blame the poor things for being rather peculiar. She hoped it wouldn't have any lasting effect on Stephanie, who was sitting on a low chair with the arresting habit of repeatedly crossing her legs then nervously tugging her hem over the knee of her lisle stockings. Her mother had instructed her sternly to treat the guests as perfectly normal. Her boarding-school had instructed her even more sternly how to carry such things through. As she chatted haltingly it amused Bluey to see her struggling to pretend they were ordinary-looking individuals. She'd be a virgin for sure, he decided, though might make a satisfactory bang if touched up enough first.

'Why don't you come back to Australia with me after the war, Stephanie?'

'I'd love to, really! Honestly, I would. I've heard it's a super place.'

'It's not bad. All the good things are free—surfing, lying on the beach, Sunday picnics, riding round the station. Australia's got space. You can get lost in it. There's no one to bother you. No one to stare at you.'

He stopped, realizing he had unthinkingly let show the raw edge of his feelings. The sergeant, whom Bluey always irritated, took advantage of the silence to compliment Mrs Sedgewick-Smith on the sandwiches.

'I'm so glad you like them. I made the paste myself, you know, from leftovers. I got the recipe from a magazine—the food facts are so helpful these days, aren't they? I would have done you a carrot flan as well, but of course that needs a lemon jelly for the glazing, and there just isn't *one* in the shops.'

Food at the time was starting to replace sex as the basis of most adult conversation.

'You're quite right about your daughter,' the sergeant continued. 'It's hard to miss the enjoyments of youth. You can't store them away like your pretty frocks for use after the war. They won't fit any more.'

Mrs Sedgewick-Smith gave a faintly puzzled smile. Behind

the bandages was he young or old? Serious or mocking? Just a sergeant, or a gentleman?

'There's an exact moment in life for your first taste of wine and of love,' the sergeant went on. 'You'll always remember it, and never succeed in recapturing the flavour of either.'

'You know, I think I read something like that in a book,' exclaimed Mrs Sedgewick-Smith.

'Probably one of mine,' said the sergeant, who had been desperate to make some such remark. Before the war he had written a couple of novels, which though noticed kindly by James Agate had not been noticed by his present companions at all. Mrs Sedgewick-Smith, a three-volume-a-week woman with Boot's, became agreeably flustered to find herself in the company of a man of letters. It also kept Bluey out of the conversation, which continued at a genteel literary level until they had finished the last pale dry crumbs of the tasteless cake. Then Bluey, resentful at his ousting from the centre of attention, demanded abruptly, 'Where is it?'

'I beg your pardon?' said Mrs Sedgewick-Smith.

'The doings. I want to go. Tea runs through me like a dose of salts.'

'You mean the smallest room?' his hostess interpreted coyly. She rose helpfully. 'I'll show you the way.'

'I'll need some assistance with the buttons.'

'Oh,' said Mrs Sedgewick-Smith.

Bluey fixed Stephanie with his eye. 'Perhaps the young lady will oblige?'

'The young lady will certainly not oblige,' snapped her mother.

'Didn't she say she was thinking of being a nurse?' asked Bluey innocently. 'The nurses do it for us in the annex.'

Mrs Sedgewick-Smith looked round desperately. None of the others gave any indication of volunteering. They found the situation only something to grin about. The literary sergeant might have saved her embarrassment, but he was damned if he were going to handle Bluey's private parts. Mrs. Sedgewick-Smith drew herself up. It was too bad. Even the lunatics hadn't

offered such problems. 'If you will come with me, I shall do all
that is necessary.'

'Good on you,' said Bluey amiably. He hadn't really expected
to get away with Stephanie. Well, it might be funny watching
the old bag fumbling with him. She didn't look as if anyone had
put a prick in her hand for a good many years. It was only the
embarrassment he could provoke in others which made bearable his humiliation at needing such attention at all.

'I'm sorry, but it's a social disability I rather overlooked,'
Graham laughed when Mrs Sedgewick-Smith explained the
predicament the next morning. 'Those buttons are a terrible
obstacle for the boys' hands. But I really can't think what to do,
apart from sending them out in kilts.'

Mrs Sedgewick-Smith hesitated. She wanted to edge away
from the subject as soon as possible, but persevered bravely, 'I
don't know if you would welcome a suggestion, Mr Trevose.
But when my husband came home from America before the
war, he was wearing a suit . . . equipped with a zip-
fastener.'

'Yes, of course.' Graham snapped his fingers. 'I remember
seeing them there myself. It's a sound idea. If only, of course,
I can get a supply of zips.'

It struck him that a beleaguered country could hardly be
expected to continue manufacturing such metallic frivolities.
There were certainly none in the shops at Maiden Cross. You
probably needed as much influence to lay your hands on some
zip-fasteners as to lay them on a case of Scotch or a few gallons
of petrol. But he had still one friend who might be expected to
perform miracles, and the provision of patients' flies was a
minor miracle indeed. Graham telephoned the *Daily Press*
office in Fleet Street, and found himself asked up to lunch.

Graham had a standing invitation to visit Lord Arlott, but
hadn't taken advantage of it partly because he was too busy at
the annex, and partly because of a vague desire to keep his prewar life disconnected from his new one. At seventy, Valentine
Arlott continued to conduct his newspaper with undiminished
energy and interference. He was a small, lively man in rimless

62

glasses, the fiery red hair which Graham well remembered long ago turned grey, but his Australian accent was as fierce as ever, to be dimmed or intensified according to how it suited to illuminate a particular argument. The *Press* was continuing in the Second War its policy of the First, bringing the exploits of Lord Arlott's countrymen repeatedly and enthusiastically to the attention of the British public. Its office was by then more or less roofless, weatherproofed by tarpaulins, standing amid buildings apparently gnawed by giant rats, or simply replaced by holes in the ground, or revealing themselves on a second glance as blackened shells like burnt-out fireworks. Graham found Lord Arlott had installed himself in a shored-up room in the basement, which he had fitted out like a military headquarters with telephones of various colours, charts, and large maps, all of great complexity. Val Arlott liked to spread the notion that the *Press* could manipulate any national movement of importance, from which he saw no reason to exclude the war.

'Zip-fasteners?' Val exclaimed, Graham coming to the point of his visit at once. His thick grey eyebrows shot up. 'What the hell would you want those for?'

Graham explained.

'Sounds like a good cause,' said Val. 'Fix it up, Geoff, will you?'

'Certainly, Val.'

There was a third person in the basement room, who from the humility with which he conducted himself Graham passed off as some sort of secretary. He was startled to discover a little later that the man was the paper's editor.

'Well, Graham—how are you going along?' Val Arlott leaned back in his swivel-chair, smiling but eyeing Graham with a shrewdness he turned impartially on prime ministers and messenger boys. 'By God, you're looking fit. And ten years younger.'

Graham laughed. 'It's the simple country life. Think what a fortune it would have cost to enjoy before the war.'

'Don't you get bored?'

'Not much. I just work and sleep.'

63

'You must notice the change—patching up our national heroes instead of our national beauties.'

'I do. It's much more gratifying.'

'I suppose it should be gratifying to me, too. I'm the one who gave you your start, aren't I?'

'Of course—no Val Arlott, no Graham Trevose.'

In the nineteen-twenties Val had run a crusade in the *Press* to install not only London's first plastic surgery unit in near-by Blackfriars Hospital, but its first plastic surgeon embodied in Graham Trevose. Graham's father-in-law had owned half the paper, which stimulated the benevolence. But Val's interest had quickly turned to some other campaign for lightening the burden of humanity—the opening of cinemas on Sundays, if Graham remembered aright.

'Making much money?' asked Val.

'No, but there's nothing to spend it on.'

'That's true. Not these days.'

'You must have had a pretty bad time of it up here in London,' observed Graham.

'It certainly hasn't been a picnic. Any bombing down your way?'

'Our only casualty has been a cow. I think they mistook us for Biggin Hill.'

'Now the bastards are turning their attention to the provinces. Swansea had a nasty time of it last night.'

'Is the damage serious?' It warmed Graham to talk again to someone important, a man who not only knew the inside story of the war but who, from the look of the room at least, might even affect the turn of the plot. 'I mean, taking the country as a whole.'

'It could be worse. They get the railways running again pretty smartly, and production all round has been hit much less than we feared. The U-boats are a stickier problem, between you and me. But civilian morale has stood up to it. It might have gone the other way, you know. Could have been panic, demands for peace. He confided in me he's genuinely relieved about that.'

64

'Who is?' asked Graham.

Val Arlott seemed surprised at the question. 'Churchill.' His look turned to annoyance as Graham gave a laugh. 'What's funny?'

'Nothing, Val, nothing.' The Captain Piles and Mrs Sedgewick-Smiths of Graham's new world shrank into their true inconsequence. 'I don't move in such circles, I'm afraid.'

'Geoff, fix up some drinks, will you?' ordered Val Arlott.

'Certainly, Val.'

When they were alone, Val asked Graham, 'How's your wife taking the war?'

'Maria wouldn't begin to understand. The clock of her mind stopped somewhere in the thirties.'

'I ran into her brother the other day.'

'The second Lord Cazalay?'

'Yes, God help us. There was some unpleasantness between the pair of you, I gather?'

'Yes. Cazalay and that fellow Haileybury were in it together, trying to get me struck off.'

'You mean about the actress? What's her name—Stella Garrod?'

Graham nodded. 'I'll concede that Haileybury moved against me through his usual high-mindedness or his hypocrisy—I've never really decided which it is. But I can't understand why Cazalay started him off. Through spite, I suppose.'

'Did you know he's got himself some sort of job in the censorship? Through the title, doubtless. I can't think of any other qualifications.'

'I wouldn't trust him even to deliver the morning post,' Graham said sourly.

'Yes, they're twisters, the Cazalays, all of them,' Val said amiably. 'Though it was sad about the father. To be reviled and ruined after enjoying power is bad enough. To face death in exile is heartbreaking. Even the sick rabbit can crawl back to its own burrow. I suppose it can all be forgotten now. Even the muddiest little eddies in our history have been submerged by the tidal wave. Not that I came out of the Cazalay crash badly,' he continued more cheerfully. 'I picked up his share of this paper dirt cheap. I suppose you've some pretty little girl tucked away there in the country?' he added.

'No.'

'You've turned over a new leaf? I don't believe it.'

'Let's say I haven't time. I'm worked off my feet, you know. I've a hell of a lot of worry. Particularly over one of your compatriots—Bluey Jardine.'

Val frowned. 'I wondered what had happened to him. He just dropped out of the news. Badly smashed up?'

'With patience on both sides and a couple of years I'll get him looking human.'

'Poor bastard.' Val rubbed his chin. 'How about our doing a story on your little show? I'd like to remind people about Bluey.'

Graham looked doubtful. 'Would anyone be interested? Plenty of men have suffered worse. And my boys aren't particularly pretty objects to come across in your morning paper.'

'Yes, people *would* be interested,' said Val decisively. 'We could send down Martha Raymond. Do you know Martha?'

'She wrote a bitterly unkind story about me and Stella Garrod in your gossip column before the war.'

Val shrugged his shoulders. 'These things happen. She's a game kid.'

Martha Raymond's physical courage matching the flintiness of her mind, she was then scaling cliffs with the newly raised Commandos, defusing unexploded parachute mines with the Royal Engineers, flying in the empty bomb-bay of Wellingtons with the R.A.F., or diving into the waters of Weymouth harbour with the Navy, all for the enlightenment and entertainment of Val Arlott's readers. But Graham wondered if even she would be game enough to drag a story from his patients.

'Geoff, what's Martha doing?' Val asked, as the editor reappeared.

'On an Army cookery course, Val.'

'Fix her to meet Graham when she's free.'

'Certainly, Val.'

66

'I hope my boys won't resent her,' said Graham doubtfully. 'They can be prickly with strangers.'

'Martha's a real professional, Graham. She can get round anyone. Like you.'

'Then I only hope the zips arrive first,' Graham added. 'Otherwise Bluey might feel inclined to provide the girl with rather too colourful copy.'

## 10

'I SEE GRAHAM'S getting up to his old tricks again,' remarked Denise Bickley, putting down her coffee cup.

'Eh? What's that? Old tricks? What old tricks?' Her host, Mr Claude Cramphorn, F.R.C.S., paused in lighting his pipe. 'He had plenty of them, as far as my memory serves.'

'Didn't you see this morning's *Press*, Crampers?'

Mr Cramphorn shook his head.

'There was an enormous article by some woman about the annex. Pictures and all. As a matter of fact,' she added casually, 'I happened to cut it out.'

Denise felt in her handbag and produced a strip of grey wartime newsprint, which she handed to her husband beside her on the sofa. 'It's wildly inaccurate, of course,' smiled John Bickley, passing the cutting on. 'The newspapers never seem to get anything right.'

Mr Cramphorn took it with a grunt. He was a fiery little surgeon given to pepper-and-salt suits, brown boots, half-moon glasses, briskly puffed pipes, and clipped sentences, a bachelor who had retired from the consultant staff of Blackfriars before the war to a farm which by chance lay within sight of the minarets of Smithers Botham. Nobody seemed to know how old he was, but no ageing general dug out to sit behind a ministry desk accepted his invitation to reactivity as eagerly as Mr Cramphorn—if he had ever been invited at all. When overlooked by the authorities at the beginning of the war, unlike Graham, who was inclined to take a neurotic view of every-

68

thing, Mr Cramphorn had simply ignored the slight. He had appeared on the Smithers Botham portico puffing his pipe, rubbing his hands, and declaring, 'Work to do? I'm willing and ready. Boys to teach? I'll teach 'em?' He marched in, discovered his old ward sister, herself recalled from helping a cousin run a boarding house at Bexhill, appropriated a dozen of the empty beds, and set up shop.

Mr Cramphorn did teach very well, the surgery of the First World War. He had lived through all the fashions. From the twenties, with short skirts and the surgical vogue of removing as many internal organs as possible compatible with the continuance of life, through the thirties with their padded shoulders and the enthusiastic tacking of floating kidneys, spleens, colons, and the like the more firmly into place, to the forties with their slacks and headscarves and 'septic foci'. Nobody knew exactly what these malevolent foci did, nor even what they were, but Mr Cramphorn removed them just the same.

It never crossed his mind to explain his methods to his patients, whom he treated as a well-mannered squire his tenants. To Mr Cramphorn a hospital was a charitable institution, and a man begging bread at your door had no business enquiring the ability of your baker. For a disgruntled sufferer to threaten litigation was to him as unthinkable as for his gardener to threaten joining his dinner-table. He was an individualist, and like the British generals facing up to the aeroplane, distrustful of such comparatively new-fangled devices as asepsis coming between himself and the pure exercise of his art. His gloved fingers often strayed absently during operations to the pocket of his pepper-and-salt trousers under his gown, to produce a large yellow handkerchief on which he would blow his nose. He frequently puffed his pipe over the scrubbing-up basin, laying it aside with his freshly sterilized hand. But whatever operation he performed, whatever its chances of doing good or ill (they stood about fifty-fifty), it was a superb piece of surgical handicraft. Mr Cramphorn was a real professional.

'H'm,' said Mr Cramphorn, finishing reading the cutting. He

liked the company of good-looking women, and had asked the Bickleys across that April evening for dinner. He had bagged a couple of precious rabbits, though he often complained the war had quite ruined the shooting. 'What d'you think of that, Pomfrey?'

He passed the cutting to the fourth sharer of the feast, a Blackfriars physician at Smithers Botham, Dr Paul Pomfrey, who observed mildly, 'I do hope it's nothing disgraceful.'

Dr Pomfrey was a distinguished elderly neurologist, a collector of butterflies, a player of the 'cello, an addict of crossword puzzles, his mind too fine a key to unlock such current mysteries as ration books, identity cards, and stirrup-pumps. He was under Mr Cramphorn's thumb through living with him. When the war started, Mr Cramphorn instructed his housekeeper to open his doors to the expectant mothers who arrived from London, much fortified by vicars and vitamins, but his brisk behaviour so induced fears of premature labour, the women were replaced by evacuee children—according to himself the nastiest available, through the billeting officer's personal spite. These guests, too, Mr Cramphorn was shortly relieved of, after insisting on treating their nits in the sheep-dip. Dr Pomfrey was conscripted to fill the spare room, and so put an end to such rude intrusions into a professional man's privacy.

'Oh dear,' added Dr Pomfrey, reading. 'We did have so much trouble with young Trevose at Blackfriars before the war. He always seemed to be getting into the papers. People must have gained the impression that plastic surgery was the only work our hospital was capable of.'

'It doesn't actually mention Graham by name,' said John, coming to his surgeon's defence.

'He'd be much too fly for that,' laughed Mr Cramphorn, puffing briskly.

' "This wonderful work",' Dr Pomfrey read out hollowly, "is being performed by the brilliant plastic surgery expert who gave hope and beauty to stage and society in London before the war". I suppose that would sink in with a good many people—eh, Crampers?'

70

'Of course, Graham *is* doing wonderful work,' admitted Denise. 'But I don't see why he should take all the credit. John comes home utterly exhausted most nights. Don't you, darling? And Tudor Beverley's rushed off his feet. Besides, there're plenty of others in the hospital who deserve being taken notice of. Quite as much as Graham. They haven't his flair for publicity, that's all. I met Babs Twelvetrees while I was buying the rations this morning, and she was dreadfully upset.'

She was the wife of Mr Alan Twelvetrees, a young Blackfriars consultant surgeon who had been invalided out of the Royal Army Medical Corps. He had expected to be treated at Smithers Botham as a returning hero, but was disconcerted to find himself resented as an intruder who hadn't suffered the earlier disorganization and inconveniences, to be given the worst wards, the surliest sisters, and the most awkward hours for operating.

'Graham didn't instigate the article,' John pointed out. 'The paper suggested it. They're always looking for odd corners of the war to write up. It's good for morale, I suppose, the more people read of what's being done.'

'You know perfectly well Graham would go to any lengths to get himself known,' his wife told him briskly.

'Mustn't give a dog a bad name, my dear,' Mr Cramphorn told her. 'Otherwise you can't blame him if he bites you.'

'I don't think Graham would bite anyone, Crampers,' she said. 'Of course he's utterly charming and such fun, and John and I love him. But he is so dreadfully weak. Look at those awful women who had him round their little fingers.'

'What do you think I should do, Crampers?' asked Dr Pomfrey helplessly. He asked Mr Cramphorn's opinion on everything. He was more under his thumb than ever at the time, through the surgeon teaching him to drive, which he performed as he operated, very fast and impatient of obstacles. After Dr Pomfrey's chauffeur had been called up the motor-car presented him with severer difficulties than the most elusive neurological diagnosis, the physician driving across lawns and flower-beds, on the wrong side of the road, and frequently within inches of Captain Pile. 'Perhaps you'd care to take it up with Graham?' he suggested hopefully.

'Not me,' said Mr Cramphorn. He disliked being drawn into the animosities of others. He had enough in the hospital of his own, complaining almost daily to Captain Pile about the quality of everything from the operating equipment to the food, and appearing regularly in his office with the shepherd's pie. 'Why don't you have a friendly word in his ear, John? You're nearest to him.'

John Bickley tried to find an excuse, but Dr Pomfrey looked at his watch and hastily switched on the wireless. The nine o'clock news brought an end to the conversation, as it did to almost every other in the country.

John had his friendly word with Graham in the annex the following morning. His wife had insisted on it. But Graham only laughed and said, 'Well, I half expected something like this. Who's kicking up the fuss?'

'Pomfrey, in his own sort of way. And a few of the others.'

'Twelvetrees, I'll bet?' John said nothing. 'Will they never learn? Things are so different now. There's no one to benefit except the boys. It cheered them up, someone taking an interest in them, particularly a pretty girl. Though God knows I deserve some sort of encouragement. I haven't had much since the war started.'

'I know all that, of course, Graham. But you must be aware how sticky the others can be about publicity.'

'I don't give a damn.' They were standing outside the wash-house, and Graham started towards the ward. 'I cared little enough in peacetime what my professional brethren thought of me. Now I don't care at all. Anyway, they've a nice surprise in store. As a result of the article, that American fellow's coming down—what's his name, always being photographed in a tin hat coming out of shelters? Hugo Kirkham. His stuff's syndicated right across the States, and they aren't coy over there about hushing up the doctors' names. A nice little flutter that'll cause when the cuttings get back here.' Graham began to sound annoyed. 'I'm not trying to attract attention to myself. I'm

72

trying to attract attention to the annex, which is quite a different thing.'

Anxious to change the conversation, John asked, 'Are you going to have a look at that fellow with the post-operative chest?'

'Later, old man, if that's all right?' Graham excused himself hastily. 'I've got to have a word with sister.'

Sister Mills occupied a partitioned office the size of a largish cupboard beside the ward door. She had been on the unit for three months, and Graham was astounded at her success. She seemed to have the right touch with unruly patients. There was less drunkenness, less swearing, fewer nurses asking for transfers. Even Bluey seemed to be behaving himself. Graham felt smugly gratified at the perspicacity of his choice. On the mornings when he wasn't operating, he exercised his prerogative as 'The Chief' by taking with her a cup of the tasteless khaki liquid passing at Smithers Botham for coffee. He was not usually one for fraternizing with his nursing staff. He generally treated them brusquely, partly through fussiness over the smallest details of treatment, and partly as a defence reaction. For the sake of his patients he tried to fill his wards with the prettiest girls going, and though some of them fired his imagination, particularly in his present monkish existence, he was careful to avoid any entanglements. He didn't care to foul his own doorstep. Besides, he was something of a sexual snob. The man who before the war had got himself into bed with Stella Garrod might find the joys of common-or-garden girls something of a come-down. And anyway, he told himself sharply, he was getting far too old for them.

'You look in a mood,' Sister Mills smiled, as Graham squeezed himself into the spare chair.

'It's a passing irritation. Some of the others are grousing about that article yesterday. They still can't forgive me for getting my name in the papers before the war.'

She handed him a thick chipped cup and said, 'Yes, I remember reading some of the things they said about you.'

'I hope they were nice things. Many of them weren't. But you

73

must have been only an impressionable schoolgirl at the time.'

It always put him in a better humour talking to Sister Mills. And he noticed she had become less solemn, less nervous of him. A sympathetic ear was a luxury when he was expected to bear the troubles of everyone in the annex.

'My father was always interested in your activities,' she told him.

'Is he a doctor?' He had never asked about her background before.

'No, he's a commercial artist. Not a particularly successful one, I'm afraid to say. Now he's working for the Ministry of Aircraft Production.'

'I used to paint at week-ends before the war. I don't think I was much good at it. I used to delude myself it was based on the same principles as my surgery. But it isn't. My job's more like plumbing, really. Whatever the look of the result, everything's got to join up the right way underneath.'

'Your own father was at Blackfriars, wasn't he?'

'Yes, the formidable old boy was the professor of anatomy,' Graham said fondly. 'He wrote an erudite volume about the synovial membranes, so erudite that only about fifty people in the country understood it. We've always been doctors of a sort. My grandfather was a semi-educated bonesetter. My great-grandfather wasn't educated at all, but an out-and-out quack. He left a fortune. He could diagnose everything known to medical science, and a good deal that wasn't, by merely inspecting the patient's urine in a flask. What's called a piss-prophet.'

She smiled. 'Quite a weight of medical tradition to carry.'

'The family business, I suppose. My son Desmond's going in for it. You must meet him when he comes down from Cambridge. He stays with me at the pub, and I let him mess about here trying his hand at being anything from assistant anaesthetist to theatre porter. You'll like him. He's a charmer.'

'I'm sure I shall. I'll look forward to it.'

Graham fell silent. He had a vague uneasiness about men-

74

tioning Desmond. 'The fuss about the newspaper will soon blow over,' he went on.

'*We*'re proud of you on the unit, anyway.'

' "The Wizz".' He laughed and got up. 'If I'm making a reputation I'd better live up to it, by doing some work. I've got to see a pneumonia John Bickley's inflicted. The fellow uses far too much ether.'

Despite his protestations, the realist in Graham admitted readily enough that he enjoyed recapturing the glory of print. He was an exhibitionist in a neurotically self-effacing profession, and finding himself so long in a surgical backwater where nobody was inclined to wander had been galling. But it was more gratifying still to find the article reviving Val Arlott's twenty-years-old interest in plastic surgery. He telephoned asking if Graham lacked equipment, promising to jolt action out of the authorities. The longed-for extra huts seemed at last likely to appear. Val even suggested a fund to provide the annex with 'comforts'—an excellent idea, Graham thought, it would keep the place in the public eye for months. But the best news of all was Peter Thomas becoming engaged to marry one of the nurses. He still looked a mess, but there he was, to marry in the merry month of May. It put up morale in the annex wonderfully. If a girl could sleep with Peter Thomas looking like that, Bluey declared, then he was off to pick up a bloody harem.

The wedding was to be at Chelsea registry office on May the twelfth, a Monday. On the Saturday night London had its last bad raid of the war, and an unexpected guest, Rudolph Hess, floated by parachute into Scotland. While the Deputy Führer's fractured ankle was being attended by a British military doctor, a younger German flier, steadfastly doing his duty above the Thames, made a mistake in his bomb-aiming and blew most of Blackfriars Hospital to pieces. Luckily, the casualties were light, the patients being at Smithers Botham and the wooden props in the basement being stronger than everyone gloomily believed. But the firemen were still working thirty-six hours later, when Graham stood with a carnation in his buttonhole

75

soulfully inspecting the wreckage before making across battered London to the registry office. The Arlott Wing, where he had worked before the war, had simply disappeared. The rest of the building, which he could remember standing in apparently unshakeable dignity when his father had shown it off as a childhood treat, was a hardly recognizable ruin. But the pavements were still busy. The bowler hat was still worn. The tramlines still ran down the Embankment. London had shrugged off fire and plague before. The smashed eighteenth-century masonry was a shame, but what was the loss of the most splendid building, he asked himself, compared with that of the most miserable of lives?

'Graham—'

He turned. He didn't recognize her for a moment. She was small and gingery, with a scarf round her head, staring at him.

'Sheila Raleigh—' he held out his hand, smiling. 'How's Tom?'

'Didn't you hear? He was killed.' He looked blank, hand outstretched and untaken. She bit her lip. 'In Greece. He was one of the last.'

'Sheila, what can I say—'

'Don't say anything, Graham. Please don't.'

'But Sheila, I'm so dreadfully sorry. It's a terrible shock. I mean, Tom was my houseman, my registrar, my partner. We worked together for ten years. He was such a wonderful chap.'

'Then why didn't you keep him?' she demanded savagely. 'If you'd wanted, he'd be safe with you now in the country. But you didn't. You rejected him. Because you really hated him. Because you were jealous of him. Because he wasn't of use to you any more. That's the truth, isn't it? Now you know exactly what you've done.'

For a moment Graham could say nothing. 'How can you accuse me of that?' he managed to ask weakly. 'It isn't right, you know. It just isn't true at all. Honestly, I'm heartbroken at the news. Surely there's something I can do to help? For the children? Isn't there anything? If there's some sort of assistance I can give, financial assistance—'

'I wouldn't take a penny from a murderer.'

She shrugged her shoulders, turned, and abruptly walked off. Graham watched her disappear, picking her way among the fire-hoses.

The wedding was to Graham as joyless as a funeral. He found it impossible to be even faintly amiable afterwards. He pleaded work, and drove straight back to Smithers Botham. He knew that everything Sheila said was perfectly correct. To come face to face with his old self was harrowing. Things had so changed. Or had they? His egotism and jealousy, which had cost poor Tom his partnership and then his life, he supposed must still be in his system somewhere. Perhaps he was merely redirecting them to temporarily more acceptable ends, like some thug given a rifle and praised for killing Germans? Was it too much to hope he really was becoming a better sort of man? How could he tell? There was no one near enough to ask.

At Smithers Botham he made for his office. He had to find some work, anything to occupy himself, to stop his self-inflicted mental wounds. He paused in the doorway, surprised to find Sister Mills at his desk. Then he remembered he'd asked her to collect case reports of something—what was it? Maxillary fractures. He was about to ask her to go when she noticed his face and jumped up, exclaiming, 'What's the matter? Was it something in the blitz?'

He shut the door behind him.

'I killed a man,' he said wearily. 'Unwittingly and indirectly, but I killed him. Tom Raleigh— did I ever mention him? He was my partner. We had a row. He should have been working with me out here on the unit. I wouldn't take him. So instead, he was killed in Greece.'

He sat in a chair by the desk.

'I'm so sorry,' said Sister Mills quietly. 'It must have been terrible news.'

'Particularly as I got it from his widow. Who knew exactly what the facts were.' He stretched out his legs. 'She told me what she thought of me. She was perfectly right. To her, I

77

couldn't be anything but the vilest and wickedest creature in the world.'

'She'd be feeling emotional. She let her tongue run away with her.'

'I'd like to think so. But my whole life before the war doesn't stand much examination.'

'Doesn't it? You brought a lot of happiness to people.'

'At a price.'

'Well, why not?' she asked simply. 'What is the price of happiness?'

'Anyway, I didn't give a damn about the happiness. Only the guineas.'

'That's quite impossible to believe. Not after all I've seen here.'

He sat staring in front of him. Then he noticed she was crying.

'I must apologize.' He got up abruptly. 'All these troubles I've brought back are upsetting you. I shouldn't have mentioned them. I've no right asking you to share them.'

'I'm crying for you,' she told him. 'You're so much the nicest person in the world, and you fight so terribly hard against it.'

Then he had her in his arms, and she was kissing him with a passion even he found exciting.

Meanwhile, Mrs Sedgewick-Smith was holding another of her regular Monday afternoon tea-parties. She had told Stephanie severely that she mustn't keep crossing her legs like that. After all, she was really getting quite a big girl.

## 11

ON SUNDAY MORNINGS Graham would lie in bed, reading the papers, *Picture Post*, the *Strand Magazine*, a novel, anything unconnected with the annex. It was only the bad doctor, he reflected, who killed himself to cure his patients.

By that November Sunday of 1942 the posters in the Smithers Botham entrance hall had changed from the ringing warning YOUR FREEDOM IS IN PERIL to the more sophisticated COUGHS AND SNEEZES SPREAD DISEASES and IS YOUR JOURNEY REALLY NECESSARY? The place was by then more than simply a hospital. It was another of the countless closed communities stretching across the globe from Spitzbergen to the Falklands, all more interested in themselves than in the war which had fathered them. There was always something going on there. The fashion of the times provided the staff with bountiful opportunity for self-expression, self-examination, and self-instruction, with dramatics and debating, brains trusts of varying trustworthiness, lectures on everything from Britain's War Aims to Milk Production, plus E.N.S.A., A.B.C.A., and I.T.M.A. Conversation in the long corridors never lacked an interesting case or an interesting scandal. The housemen continued to entertain the nurses. The matron continued to entertain doubts.

The war had swept a remarkable assortment of illnesses and injuries into the vast wards. It was an Aladdin's cave of clinical medicine, if only the students had bothered to rub the lamp of learning. There were special units for surgery of the head, the chest, the limbs, and the arteries, created not through the benevolence of some millionaire but through the malevolence of Adolf Hitler. Its beds contained Free French, Free Poles, Free Norwegians, Free Dutch, Free Czechs, and unfree Germans (who made model patients, there being nothing like several years' Nazi indoctrination for fitting in with the ideas of an old-fashioned British ward sister). Captain Pile was still there, and still a captain. Corporal Honeyman was still there, and still a corporal. Dr Pomfrey, after a baffled half-hour with his car at full throttle, unaware that his rear bumper was enmeshed in the stout railings of the coal store, had decided to settle for a second-hand bicycle. But to anyone who read the newspapers, Smithers Botham in 1942 was the place where a man called Graham Trevose performed his miracles.

The annex was no longer a sideshow but one of the busiest surgical units in the country. The huts in the grounds had doubled and the staff had trebled. Graham was receiving more patients from the R.A.F. than he could handle. His work had attracted surgeons—and journalists with their photographers— from every Allied nation, even the Russians. Women in fish-queues could talk to each other about Graham Trevose. Every morning brought a letter or two, generally badly written and spelt, with a few shillings towards the comforts fund. Graham thought this the most rewarding recognition of all. And it had all started because he had gone to Val Arlott seeking some zips for trousers.

An unaccustomed sound crept across the misty morning. Church bells in the distance. For more than two years these accompaniments of Christian joys and sorrows had been silenced, reserved by the Government to herald not the coming of the Lord but of the German armies.

'Listen.' Graham slipped his hands between his head and the pillow. 'I remember in the last war they rang the bells after Cambrai. It was when we used tanks for the first time, and broke the German lines. In a week or two we were back where we started, of course. It always seemed the case in those days. Let's hope this Alamein affair is more permanent.'

Clare Mills slipped her hand into the jacket of his pyjamas, which were pure silk, prewar, made to measure in Jermyn Street. The poor lamb really was terribly thin. It was like being in bed with a skeleton beside you. 'Happy?'

'This is probably a terrible confession, but the war's been the happiest time of my life.'

'Is it so terrible?' she asked gently. 'Surely the misery needn't go undiluted?'

'I suppose happiness is a well-insulated state of mind. Most of the boys are perfectly happy, and God knows they haven't got much to justify it. Even Bluey seems happy enough these days.'

'Perhaps he's found a new girl-friend.' She ran her hand down Graham's chest. It was so smooth, the ribs standing out like the black notes on a piano. No wonder he'd once suffered from tuberculosis.

'Why do I attract you?' he asked.

She pouted thoughtfully. 'You're different. From any other surgeon.'

'Different from old Cramphorn, you mean?'

Clare laughed. 'You're gentle, you're amusing, you're kind, you understand women. And I love you. Besides, you had a tremendous build-up. I'd read so much about you. It's like being with a star you've only seen on the flicks.'

'Don't tell me I've got to match up to Clark Gable?' he asked, though feeling flattered.

She touched his small hard nipple with the tip of her fore-finger. 'Tell me why I attract *you*.'

'You're a good housewife.'

'I thought that was it.'

'Do you realize, darling, this is the first time in my life I've had a home I could call my own? I mean a place where I could do as I pleased, without it being run by a lot of servants. Where I didn't feel I had to put on a show, to impress the world with my importance.' He looked round the room, which was hardly big enough to take the bed. The beige wallpaper had galleons sailing across it, a fumed-oak dressing table was squeezed into a corner, there were faded pink curtains, an angular hanging mirror, and a coloured print of Tower Bridge, pre-blitz. They lived in a bungalow, rented furnished in the country some ten miles from Smithers Botham, with four small rooms and a kitchen, a bath with an alarming geyser, and the name of 'Cosy Cot'.

Graham felt he would have been happy with Clare even living in a Nissen hut. She shared his new liking for books and for the concerts on the wireless. She cooked agreeably and mended his clothes with her painstaking nurse's stitches. He had enjoyed himself teaching her to dress properly, pulling her out of those awful tweeds and putting her into frocks, though the fun had been officially dimmed by the coming of clothes' rationing. She was the most adoring woman he had known, which he sometimes wryly reflected accounted for their harmony. They had always the annex to fall back on as a common interest, Graham insisting she continued with her job, declaring the ward would fall into anarchy otherwise. As for their other common interest, Graham decided she enjoyed a greater talent than any woman he had met for copulation, with all its ancillaries, which he was apt to describe as 'novelties'.

As the church bells died away he said, 'You've given me something to live for, darling. A unique gift.'

'You always had your work.'

'Only a fool or a saint lives for his vocation. Do you know, before you came along I was the prey to horrible and gloomy thoughts. Doom, impending death, extinction. Most uncomfortable. Such things don't even enter my mind now. You've exorcised the ghosts. Perhaps the magic charm is finding myself with a girl of your age. Or perhaps it's just the flattery.'

She gently kissed his unshaven cheek. 'It isn't flattery.'

'Is the distinction important? At my age, flattery's a workable substitute for love.'

'Now you're being silly.'

'Yes, I hope I am.' He looked up at the ceiling, which had a large crack running across it. 'Do you think we should have another week at that place in Wales?'

'They were awfully awkward about our identity cards.'

'They might have grown more accustomed to such irregularities by now.'

He had taken her to a village hotel, remembered from before the war, for what he liked to remember as their honeymoon. Their first sudden contact in the office, the day he had met Sheila Raleigh, he told himself was like the unexpected symptom of some smouldering disease. He had been attracted to Clare almost since setting eyes on her. But he was immediately disconcerted to discover there was another—a Royal Marine lieutenant, stationed in India, to whom she was unofficially pledged. Graham declared to himself hastily that any monkey business was out of the question. Her lieutenant was abroad in the service of his country, like the Crusades, exactly the same principle. A man of his own standing couldn't possibly stoop to such things. But he wondered how strong the psychological chastity belt was. It might be fun to try the lock. In the end it sprang open with an ease which surprised both of them, the severest difficulty being the locale. His house in Mayfair was bomb-damaged beyond habitation, and he could hardly smuggle Clare upstairs in the pub like one of the students. It occurred to him he hadn't taken a holiday since the war started. Afterwards, she declared she couldn't possibly go back to the nurses' home. In a place like Smithers Botham, everyone would know of their adventure. The other sisters were unkindly enough already, and anyway had a tendency to kiss each other good-night. They moved into Cosy Cot, and she wrote to her Royal Marine, a dreaded epistle known as a 'Dear John'.

The rest of the Smithers Botham staff thought sharing a bungalow with your ward sister rather rich, even for Graham. He didn't care. It never occurred to him to ask if Clare did. Denise Bickley was particularly outraged, about which Graham cared even less. In peacetime, Graham's goodwill represented a large slice of her husband's income, and Graham reflected grimly the war couldn't go on for ever. As for Clare's parents, who lived in Bristol, they were gratified to learn from her letters that their daughter had moved from the hospital to comfortable and apparently altogether satisfactory lodgings.

83

'Why don't we have our own celebration of the victory in the Desert?' Graham asked her from the pillow. 'We're alone in the house, no one's likely to call and disturb us.'

Clare laughed and got out of bed, throwing back her blonde hair and starting to take off her red-and-yellow spotted cotton pyjamas. She really had an admirable figure, Graham reflected. Her breasts were wonderful. He couldn't have made anything better himself.

'Must I keep using this toothpaste stuff?' she asked, squatting to insert her diaphragm.

'My God, yes,' said Graham hastily. 'It's terribly risky without the spermicidal jelly. All that cap does is to hold it round the cervix.'

'It's awfully messy.'

'You can't have everything, my love,' he told her, a shade primly.

'And I shall have to keep it in half the day, won't I? It'll give me backache.'

'I'll sit rubbing it with Sloan's liniment.'

She laughed again, and came back to him.

In the sexual line Graham was, as Haileybury would have put it, an enthusiast. After all, he told himself, he had a deep knowledge of the apparatus concerned, and he might as well put the information to fullest use. He often recalled with satisfaction Balzac's exhortation for no man to marry before dissecting at least one female pelvis. But he could never bring himself to feel the business more than 'a sneeze in the loins'. It was only a reflex, centred in the humblest lower segments of the spinal cord, transmitted across the pelvic basin by fibres hiding under their Latinized name 'the nerve of shame'. Even a real sneeze was a more cerebral occurrence, conducted by fine-sounding aristocratic nerves springing out of the brain itself. Of course, women took a different view. However many men sneezed in their loins, they invested it with some mystical significance. He supposed it was mainly through their fear of appearing tarts.

'You look sad,' she said teasingly afterwards.

84

'Do I? It's physiological after an orgasm. Isn't there a classical tag? Though the single one I can remember is *calor, rubor, tumor, dolor*, and that's only inflammation.'

She ran the tip of her finger round his umbilicus. 'That's a strange thing we have.'

'It's only a cicatrix, a scar.'

'What's inside it?'

'Nothing. The remains of the blood-vessels which fed us before we were born.'

'It's quite pretty, really, like a flower. A budding rose.'

'Most are like cabbages.'

Her hand slipped down to his penis, off duty in the at-ease position. 'It's full of tissue like a sponge, isn't it? I remember from our anatomy lectures. It was awfully funny, the sister-tutor was a terribly dried-up old thing. She told us all about an erection, with diagrams on the blackboard, as though she was talking about the moon. She could never have seen one in her life.'

'It's a really most interesting organ. The arteries dilate enormously, quite unlike any others in the body.'

'It must be fascinating to have one.'

'According to the psychiatrists, all women think so. Penis-envy. Though quite where that interesting discovery gets us, I don't know.'

'Did all your women want one?' He felt this reference, under the circumstances, in rather bad taste, and said nothing. 'Have you had an awful lot of women, Graham?'

'You know I'm a married man.' As she gave a small pout he went on, 'My sex life with Maria pretty well ended with the honeymoon. You could hardly blame me for seeking out others, particularly when she went off her head. But none of them meant anything, not one.'

'Not even Stella Garrod?'

'Particularly Stella Garrod.'

'How about Edith?'

'That's rather going into ancient history,' he said quickly.

'Graham, darling, perhaps I'd better give up the annex.'

85

'Unthinkable!'

'Staff-nurse Jones could easily take over. She's awfully good with the boys.'

'But why this sudden change of heart? I thought you liked the work. You'd get bored all day here.'

'I haven't used the toothpaste once or twice. I didn't think it would matter. I haven't seen anything now for a fortnight. Of course, it may be perfectly all right. Just a delayed period.'

His large eyes stared at her across the pillow.

'If it isn't all right, will you be pleased?' she asked timidly. 'No, don't answer. Wait till we know.' She kissed him and got out of bed abruptly. 'It's Sunday. That means fried eggs for lunch. Something lovely to look forward to, isn't it?'

## 12

TO FIND HIMSELF confronted with fatherhood on a second occasion filled Graham with the same numb shock as on the first, almost exactly twenty-two years previously. With Maria, their sexual endeavours were so beset with difficulties he somehow felt her reproductive system too inefficient for conception. With Clare, he had put a touching faith in science. As usual, the human element had let him down. It was the same in the annex, when they got a run of infection after the nurses forgot to sterilize the needles properly in carbolic.

Monday was Mr Tim O'Rory's day at Smithers Botham. Graham caught the gynaecologist at lunch in the medical officers' mess and invited him for a stroll on the lawn.

'It's Clare,' he said, once out of earshot. 'I think she's pregnant.'

'Well, now,' said Mr O'Rory. A thick-set, dark-haired, red-faced, humorous Irishman, he looked kindly on feminine failings through his heavily rimmed glasses and seemed to find them an endless source of innocent merriment. 'And what gives rise to this little suspicion?'

'She's a fortnight overdue. She's always been as regular as clockwork before. Of course, it might be a chill, something like that, mightn't it?'

'Sitting on a damp park bench, doctor?' Mr O'Rory chuckled. 'Maybe so.'

'You don't think that's a possibility?'

'You know my low mind, Graham. Any woman outside a

nunnery, who misses a period between the ages of fifteen and fifty, must be assumed pregnant until proved otherwise. And I'm not so sure about the nunnery these days, either.'

Graham was in no mood for professional pleasantries. 'Can you do a test in the lab?' he asked irritatedly.

'I will certainly invoke the assistance of a small frog, Graham, if you want. I'll be needing a specimen of the lady's urine.'

'I've got one in the car.'

'But don't get too alarmed,' Mr O'Rory added amiably. 'The lady may have made a mistake in her dates. It's remarkable how unreliable the feminine gender is at its fundamental calculations.'

The telephone at Cosy Cot rang the following evening.

'That was Tim,' said Graham, putting down the receiver. 'It's on.'

Clare turned her eyes back to her sewing. Graham stuck his hands in his pockets and stood in the middle of the small sitting-room, which was filled with books, medical journals, files of notes, photographs of his patients, and had a coloured picture of Bubbles over the fireplace.

'It's wonderful news, isn't it?' he declared.

She looked up again. 'Are you sure you want it?'

'But of course I do! As long as you do?'

'More than anything.'

Graham perched on the edge of her chair and put his arm round her tightly. So, he thought, one of my wriggling little spermatozoa has threshed with its hair-like tail across the black mucoid depths of Clare's pelvis, to sink itself joyfully into the speck of jelly comprising her ovum. The stark object of the most fashionable wedding, with all its elaborate trimmings of an ecclesiastical, legal, floral, and emotional nature, had been simply achieved. No trouble at all. The human race really did surround itself with a lot of fuss over its reproduction. Clare wondered what he was going to say. At least he'd declared he wanted the child, she thought. She didn't dare to question whether he really meant it. Living with Graham, she rarely dared to question whether he really meant anything.

88

'There'll be a terrible lot of practical details to settle,' Graham announced.

He immediately threw himself vigorously into solving the varied problems set by the new pregnancy. He decided Clare must leave the annex at once. Staff-nurse Jones could enjoy unexpected promotion, he must find someone to succeed the girl as staff-nurse. Appointments must be made with Mr O'Rory. Specimens must be collected. A woman must be sought to help in the bungalow. They would go away for the holiday in Wales, it would do Clare good. Her ration-book must be exchanged at the Food Office for a pregnant woman's green one. Extra milk and vitamins must be applied for, with a dozen Government forms. Pregnancy struck Graham as a highly complicated item of official business. It had been so much simpler last time. Which reminded him, he really must do something about Maria.

Graham had been meaning to do something about Maria for over a year. But there had always seemed a last-minute snag. Whenever he steeled himself to start instructing his lawyers there was somehow a rush of work in the annex, keeping his mind occupied for weeks. The solicitors had anyway been bombed out of the City, and re-established themselves at some inaccessible address near Southend-on-Sea. There seemed then no urgency. Clare appeared perfectly content with their arrangement. Graham couldn't see how ten minutes in a registry office would make the slightest difference to the pair of them. Or perhaps, he sometimes suspected, he still had his lingering reluctance about disowning Maria for good. Or perhaps . . . perhaps he was afraid of committing himself wholly to Clare? It was too difficult to think about, and the problems of the annex came first. Clare certainly raised the topic of a divorce. He felt it only to be expected, but she never harped on it for long. It never occurred to Graham that she saw how much it distressed him, nor that her silence was the expression of her terror of losing him.

But now the solicitors were written to. A divorce was imperative, the wheels of the law must be geared to the rapid

89

process of reproductive physiology. The solicitors wrote back with a promise of doing their best, explaining the Court would doubtless be sympathetic, but there were innumerable difficulties in wartime. He fixed a visit to Southend for the end of the month. He also agreed at last to see Clare's parents in Bristol. It was a glum prospect, even his charm might not prove an antidote to all unpleasantness, particularly as Mr Mills was hardly older than himself. Besides, a journey in the crowded, slow, and foodless wartime trains would be terrible.

First of all he must put matters to his son Desmond.

Something seemed to have gone wrong with Desmond. At Cambridge he had taken a fair degree in Part I of his Tripos, stayed on a year to breathe the rarefied academic atmosphere of the Part II, and done rather badly. From a gay if self-centred schoolboy he was turning into a reticent and solemn young man, wearing a dignity as unfitting for his years as a middle-age spread. He was even something of a prig. When he had left Cambridge that summer to start his three years' clinical course at Smithers Botham, Graham had assumed he would move in with them at Cosy Cot. But Desmond was reluctant. He suggested it might somehow hold him up to ridicule, particularly in the eyes of his cousin Alec, Edith's child, who was arriving to study at Smithers Botham the same autumn. Desmond arranged to live in the hospital itself, as one of the dozen-strong students' 'Emergency Squad' under the direct orders of Captain Pile—though for what emergency this squad was held in readiness, and how it would tackle it when it arose, everyone had long ago forgotten.

Graham dismissed all this as the self-dramatization to which the young were so distressingly liable. Desmond had probably been mixing with the wrong sort of people at college. Though perhaps the son's disinterest was partly the father's fault, Graham admitted. He had never taken overmuch care in Desmond's upbringing. Before the war he was too busy making money and amusing himself. During it he was too busy with the annex. Anyway, the lad seemed to step along confidently enough by himself. But now there was another factor. The war would certainly be grinding along in 1945, when Desmond was due to qualify, to sweep him with the others into the medical branches of the Forces. Why, he might even find himself under the orders of Haileybury! Somehow, Graham determined, he must get the young man into the Navy.

Graham set the scene of Desmond's enlightenment carefully. He had anyway been remiss about standing the boy treats. He made the effort of booking a couple of stalls for *Blithe Spirit*— as Russians were then being bombed instead of Britons, a seat in a London theatre was as hard to come by as a seat in a long-distance express. After the show they went to an Italian restaurant in Soho. In the first black nights of the war Graham had sometimes cheered himself up there by toasting Allied victory in Chianti at the insistence of the proprietor, who by 1942 had been caged up for a couple of years in the Isle of Man. But the elderly head waiter remembered him, and even laid the establishment open to immediate prosecution by letting them consume not only soup and chicken but a slice of fish as well.

Over the meal, they talked about their work. Now Desmond was growing up in medicine, Graham could enjoy the singular satisfaction of a medical parent in watching his child emerge as a professional colleague. They met often enough at Smithers Botham on perfectly easy terms, though coming to talk less of personal things than their cases, or to dissect the characters, abilities, and errors of the other consultants.

'Anything interesting in the annex at the moment, Dad?' Desmond asked across their corner table in the restaurant.

'A lot of oddments. The by-products of the war, mostly. There's a man from the Desert who gave himself a rub-down with petrol—they're short of water, you understand. Then the idiot lit a cigarette. He was an awful mess. There's a naval rating who was working in the engine-room of a destroyer when some fool turned on the superheated steam. Tragic cases. There's not much glory in being run over by your own tank. Anyway, war's a horrible business.'

'Are you getting sick of it?'

'I've never had time to pause and think. I suppose when I get back to bobbing noses, it'll be a relief knowing the patients' real suffering is only in the pocket.' Graham added after a moment, 'Sometimes it's difficult for me to realize our present highly abnormal form of life won't go on for ever. I suppose the same goes for all our generals.'

'Do you expect a lot of changes after the war?'

'I can tell you one.' Graham picked up his small glass of sloe gin, doing wartime duty for cognac. 'I'm going to obtain a divorce from your mother.'

Desmond considered this for some moments. 'That comes as something of a surprise, I must say. After all this time.'

'But surely my decision doesn't mean much to you, does it?' Graham asked, rather over-anxiously. 'Your mother's been ill for so long. You were only a child when she first had to go into hospital. You can hardly remember her when she was . . . well, as she used to be.'

Desmond said nothing. Graham wondered what Maria would be like had she kept her wits and her money. Doing something energetic in the war, doubtless. She was always the busy type.

'She's a complete wreck of her former self,' Graham added. 'Only I can appreciate the change.'

'She's not in very good shape, admittedly.'

'That's a mild way of putting it, Desmond. I assure you it makes not the slightest difference to your mother if I remain her husband or not. The whole conception of marriage is far beyond her ability to grasp. She's certified, you understand—certified as insane. Of course, I'll see she's looked after. Just as I do now. She'll stay in that home in comfort until the end of her days.'

'But *why*, Dad?' Desmond looked more solemn than ever. 'Why this sudden decision?'

'Because I'm going to marry Clare. Surely you must have expected that?'

'No. Not really. I didn't think you felt it necessary.'

'It's decidedly necessary,' said Graham, nettled by the remark. 'Clare's pregnant.'

Desmond stared at him.

'It's going to call for a measure of mental readjustment in both of us,' Graham continued. 'But it's a demonstrable fact.

The embryo has been created. Your baby half-brother or sister already exists, ectoderm, endoderm, mesoderm, yolk-sac, amnion, the lot. Two or three millimetres long, snug in the mucosa of Clare's uterus. We can't get away from that.'

'What's Alec going to say?'

'Why do you always bother what Alec's going to say?' Graham asked irritably.

'He's always trying to get some sort of hold over me. He's got a nasty tongue when he likes.'

'I'm sure you can cope with Alec.'

'It's bad enough his taking my money.'

'I'm certainly not going into that again now,' Graham told him promptly. 'If the cost of his education is coming from your trust fund, it was the least I could do for both the family and for Aunt Edith.'

Alec's father, the medical missionary, had maintained that the rewards of his vocation were to be found not in this world but the next, where presumably he had been enjoying them for seven years since dying, flat broke, in Malaya.

'Anyway, it's only a loan,' Graham pointed out. 'Alec's supposed to pay it all back once he's qualified. In the end you'll be no worse off.'

'What do you suppose Aunt Edith is going to say about your marrying again?'

Graham raised his eyebrows. That delicate little complication hadn't occurred to him. 'Desmond, I'm afraid I've got to go ahead with this divorce. I hope you'll come to see it as the right step.'

'I only see it as being rather hard on mother.'

'That's ridiculous.' Graham became angry. 'You know perfectly well most of the time your mother hasn't even the first idea who I am.'

'Still, she is my mother. I feel sorry for her.'

He really had little affection for his mother. But he was desperately frightened about doing the 'wrong thing'. He was becoming aware of inner forces which could drive him along the same devious paths as his father, and *that* must be avoided

93

at all costs. Graham's life had already made his son an easy target for ridicule, not only from Alec but from any of the other students disposed to a bit of ragging. For security he must fly into conventionality.

'Now you're just being pompous,' said Graham curtly. Desmond turned red, and Graham rebuked himself. He'd been too savage. Desmond was really very young, and confused with the ways of the world. Just as he had been himself at the same age. 'Come, Desmond,' he added more kindly. 'Try and adjust yourself. Clare won't be more to you than a stepmother in name. She'll be terribly tactful. I promise you that. You'll come to like her tremendously.'

Desmond hesitated, and said, 'I think I prefer to make up my own mind about people, Dad.'

Graham called for the bill. Desmond really could be terribly difficult when he wanted. Just like Maria.

Everyone at Smithers Botham seemed to know about the baby from its conception. Graham had confided in John Bickley, and he supposed Denise had spread the news with enthusiasm. Crampers had grunted something at him—congratulatory, Graham hoped. Even Captain Pile had made the point of repeating that no woman whatever was permitted to give birth within the hospital's glass-topped walls. Graham didn't care about the notoriety. He rather enjoyed it. He told himself more forcibly every day he was delighted with their child. A young life, something to perpetuate himself right to the end of the century, was an anodyne for any painfully intruding ideas about death and extinction. He could have no possible reservations about it whatever, he decided. And it would be wonderful for Clare. He treated her with the greatest tenderness, physical and mental. As for the effect on the mother-to-be of her circumstances in general, and her standing in the eyes of everybody at Smithers Botham in particular, it never crossed his mind to enquire.

All this happened in the busy fortnight following the Sunday when they rang the church bells. Then he had a letter from the Ministry terminating his contract at the annex.

94

## 13

'I WANT TO SEE Brigadier Haileybury,' said Graham to the
sergeant in the hall. 'My name's Trevose. I'm a surgeon. The
brigadier knows me well.'

'Have you an appointment, sir?'

'No. But I'm aware that he's in the building and I don't intend to leave until he gives me an interview.'

The sergeant looked uneasy. The wild-eyed civilian seemed
an unlikely crony of the austere brigadier. 'If you'll wait here,
sir, I can but pass on your message.'

'Please do.'

He left Graham alone in the hall, which like the inside of all
requisitioned houses had bare walls and floor, was furnished
with trestle-tables and fire-extinguishers, and had the decorations badly knocked about. Haileybury now held sway in a
country mansion fronting the River Itchen south of Winchester,
in preparation for the 'Second Front', Graham supposed,
whenever that might be established. Within a minute the sergeant came clattering down the oak staircase, announcing that
the brigadier would be delighted to receive his visitor at once.

The office upstairs was large, warm, and bright, overlooking
the river, where in season Haileybury amused himself fishing
for trout. There was a neat, busy-looking desk, filing cabinets,
maps and charts on the wall. A lieutenant with twined-serpent
R.A.M.C. badges, who hovered in attendance, was gently
waved from the presence.

Haileybury extended his large red hand. 'An unexpected pleasure, Trevose.'

'Is it so unexpected?'

The brigadier pursed his lips. 'Won't you sit down?'

Graham took a small hard chair and began, 'Haileybury, do you know the one thing the powers-that-be in this war could do with me? They couldn't court-martial me. They couldn't put me in jail. They couldn't even tell me off. The only way they could save themselves the nuisance of my existence was to sack me. They have.'

Haileybury put his finger-tips together and blew on them, rather noisily.

'You're perfectly aware of that, of course,' Graham added accusingly.

'It has come to my ears.'

'Why did you do it? Why did you throw me out?'

Haileybury looked shocked. 'I?'

'I've a certain right to know, you must admit.'

'But, my dear fellow, I couldn't possibly be responsible for your dismissal. That would be a civilian matter, quite outside my province.'

'In all the years we've been squabbling, Haileybury, you've invariably done two things that I often enough have not. Told the truth and been honest.'

There was a silence. 'I see,' said Haileybury.

He got up, crossed silently to a filing cabinet, and still without speaking removed a folder.

'Your suspicions are correct, Trevose, I must agree,' he admitted, sitting down. 'Though only partly correct. I certainly made representations to the proper authorities. And I can hardly pretend otherwise than that my views were bound to carry some weight.'

He opened the file. My God! thought Graham, he's more of my cuttings than I've collected myself. He imagined Haileybury painstakingly snipping each one out, muttering to himself and shaking his head sorrowfully.

'Very well, the annex has been getting some publicity,' said

Graham. 'And what of it? It's cheered the patients up. It's encouraged my staff to keep working flat out. It's given the civilian population something to feel proud of. Hasn't it put up the morale of your own men? At least they know there's a unit to look after them efficiently, if they get their faces smashed up. It's made a hell of a difference in the R.A.F., I happen to know for a fact.'

'That isn't the point,' said Haileybury.

'You don't imagine it's done me any personal good, do you?' demanded Graham irritably. 'I've neither the desire nor the need to push my own interests. I'm only concerned with those of my patients.'

'I think we know each other's views on these matters too well for the need of repetition. I will only emphasize that mine have remained quite unchanged by the war.'

'Oh, you're stupid, ridiculous, blind, smug. Of course I can't help getting into the papers. I'm part of the scene. Nobody objects if General Montgomery or Vera Lynn or whoever you like gets photographed for the front pages, do they?'

'I think you're putting it rather extravagantly, Trevose.'

'Then tell me why you're getting me kicked out? No, don't bother. I know. Through spite, that's all.'

Haileybury drew a deep breath. 'You must be perfectly aware,' he said calmly, 'that there has been a great weight of complaint. However understandable your enthusiasm—perhaps even commendable—you have rather created the impression . . . well, the impression that nobody else in our profession is doing anything for the war at all. It has all been brought very sharply to the notice of the Ministry and the Service departments. And to myself personally.'

'By whom?' Twelvetrees at Smithers Botham, Graham thought, perhaps even Crampers.

'You might prefer me not to name names. The last time I unwittingly did so, I understand it led to a good deal of remorse on your part.'

The reference to Tom Raleigh made Graham shift uneasily in the chair. He continued in a more subdued voice, 'You

97

might at least tell me why the Ministry should have chosen this particular moment to pounce. It couldn't have come at a more awkward time for me personally.'

Haileybury reflected that most times were awkward for Trevose personally. 'I fancy people had to decide when matters had gone a little too far,' he declared. He paused and added, 'As I have been frank, will you perhaps let me make my motives clear?'

Graham nodded curtly.

'I assure you there was no suggestion of spite on my part. Surely you don't really think that of me? Not in your heart? There was no spite on anybody's part. But medicine is entering upon difficult times. You must know that, if only from the newspapers. When we raise our eyes from the war, what do we see? The future of our profession is in the balance. The politicos are concocting a large number of recipes for cooking our goose, believe you me. There's talk of forcing us into some sort of State health scheme—pure socialism.' Haileybury seemed to shudder. 'That would never do. We should lose our professional freedom. We should become mere civil servants, with the Government our taskmaster. The doctor–patient relationship, as we have known it for centuries, would be lost for ever.'

'All that's nothing to do with me.'

'But it is.' Haileybury leaned forward earnestly, his eyes shining. 'We shall have to fight these people. Fight them at every turn. And what shall be our weapons? We shall need every scrap of dignity, of integrity, of professional correctitude that we can muster. We must make it plain to the public that we stand above the ordinary commercial motives of life, that we seek no vainglory for ourselves, that we have no thought but for the welfare of our patients. None of us must falter—or appear to falter—from the rigorous discipline we have imposed on ourselves. None of us! We must fight not as individuals, but as a profession. Oh, politicians are slippery people, Trevose. I know. I've had dealings with plenty of them. We mustn't give them the smallest stick to beat us with.'

Graham replied by holding his hands before his face. 'So that is why these must be lost to the country like a torpedoed munition ship?'

'You're taking too dramatic a view, as usual,' said Haileybury shortly. 'Your unit will continue as before. That Canadian Tudor Beverley is a perfectly sound man. You should be the first to admit that none of us are indispensable. If I may say so, in peacetime you had rather a procession of assistants. Anyway, you remain on the staff of Blackfriars. Some beds will be found for you, either at Smithers Botham or elsewhere. Perhaps the Ministry of Pensions would have something to offer. You might like to know that I have made a point of assuring myself you wouldn't be left in the cold.'

'I am not going to treat a single casualty outside the unit that I have built up.'

'Then I fear you will find little else to do. Women are not given much to having their faces remodelled these days.'

'You're wrong.' Graham got up. 'Once released from my contract, I'm allowed to take on as much private practice as I can handle. Right? Well, women are continuing to give a great deal of thought to the new area I'm treating. I've been working with O'Rory at Smithers Botham on a reconstruction procedure for congenital absence of the vagina. It isn't a particularly unusual condition, you know. The operation's extremely interesting. You dissect the pelvic tissues from below, then put in a skin-graft on a mould. Sometimes it takes, sometimes it doesn't. You have to cut the graft extra thin or you'll get a crop of hair, which would be highly uncomfortable for all concerned. So, Haileybury. You don't want me. Nobody does. I shall therefore spend the rest of the war making new pussies.'

Without another word he clattered down the oak staircase and out to his Morris. The sergeant stared after him anxiously. Whatever had happened, it seemed likely to put the brigadier in one of his moods.

Graham wanted to leave the annex as soon as possible. Tudor Beverley and his staff offered to resign *en bloc*, but Graham wouldn't hear of it. Desmond, who seemed more shocked by his father's dismissal than by his second stab at paternity, suggested he withdraw from the Blackfriars medical school—the ridicule was liable to break out afresh, he suspected inwardly. Graham told him not to be stupid. His patients suggested getting up a petition, but Graham knew that official minds couldn't be swayed by even a snowstorm of paper. Anyway, he was suddenly weary of battling with authority. He'd lost, and he wanted to leave the field, just as soon as he could tidy up his work.

Clare was wonderful. Her practical mind stood rock-like amid their sea of troubles. She decided they would move somewhere for the span of her pregnancy, perhaps up to Scotland. They could enjoy a wonderful holiday until the baby was born —Graham had no need to start work, they'd saved a bit, and she'd a little money of her own. The divorce could surely be left in the hands of the solicitors. Graham agreed with everything. He felt he wanted the child desperately. It would be an achievement, a symbol of defiance, something to show for his existence. Without a regular achievement of some sort, he doubted if he could live at all.

Then they killed Bluey.

It was stupid, unnecessary, almost criminal. A couple of years of Graham's surgery had the Australian looking more or less like a human being. Better still, his hands were mending splendidly. He had a pair of new thumbs made from chips of his hip-bone, he could light cigarettes, hold a tankard, even fondle a girl. A small operation was still needed to trim the inside of his lip. John Bickley again gave an injection, and slipped the rubber tube into his windpipe. To stop the blood from Graham's incision trickling into his patient's lungs, John packed the back of Bluey's throat with a length of oiled bandage. It was common practice, performed on the patients every operating day. Afterwards, John drew out the tube and forgot the bandage. They wheeled Bluey back to bed. The nurse who found him dusky and straining to breathe wasted away his life trying artificial respiration. John was summoned, and instantly ripped out the bandage which was suffocating him. But it was too late. Two years in hospital had so enfeebled Bluey that the survivor of a blazing Hurricane succumbed to lack of oxygen as readily as a baby.

John went back to the theatre and told Graham. The surgeon dropped his instruments, left the operation to Tudor Beverley, and strode out to sit alone in his office. John hesitated. He had better face him. At the end of the case he followed Graham to the hut, and found him in tears.

'It was a terrible mistake,' John admitted at once. 'I just don't know how it happened.'

Graham said nothing.

'I'm always so careful about the throat-packs, Graham—you know I am. I've had nightmares about leaving one in. I've been half afraid something like this might come about, ever since the unit started.'

Graham wearily moved the glass bottle containing the soldier's tattoo. 'And after all the poor devil went through,' he muttered.

'I can't begin to say how sorry I am.' Graham again made no response. 'But it's awfully difficult, you know, with two tables in the theatre. Without any proper assistants. I've told the nurses time and time again to feel for the throat-pack at the first sign of trouble afterwards. The nurse in charge of Bluey was new. She let us down.'

'If you're going to make excuses, don't shift the blame on to some poor girl who at the moment is too frightened to speak.'

'I'm not making excuses,' said John patiently. 'I'm only putting the facts.'

'Whose responsibility is it?'

John shrugged. 'Of course, mine. Ultimately, as the anaesthetist in charge of the case. I'm not denying that.'

'Of course you're making excuses,' Graham told him angrily. 'You're always making excuses, whenever you make a mess of it with a patient. If you give a perivenal injection, the vein was abnormal. If you break a needle, it was a faulty one. If your oxygen cylinder runs out, you told the orderly to change it. I only hope you'll find the coroner a more sympathetic listener.'

'I'm perfectly prepared to answer whatever the coroner feels like asking me,' John retaliated. 'I've nothing to hide.'

Graham made an impatient gesture. 'Oh, you'll come out of the inquest with your skin. Unavoidable mistake, pressure of work, patient's difficult airway. You'll continue with your job here as though nothing had happened. *I* shan't even be here to inconvenience you. You and Denise can go on putting out poisonous gossip about me, as much as you care. That probably helped to get me sacked, if you looked into it.'

'It's not fair to say that, Graham,' John told him patiently.

'It may not be, but it's the truth and you know it. Denise doesn't like me. She never has.'

'If Denise has sometimes been . . . well, indiscreet,' John admitted, 'she's been careful nothing could go further. Not outside the hospital. But now you're talking as if we were sworn enemies. Of course we're not. You're imagining things. Haven't we been friends, you and I, close friends, for years? Ever since the E.N.T. days? We've been through enough together, God knows. We've lost patients before.' He hesitated. 'We've even covered up for each other before. I wouldn't like to think that, however tragic, this incident meant the end of our personal relationship.'

'Be that as it may, but never in your life will you give another anaesthetic for me,' Graham told him angrily. 'At this particular moment, I doubt if that strikes you as much of a penalty. I'm down, I know it. But I won't stay down. When the war's over there'll be fifty anaesthetists in London breaking their necks chasing after my work. I'm going to make my fortune again. And this time you won't get ten per cent of it. Now please leave me in peace.'

That night, Clare woke with pain in her back. When she looked, she saw there was some vaginal bleeding. Graham telephoned Mr O'Rory. Then he carried her outside in a blanket, tucked her into the back of the Morris, and drove the ten miles to Smithers Botham. The gynaecologist was already waiting, greeting them with some mild joke about plastic surgeons working at the right end to avoid calls from their sleep. He put Clare into his ward, tipping up the foot of her bed on wooden blocks. He surrounded her with hot-water bottles, ordered an injection of morphine, prescribed doses of bromide, and added well-polished reassurance.

'Is she aborting?' asked Graham, outside the ward.

'Well, now, it's a threatened abortion,' Mr O'Rory said amiably. 'It's just eight weeks since the end of the lady's last menstrual period. So it wouldn't be an unheard-of occurrence at such a time, would it?'

'Could anything have caused it?' Graham asked anxiously. 'Mental distress, that sort of thing? You know what worry we've been having.'

'Oh, these things happen, they just happen. To tell the truth, none of us knows really why.'

'What's the chance of saving the foetus?'

'I'd say quite good. Yes, quite good. Though the lady will have to take life with queenly ease for quite a while afterwards.'

'That's nothing to bother about, nothing at all. . . .'

'And anyway,' smiled the gynaecologist, 'the lady isn't necessarily destined to repeat the performance on a second occasion, is she? If all is lost, there's plenty more where that one came from. Eh, Graham?'

Graham began to wonder if he really liked Tim O'Rory after all.

The bleeding went on. The following day Mr O'Rory shook his head and said he feared the lady must visit his operating theatre. They gave Clare another dose of morphine and wheeled her along the cold concrete corridor. Mr O'Rory's anaesthetist administered gas and trichorethylene, they stuck her legs in the air, Mr O'Rory settled himself comfortably on a metal stool between them, and with a curette removed Graham's latest achievement for good.

Graham spent the night alone in the bungalow. Depression was no stranger at his side, but he had never known such misery before. Everything was running against him. When he told John Bickley that he wouldn't stay down he'd meant it. But for the first time he now sensed he was finished for good. He'd never recover professionally. Not when everyone could point to him as the man who was sacked in the war. The child was lost, and in such straits they'd be insane to start another. He wondered if Clare would stay with him. He had really little to offer her, and at her age she must surely expect something rewarding from life. It never occurred to Graham how much she might love him for himself. He always expected to take so much from others, he sometimes felt obliged to offer more than he possibly could.

Haileybury would not have been surprised at this mental turmoil. He knew Graham's moods well enough. He was unaware of the pregnancy, and only faintly aware of Clare, whom he had dismissed as another of Graham's pick-ups. The following morning a car arrived at his mansion, containing a general. Haileybury knew the general well. They had been to the same public school, they belonged to the same London club, before the war they had been off golfing and mountaineering together. The general marched up to his office, saying nothing. He laid on Haileybury's desk a slip of typewritten paper, which declared simply,

*Pray, why has one of our most famous and able doctors been dismissed his post? The news of his work has vastly heartened men and women in all the Allied Services. He will be reinstated immediately. I wish to know who is responsible.*

Haileybury gave a deep sigh. It was useless to fight Trevose. When they both got to Heaven he was bound to get God on his side.

'Abortion?' said Mr Cramphorn to Denise Bickley at Smithers Botham. 'I'll bet Graham did it himself. With a knitting-needle.'

# 14

IT WAS A GLORIOUS AFTERNOON. The sun streaked the water with gold and warmed the grassy slope where twenty-two-year-old Alec Trevose lay with his face roofed by Sir Robert Muir's *Textbook of Pathology*, all 991 pages of it. The slope ran down to a white-painted hotel which had once housed holidaymakers at Southsea, near Portsmouth, but was now a makeshift hospital. Both sea and sky were for once free of men and their machinery, except for an approaching landing-craft, its silver balloon floating nonchalantly overhead, bringing smashed vehicles and possibly smashed humans back from Normandy. By mid-July both the weather and the progress of the invasion had improved noticeably. Montgomery had liberated Caen, the Americans had started moving down the eastward side of the Cherbourg Peninsula, and the coloured-headed pins stuck into maps on the walls of homes all over the country began to lose their faintly worrying immobility.

Beside Alec on the grass was his sports jacket with leather patches on the elbows, a frayed Blackfriars tie, and a semi-stiff collar. He had cast off his shoes, and his big toes poked through the holes in his socks. His striped shirt was open to display his thin chest—he suffered from asthma, an awkward complaint, liable to grip him in moments of emotion, sexual or otherwise. Alec often put down the asthma to some obscure psychological effect of having been delivered by his own father, the medical missionary, in the Malayan jungle several hundred miles from alternative professional attention. It was the first of many uncomfortable things which seemed to happen to him.

While his cousin Desmond had gone to a splendid public school, he had attended an odd establishment for the education of the sons of other missionaries, to be reared in a strong atmosphere of piety, chastisement, and carbolic soap. Even the cost of his education was being met by his Uncle Graham (or his cousin, Desmond, however you looked at it), though his bills were thankfully met by anonymous lawyers. He had started the telescoped medical course at Cambridge when the war was a year old. It wasn't much fun, he reflected, with no one to talk to except potential doctors, engineers, and clergymen, all three professions being thought essential by the Government to ensure eventual victory. But he had seen Cambridge as it should be seen, with King's Chapel shining in the pure moonlight like an iceberg, Great Court at Trinity a mystery of stones and shadows, Clare College running lightless to the river as a silver screen, the alleys returned to their rightful medieval blackness. It was Cambridge as Newton and Milton had seen it. His tutor was an ancient cleric in a purple stock encrusted with the memorials to countless college soups, who wore both gown and air-raid warden's helmet during alerts, taking seriously his responsibility for the physical as well as the moral safety of his pupils. The science dons had mostly disappeared to concoct new devilment for the enemy. On the whole, Alec thought the University rather superior about the war. It had lived through plenty before with fitting scientific detachment. The church clock still stood at ten to three, and for most of the time honey was off the ration.

That sunny afternoon by the sea he was still officially studying clinical medicine at Smithers Botham, where he had occupied almost a dozen lodgings in the surrounding countryside. However agreeable his hosts, however tasty the Woolton pie, however hot the officially permitted few inches of bathwater, Alec was always convinced of being happier at the next stop. It was a strange restlessness which applied to his hobbies, his friends, his enthusiasm for the various subjects he studied, and his views of life in general. He had finally asked his uncle Graham to get him into the Emergency Squad. He felt he got on rather well with his uncle Graham. Physically they were much alike. Alec supposed when the family genes had been shuffled at their separate conceptions, they had drawn much the same hand.

The Emergency Squad at Smithers Botham occupied a low two-storey block which in peacetime had housed the better-class lunatic, who could afford to pay for his own incarceration. It was comfortable enough, it saved paying rent, and you could always risk smuggling in a girl. The Squad's existence was at last justified on D-Day, when they were abruptly dispatched by lorry across the face of signpostless England to the converted hotel at Southsea, which they found in charge of a Polish civilian doctor who was unable to speak much English, and who seemed uncertain if they were a party of top-flight specialists from London or the men come to mend the boiler. No one knew what cases the hospital was created to take, because none ever appeared. Everyone seemed to have forgotten about them. Their only contact with authority was Brigadier Haileybury, who one afternoon had arrived unheralded to inspect them. 'I believe I know you, don't I?' he had asked Desmond.

'Yes, sir. We met once before the war. In my father's place in London. My name's Trevose.'

Haileybury nodded. 'Your father is certainly making a name for himself.'

'Deservedly, I hope, sir?'

'Of that I have no doubt. I hope you inherit a share of his remarkable talents, young man. You could look forward to a brilliant career.'

The brigadier disappeared. They all noticed he had a wonderfully pretty A.T.S. driver.

Alec slid the pathology textbook from his nose, aware that someone was approaching up the slope. It was Desmond, dressed in a grey flannel suit. His cousin sat down silently beside him, picked a stalk of grass, and stuck the end between his teeth.

'Anything doing in the wards?' Alec asked.

'No. What are you reading?'

'Muir.'

'I mean this other book,' Desmond picked up an open volume from the grass. He turned the pages frowning, and after a moment read aloud,

> *'Behold me waiting—waiting for the knife.*
> *A little while, and at a leap I storm*
> *The thick, sweet mystery of chloroform,*
> *The drunken dark, the little death-in-life.'*

He tossed the book down and asked, 'What are you reading that sort of stuff for?'

'It's too hot for pathology.'

'It's a rather flamboyant bit of verse, isn't it?'

'No, I don't think so. Doesn't it put a patient's feelings well? God knows how many think the same thing. They aren't articulate enough to express themselves, that's all.'

'Nobody uses chloroform any more,' said Desmond briefly. 'Who wrote it?'

'Henley. When he was in Edinburgh Infirmary, waiting for them to chop his foot off.'

'Why have you taken to poetry?'

'Why not? Don't you realize, we're totally uneducated. All of us. At Blackfriars they simply drown us intellectually in a torrent of facts, mostly extremely dull. What chance have we got to equip ourselves with some knowledge of literature, the arts, philosophy?' he added grandly.

'I daresay.' Desmond bit a piece of grass then spat it away. 'Unfortunately, they don't ask questions on those subjects in the finals.'

'I think we should be more interested in being well-educated doctors than getting through our finals.'

'Oh, this is just another of your crazes,' Desmond dismissed his cousin's cultural ambitions. 'I've got to go back to London this evening.'

'What's this? A night out?'

'No, it's my mother,' Desmond told him with careful casualness. 'I've just heard. She's had a stroke. Quite a severe one, I gather.'

'I say, I'm sorry.'

'So am I. But these vascular accidents happen.' Desmond got up. 'Shouldn't you try and find someone to mend your socks?'

It would never do to display emotion, or even concern, especially in front of Alec.

The news telephoned from Sussex that morning was hardly a surprise to Graham. For a year Maria's blood-pressure had been steadily mounting, as she became fatter than ever. He still hadn't divorced her. The plan had somehow been overlooked in the flurry of his reinstatement at the annex. He told Clare—as he told himself—the episode of his sacking must be taken as a warning. For the patients to continue benefiting from his abilities, he must be careful about publicity in the future. A divorce case in the papers certainly wouldn't help his standing in the eyes of the Ministry. Such distressing tangles were perhaps best unravelled after the war, when he was his own master again. Clare agreed. The subject was dropped. So was that of a second excursion into pregnancy. Among any affectionate couple the matters never mentioned are generally the important ones.

Their domestic bliss at Cosy Cot continued. Clare didn't go back to her work at the annex, but stayed at home to look after the house, grow radishes and lettuces in the garden, and cook the rations. They were frequently indebted to Mr Cramphorn, who seemed to have taken to them after Graham's brush with authority, and would appear at the door with a rabbit he had shot, or a pigeon, or a rook, or even a squirrel, which he proclaimed excellent eating if roasted with a strip of bacon, as inclined to be rather dry. The food situation was trying. Graham himself sometimes guiltily brought liquid paraffin from the hospital to eke out the cooking fat, until the Ministry tumbled to this regrettably widespread practice and added the chemical phenolphthalein, which turned the fried fish bright pink.

'What's Maria's prognosis, Graham?' Clare asked.

They were sitting on the handkerchief of a lawn in the garden that evening, waiting for Desmond. Graham had managed to buy a bottle of Pimm's No. 1, which he prepared with great enthusiasm, adding bits of apple, cucumber rind, mint, and even carrot. 'It's difficult to say. She may recover, more or less completely. She may end up with a hemiplegia, half-paralyzed—and dumb, of course, if her speech centre's gone. She may go on having small strokes for months, even years. On the other hand she may develop broncho-pneumonia and die in a week. These patients get bedsores, sepsis, you know. Sometimes they just fade out.'

Clare said nothing. If Maria died, the last obstacle to their marriage would die with her. Well, the last excuse, anyway. Sensing her thoughts, Graham added, 'I should have gone ahead with that divorce.' He reached out and took her hand. 'I know how you feel, and it must be awful. Stepping into a dead woman's shoes.'

'No, I don't feel that at all, darling. Maria's never been more than an abstract quality to me.'

'You should have made me do something about those lawyers.'

'You'd have said I was nagging.' She laughed. 'You might have left me.'

He squeezed her hand and said, 'Don't be silly. You know perfectly well—'

He broke off. A noise. A motor bike in the sky, coming nearer.

'Is that one?' he asked anxiously.

'Yes, I rather think it is.'

'Crampers told me the one which fell in Maiden Cross yesterday killed about twenty people.'

The engine stopped.

'It's a long way off,' he said, still sounding uncomfortable.

They stared at each other. The silence seemed to last for an age. Finally there was an explosion far in the distance.

'Some of them glide on for miles,' Graham observed. The flying-bombs had taken on an ill-natured personality of their own. They were malevolent, winged, fire-spitting beasts, impossible to relate to the busy grey-uniformed squads dispatching them. 'I hope Desmond's all right,' he added in a worried voice.

But Desmond arrived unaware of his peril. He spent the night in the bungalow, setting off early the next morning with Graham in the Morris. The nursing-home where Maria lay ill catered for a more genteel mental sufferer than once found themselves in Smithers Botham. It was a manor house providing seclusion, fresh vegetables from the garden, and nursing which was unfailingly kindly if not particularly skilful. They were received by the matron, a stout, blue-uniformed north-countrywoman, radiating cheerfulness. 'The poor soul's poorly, of that there's no doubt,' she greeted Graham. 'If she went, we'd quite miss her, you know. She's been with us longer than anyone.'

Graham was familiar enough with Maria's room. She had occupied the same one since he had her shut up in the place ten years ago. It was small, bright in the sunshine, with a vase of pink roses beside the bed. Maria was unconscious, breathing noisily. It was too soon after the haemorrhage, which had sprung from a brittle artery amid the microscopic telephone-cables of her brain, to tell the extent of her coming paralysis. Graham noticed she suffered the indignity of a large fly crawling unmolested across her cheek. Her grey hair lay neatly on the pillow in two plaits, each tied with a pink bow, like a schoolgirl's.

Desmond stood in the background, looking solemn. However much he had prepared himself, however often he had observed the same clinical state in others, however little he felt for his insane mother, it was a shock to see her like that. Graham went to the bed and felt her pulse. His fingers slipped down to take her flaccid hand. It reminded him of the night when her troubles had started, when she tried to kill herself with an overdose of sleeping-draught and had been saved by the skill of John Bickley. He suddenly felt himself touched. Now his wife lay under his eyes as a dying wreck, he felt a surge of love for her. It was stronger than any he could remember in his life, even before he had married her.

III

'Isn't her breathing rather obstructed?' he complained mildly.

'The doctor will be along by and by,' the matron told him comfortably. 'Doubtless he'll deal with it.'

Graham nodded. He supposed at that stage it didn't make twopence worth of difference. 'Perhaps you'll ring me at Smithers Botham, Matron, if she takes a turn for the worse?'

'I will that, Mr Trevose.' In the corridor outside she went on cheerfully, 'It's sad, isn't it, your poor wife should be smitten when there're such good news on the wireless this morning.' As Graham looked at her blankly she explained, 'Haven't you heard? They've tried to blow up Hitler with a bomb. The Germans themselves. It won't be long now till it's all over and done with, you mark my words.'

As they drove away, Graham said to Desmond, 'I suppose there're people who ought to know. You'd better try and get hold of your uncle Charles. You can probably find his whereabouts if you telephone Val Arlott's office at the *Press*. Say it's on my behalf. God knows where her other brother's got to.'

'Do you want to speak to Uncle Charles yourself, Dad?'

'I most certainly do not.' Graham drove in silence for a mile. 'So they tried to liquidate *Der Führer*, did they? Perhaps they'll end up with a revolution in Berlin, like last time. It could all be over by Christmas.'

Graham hardly said anything for the rest of the journey. The shadow of death that hung over both Hitler and Maria was bringing to the front of his mind difficult problems.

## 15

MARIA'S FUNERAL caused a frightful fuss. She lingered a week, regaining consciousness, her hand groping the air, her eyes askew, speechless. During the days she was passive enough, but at nights she grew restless, clawing at her sheets, trying to get out of bed. The nurses were perfectly used to such behaviour. They brought long boards to slot along the sides of her bed, as though she were in her coffin already. On the Thursday morning she had another cerebral haemorrhage, and left life as she had entered it, with a gasp.

When they telephoned Graham at Smithers Botham he shrugged his shoulders. But he was surprised at his inner distress. It is a merciful quality of the human mind never completely to expect the inevitable. There were practical details again. He knew his wife wished to be buried at Biddenden, in more glorious days the Cazalay family's country 'place'. She had told him as much when her life was in danger once before, at the stormy birth of Desmond. But Biddenden was in Kent, and since the opening of the second front a military area. Graham seemed to remember that permits were needed to venture there. He approached Captain Pile, who confessed it outside his authority—though he had taken to Graham since the surgeon had become a national figure, often boasting to his cronies of association with this wonderful work. The undertakers finally sorted things out, and the following Wednesday morning Graham set off in the Morris again with Desmond. They started late, Graham having been called to a soldier brought into the annex from a bad road smash. In an age infested with priorities, he supposed that the dying could claim precedence over the already dead.

Graham remembered the Cazalays' old house well enough. It was a mile or two from Biddenden, near another village with a few houses, a pub, and the church. You first caught sight of it as the road turned on the hill, through a gap in the trees—but the trees had grown. Graham tried to remember the last time he'd been invited to spend a night in its spacious and chilly bedrooms. It was not really an old house, its twisted chimneys, leaded windows, and timbered gables going no farther back than the reign of King Edward the Seventh. It was rather vulgar, really, like the late Lord Cazalay himself. He wondered how the famous glasshouses were, the airfields in the area having been plastered by the Germans generously. As he drove past the lodge gates he saw a notice announcing HEAD-QUARTERS—FORCES AND WORKERS ENTERTAINMENT SERVICE. Well, he supposed, that was carrying on the first Lord Cazalay's tradition.

'Did you ever visit the place?' Graham asked Desmond.

'I don't know. I could hardly remember, could I? I was too young before the family disgrace.'

Graham grunted. He disliked to think of the disgrace spilling on to his own family. He had brought nothing but honour to the Cazalay tree. 'We're late,' he said, as the church came in sight. 'Everyone's gone in.'

They hurried inside, making for the front pew. Graham found himself beside a fat man with the bar of a black moustache across his red face—Maria's brother Charles, the second Lord Cazalay. They inclined their heads gravely. The elderly clergyman rose. A familiar noise intruded into the church, a phut-phut-phut coming steadily nearer. Graham shifted his feet uncomfortably. Now they had moved the anti-aircraft guns to the coast and left the Spitfires and Hurricanes to prowl inshore, most of the flying-bombs were being shot down. It occurred to him they were standing in the middle of the area proscribed by the Air Ministry for exactly this purpose.

The noise grew closer. The clergyman stood with his mouth open. Graham noticed the church windows had already been blown out and boarded up. It would be a strange end, to be buried alive at his wife's funeral. The engine cut out. Silence. Then an explosion which shook the earth under them. The clergyman started the burial service in a tone of deep relief.

It was all mumbo-jumbo, Graham thought. The only difference between a human body alive and a human body dead was that between an engine running and switched off, though the stopped engine didn't inconveniently rot to pieces. There were a surprising number of people in the church, twenty or thirty. Old friends of Maria's, he supposed. Living ghosts, come to clank the rusty chains of their memories in his ears. He hoped the old clergyman would get it all over quickly. He probably would, there was always the chance of another flying-bomb.

As they wheeled Maria out, Graham noticed the route to the graveside passed a row of elaborate memorials to others of the Cazalay family. Though not her father and mother, who had died in the arid air of Venezuela, a destination recommending itself for Lord Cazalay's retirement through its lack of an extradition treaty with Great Britain. As Maria's remains were lowered from sight another flying-bomb came out of the distance. As the engine stopped, heads turned heavenwards in anxiety rather than supplication. It exploded with a distant thump. Graham wondered idly who was unfortunate enough to be underneath it.

'Mr Trevose, you must remember me,' said an old lady in a velvet hat, voice conscientiously hushed.

'Of course I do,' Graham lied.

'I was on the committee of the Sunshine League and the Free Medicine Club with your dear wife, you know.'

The Sunshine League! Well, the war had relieved the rich of the painful necessity of lightening the burdens of the poor. Graham found himself facing a thin old man with two sticks, whom he recognized after a moment as Sir John Blazey. He'd been chairman of the small hospital at Uxbridge which Graham

115

had used as his first step to success in plastic surgery—rather unscrupulously, he supposed. He thought the fellow had died long ago.

'Your wife was a great woman, Trevose.' The old man shook his head reflectively. 'She was quite unsparing in her sense of duty to others. We shall never know how many unfortunate people have had cause to be grateful to her.'

Graham thanked him. He had almost forgotten the Maria of the busy committees, with her picture in the *Illustrated London News* and the *Bystander*. Now the glories of her past began to draw his eye from the shadows of her later poverty and insanity. Well, it's good to know she died a credit to me, he thought. He found himself shaking hands with Val Arlott.

'Why did you come?' Graham asked, looking surprised. 'I didn't notice you in the church.'

'Have you a moment for a stroll?'

They walked together in the country lane outside the church-yard. 'I can't say why I came, exactly,' Val told him. 'I've been wondering. Perhaps it's to make up for missing the burial of her father. I was fond of old Cazalay. In some measure, I suppose I was responsible for his plight.' Graham made an unbelieving gesture. 'It's difficult to know. There are things I might have said or done to check his recklessness. Perhaps I'm suffering unconscious feelings of guilt towards the family. This is my penance. You'd know about such matters, wouldn't you? How are things going?'

'At the annex? We're still busy. Though the excitement's gone. We're an institution now. Like all institutions we've lost the fun of getting greater and grander, we've only the worry of seeing ourselves slipping.'

'I wish I'd done more for you medical people. Particularly now I'm getting so old and infirm. Look at Nuffield—given millions, set up professors, all manner of things.'

'You know they tried to sack me?'

'Yes, I got the P.M. to scotch it.'

Graham looked faintly put out. He had imagined the inter-vention a tribute to his own personality. 'After the war you'll have plenty of room for your charity, I should imagine, Val. These ideas about State medicine and so on, nothing will come of them, surely?'

'Don't you believe it. When the fighting stops we'll get a socialist government.'

'Surely you're not telling me the country's going to reject Churchill?'

'Why not? What stopped us giving in after Dunkirk? Our national streak of perversity.'

Graham looked glum. 'That'll make it tough for me, trying to build up again.'

'You've got a wonderful reputation.'

'I can't eat it.'

'No, but it helps. There'll be a lot of goodies and gongs going after the war, Graham. I don't see why you should be passed by. I take it you'd be agreeable if I put you in for something?'

Graham gave a faint smile. 'Haven't I been too gay a dog to be given an official collar?'

'The war's altered a lot of that. After all, if you're brave enough to win the V.C. nobody gives a damn how many women you've screwed.'

'It's certainly an attractive proposition—' He broke off, listening 'No, it's only a motor-bike somewhere. Those doodlebugs are damn scaring. I thought that one in church was going to blow the lot of us up, corpse and all.'

'Don't worry. Duncan Sandys says we've got them licked. Only about one in five get through now.'

'When's the war going to be over?'

'Against the Germans, by Christmas. Against the Japs, in a couple of years. Against the Russians, God knows.'

With this deep and disquieting observation, Val Arlott shook hands, entered his chauffeur-driven car, and made off.

Graham felt he needed a drink.

The other mourners were cramming themselves with some agitation into three or four taxis parked off the lane. His son was standing alone, looking awkward by the lych gate. 'I expect you could do with a stiff one, Desmond, couldn't you?'

'Yes, it wouldn't come amiss.'

'We'll try our luck in the pub.'

They walked a quarter-mile down the lane in silence. The funeral had already been displaced from Graham's mind by his talk with Val. Some sort of 'gong'. What sort? They could hardly hand him the O.B.E., like some zealous food official. A K.B.E. would make him Sir Graham, which would sound very pretty. But he doubted if even Val could push him into the pure light of official favour. The bigwigs in the medical profession would certainly have a say in it, and they had always mistrusted him. Someone would be resentful he won his fight over the sacking, and eager to express it practically. And Haileybury would be against him. No, not Haileybury, Graham decided, after a moment's thought. Haileybury was far too stupidly righteous to take the chance of such easy revenge. Anyway, he didn't care. He had never let official honours flicker among the varied ambitions which had burned inside him. He knew medical knights enough, and he thought most of them horribly dreary.

They pushed open the door of the little saloon bar, to hear a loud voice declaring, 'But of course you must have some whisky. Come along, be a good fellow, look out a bottle from under the counter. Don't you understand, I've just been to a funeral?'

Graham hesitated, but it was too late to withdraw. He had never liked Maria's brother. The man had laughed at him as her suitor, paining young Graham with the discovery that in 'society' medical people were seen with the eye of fifty years previously, when the healer was admitted only via the tradesmen's entrance—though Graham had acted afterwards on this brutal realization, most profitably. He was also rather afraid of Charles Cazalay. He had the unscrupulousness of his father, if not the intelligence which made the most of it. He had tried to damage Graham once, and wouldn't hesitate to try again if it suited him.

'Don't you know who I am?' Lord Cazalay continued to the landlord, half-chaffing and half-hectoring. 'You should, you know. I'm Lord Cazalay. I used to live in the house. Before your day. I remember the fellow who kept this place, man called Greensmith. Greensmith would have found something for me, I don't mind telling you. Now run along and see what you can do.'

Overcome either by the materialization of the local legend or the solemnity of his errand, the landlord departed anxiously to search his cellar. Graham approached and said, 'It must be twenty years since we met.'

'Graham, I'm delighted to see you again,' Lord Cazalay greeted him affably. 'I'm sorry it should be on such a sad occasion.'

Graham introduced his son. 'You can't have set eyes on Desmond since he was a baby.'

Lord Cazalay briskly brushed his moustache and remarked, 'He's grown into a fine lad. As you know, I decided to make my home for some years in France.' He lowered his voice respectfully. 'It was very distressing about Maria, Graham. I know how you must feel. Her life was such a waste, shut out of the world so long. It was always a comfort to me that my sister had you to care for her—a medical man.'

'Thank you,' said Graham shortly.

'Well, Graham—you've become more famous than ever. I always seem to be reading about you in the papers.'

'I'm only doing my job. Like a lot of others who don't get noticed.'

'I'm with security, you know.'

'I thought you were censoring civilian letters?'

'It's the same thing,' said Lord Cazalay, looking put out.

The landlord reappeared, holding an unopened bottle of Haig like a newborn baby. As he poured three measures Lord Cazalay went on, 'What are your plans for after the war, Graham?'

'I think it's only courting disappointment making any.'

'I wouldn't say that. It'll be every man for himself and the devil take the hindmost. Like last time. The thing is to get in early, before the mugs. There'll be pickings enough for the right people.'

'Where precisely do you intend to pick, if I may ask?'

'Travel.' Lord Cazalay swallowed his whisky and demanded another. 'People have been cooped up here all the war, they'll be bursting to get out and about. There'll be plenty of spare shipping space, Army buses, that sort of thing, if you know where to put your hands on them. I've plenty of valuable contacts in France. I doubt whether they've got into any trouble with the Germans.' He looked at his glass reflectively, and added, 'As a matter of fact, I'm starting a small company. If you're interested, I could let you have a piece of it.'

Graham thought this brazen, even for his brother-in-law. 'You're asking me for money, after having tried to get me publicly disgraced as a professional man?'

Lord Cazalay looked serious, then said, 'Graham, I'm glad you raised that business. It's been on my conscience. I'd been meaning to have a word with you, but with the war, of course, everything's been difficult. It was all a tragic misunderstanding, surely? I was simply wrongly advised. It was a relief to me nothing came of it.'

'It was to me, too.'

'Don't you trust me?' he asked, part humorously and part aggressively.

'I don't think this is quite the occasion to conduct commercial affairs.'

'No, no, perhaps you're right,' Lord Cazalay said quickly.

'Now we must be going. Desmond has to catch a train for Portsmouth.'

'We'll keep in touch,' Lord Cazalay promised. 'Yes, very much in touch.'

They left him with the bottle of whisky, which he seemed about to settle down and finish, on the estimable principle that unexpected blessings needed exploiting to the full.

## 16

'WHAT WAS IT LIKE?' asked Clare as Graham got back to the bungalow, having left Desmond at the station in Maiden Cross.

'More harrowing than I imagined.'

'Do you want some tea, darling? You can't have had anything to eat.'

'I don't think I'm hungry, really.'

He sat in an armchair in the sitting-room and picked up the *Daily Press*. He hadn't seen a paper that morning. 'The Russians seem to be doing well,' he observed. He wondered what Val Arlott had meant about a war with the Soviets. They seemed prickly customers, but at least they were on our side, and putting up a far better showing than last time.

'Did you see the brother?'

'Yes.'

'Any trouble?'

'No, he tried to borrow some money off me.'

Clare sat on the arm of his chair. 'I can see it's upset you, Graham.'

'It was all the paraphernalia—dirges, gloomy incantations, that sort of thing. Why should I be disturbed by her death in itself? It was a merciful release, overdue if anything.'

'I never met her, of course. But I thought I knew her. I've so often imagined her lying beside you.'

'That was never particularly successful or pleasurable.'

'What was she like? In her prime?'

Graham tossed the paper down. 'Active. Always busy. A

great do-gooder. On dozens of committees. She was an intelligent woman before her brain gave way. We had a rather cerebral relationship, I suppose. She was dreadfully afraid of her own emotions. The only thing in the world she was afraid of.'

'What made you marry her?'

'Who knows at such distance why they married anyone?' After a pause she asked, 'When are we going to be married ourselves, Graham?'

'There'll have to be a decent interval, naturally.'

'Of course, I appreciate that.'

'I've got to take some account of the world in general, however much I despise it. There'd be gossip if we got married tomorrow—Crampers, the Bickleys, everyone at Smithers Botham. It would probably get into the papers, certainly into the *Press*. I don't want to invite maliciousness. God knows I've had to suffer enough of it recently.'

She noticed it didn't occur to Graham even to ask her own sentiments. Clare was used to his self-centredness. She had decided there was nothing unkind or even unattractive about it. In some ways it was a virtue. His egotism, more than anything else, had made the annex what it was. If Graham could think of nobody but himself, she felt resignedly, it was perhaps because there was nobody in his acquaintance half as interesting.

'How long?' she asked.

'I really can't say off-hand, Clare. I've had no experience of the situation.'

'Do you mean six weeks or six months? A year? Two years?' For the first time she resolved to press him.

'We must allow the corpse to grow cold.'

'Well, then—six months, say?'

'I should think that would strike everyone as respectable.'

'Shall we decide on January?'

'Yes, in January. The war will be over by then.'

The sitting-room window was open, and a breeze blew some sheets of case-notes from Graham's table on to the floor. She rose to gather them. 'We'll be back in London then, as likely as not,' he told her. 'Mightn't this be the moment to start looking for a flat? My house in Mayfair would cost a fortune to put into shape. I'll need new consulting rooms, too. We might be able to combine both. Harley Street isn't a bad area to live. It's near Regent's Park and not far from the West End.'

She smiled and said, 'It's difficult to imagine myself living in London at all.'

'It'll be wonderful, once things get back to normal. Wonderful for both of us. There's scores of places I'm longing to take you—restaurants, theatres, little clubs I remember. Not all of them can have disappeared in the blitz. There's hundreds of people I want you to meet. This time they'll come back, thank God. It was different after the last war, with those awful blood-baths.'

'You won't do anything like that at all, Graham,' she chided him gently. 'You'll be too busy working.'

'I've worked hard enough during the war. I deserve a bit of relaxation. It's been five years out of my life. Do you realize that by Christmas in 1954 I'll be sixty?'

'That's a long way off. Anyway, I'll be almost forty.'

'Of course, I shall have to make a living, build up from scratch.' He gave a grin. 'I'll have a new wife to impress. I don't really believe these wild schemes for putting doctors under the State will come to anything. Supposing we all went on strike? That's a chilling prospect for the politicians. Things will go on much the same, if you ask me. You can't change England.'

'But what about the annex?'

'I suppose it will cease to exist, or become totally unimportant again, like the R.A.F. itself. I don't know. It's no concern of mine. My job there finishes with the war.'

'But Graham!' she exclaimed. 'I can't believe you could give up the annex, just like that. You created it. It's filled your thoughts, day and night. You'd be aimless without it. You can't have just lost interest in it.'

'But it's a phase in my life. Don't you see, Clare? We've all grown so used to the war we've forgotten it's a highly abnormal form of existence. I've been lotus-eating down here. I've had no worries about making money, nor about what to spend it on. A lot of the others at Smithers Botham haven't the sense to see it the same way. They're stuck in a rut, you'd imagine they thought the war was continuing for ever.' He swept his hand round the sitting-room. 'My God, I'm longing to live in a proper house. Somewhere with my own furniture, decent pictures, eating off plates without cracks in them. None of this bloody rationing, servants to do the dirty work, a bit of style again. Oh, I'll admit it, the war's been stimulating, rewarding, often amusing. But when it's over I want to forget it like an illness. I want to pick up my career again. As far as surgery goes, I'm only approaching my prime.'

She was facing him, leaning against the table, and he saw she had started to cry. Women were unaccountable. 'What's the matter?' he asked, not particularly kindly. 'I haven't said anything wrong, surely?'

'I thought the annex meant everything to you, Graham.'

'It's something I'll look back on with considerable affection.'

'Like me?'

'Why do you say that?' he asked irritably. 'You're being fanciful.'

'I'm not. It's perfectly true. I'm just part of the annex, as far as you're concerned.'

'Now you're being downright silly.'

'You don't want to marry me, do you? You don't want to at all.'

She advanced on him angrily. Graham was startled. All his life he had surrounded himself with submissive people, and it was always unsettling when they turned on him.

'Clare, you're simply saying a lot of irresponsible things which are making you overwrought.'

'I'm saying things which I should have said months ago, years ago. My God, I've been a fool. Do you imagine all this hasn't been boiling in my mind since I came here? Of course you don't want to marry me. You've always had some excuse, something to put it off. Even when you got me pregnant you didn't want me as your wife. You were scared stiff at the

124

thought. You didn't want that child either. You were as pleased as Punch when I aborted. That's the truth, isn't it?'

He stood up. 'Of course it wasn't the truth,' he told her crossly. 'I did everything I could to save it, didn't I? I was upset when we lost it, dreadfully upset. Do you think I don't know my own mind?'

'No, you don't know it at all, Graham. That's your trouble. There're plenty of wonderful things about you, and you don't recognize them. There are plenty of horrible things about you too, and you don't recognize those either. Or you won't bring yourself to face them, which is the worse for you.'

'So you're suggesting I'm going to turn you out after the war, like some camp-follower?'

'It won't come to that. We can't go on with this play-acting any longer. We've got to split up.'

'You can't mean that?' He was alarmed at this practical turn in the conversation.

'It'll only get worse if I stay.' She looked down at the threadbare carpet and went on more calmly, 'I haven't made up my mind just this minute, Graham. I decided . . . oh, months ago, I don't know when. Perhaps I didn't decide at all. It just crept up on me.'

'Clare—' He approached her, but she pushed him away. 'Supposing I said I'd marry you tomorrow?'

'No, it wouldn't do. It wouldn't work. We'd be in a worse mess than ever. Once you got back to London you'd want to be rid of me. I'm not your type. You don't love me. I don't think you could love anyone. Your attitude to women is like your attitude to the boys in the annex. So many 'construction jobs', as you say. You overlook that I've got the right to any feelings at all.'

Graham stuck his hands in his pockets. It was all most distressing. He hated emotional scenes. Perhaps they were both upset with the business of Maria. Clare would be over it tomorrow. 'Why did you take up with me in the first place?' he asked, a shade resentfully. 'You knew enough about me, about my past affairs?'

'Every woman's a heroine, I suppose. She expects to succeed where others have succumbed.'

'Possibly.' They stood looking at each other. 'You can't mean it?' he asked more quietly. 'About going away?'

'Yes, I do. I'll get a job somewhere.'

'Let's discuss it again tomorrow, when we're ourselves.'

'No,' she told him. 'There's nothing else to say.'

A week later Clare left the bungalow and Graham took a room in a London hotel, explaining to everyone at Smithers Botham that this temporary change in domestic arrangements was necessitated by his searching for a flat. The pair had parted politely, even amicably. A continued emotional tempest would have worn out both of them, and they were old enough to take such things sensibly. In the end, Graham was rather pleased. He would miss Clare, of course, but she was right. She was a simple, kindly girl, but not at all the sort to stand beside the fashionable plastic surgeon, Graham Trevose, now returning like the exiled European governments to his rightful dominions. A marriage would have been a disaster. And supposing this 'gong' materialized? Lady Trevose? Decidedly not. To fill *that* rôle he wanted someone far more intelligent, more versed in the ways of the world, more socially adept, someone of better family than the seedy commercial artist's.

Someone like Maria? he thought.

Yes, someone like Maria.

Maria in death, like Maria in life, always came out top in the end.

## 17

BY CHRISTMAS, when the fighting should have been over, the German armies broke through at the Ardennes for the second time in the war. Luckily for the Allies, the weather cleared and they could bomb them to pieces on the twisting hilly roads— which they would have saved themselves a great deal of trouble by doing in 1940, if only they'd had any aeroplanes. In London the flying-bombs were replaced by rockets, which perplexed and affronted the Government, as Lord Cherwell had worked out most carefully they were too expensive for the Germans to use. The rockets particularly harassed Alec Trevose, who was doing his two months' midwifery training at a sandbagged lying-in hospital in north London. Every time one fell the noise sent half a dozen local women into labour, and it was no fun finding your way through blacked-out back streets on a bicycle, loaded like a mule with bags of instruments and dressings, suspected by policemen of being some sort of saboteur, and wondering if the next unheralded missile had your number on it.

Alec didn't like midwifery. He was beginning to see himself as an intellectual, a man of culture, and childbirth was an extremely uncultured pursuit for all concerned. Alec hated the babies. He hated the midwife in charge of him, a sparse-bosomed Scotswoman with a vinegary tongue. She in turn seemed to hate him, and indeed men in general, which he felt was reasonable from her toilsome occupation. Only the jovial Mr O'Rory brought levity to the solemn reproductive circus with his visits twice a week. He was a Catholic, and therefore unable to perform abortions—though he stretched a point when they were natural, like Clare's miscarriage, and passed the others to his houseman, back-seat driving over his right shoulder. Female sterilization was for him, he confessed, quite out of the question. He would perform the operation to the crucial point, then demand genially of his assistant, 'Just tie a a knot in those two ligatures round the Fallopian tubes, my boy, there's a good fellow. My religion doesn't allow me to do that sort of thing at all.'

Alec rather took to Mr O'Rory. He felt he had the cultured approach.

In the spring the Nazi magnificos suddenly appeared in the papers as haggard and anxious old men, shuffling about in baggy civilian suits. It induced feelings of freakishness rather than triumph. To anyone of Alec Trevose's age, a world empty of Hitler and Mussolini was as strange as one without Mickey Mouse and Donald Duck. Himmler bit the cyanide capsule in his tooth, and vomited himself to death over the trousers of a British officer. If nobody really knew what had happened to Hitler, nobody really cared. There were rejoicings in British streets, of a seemly nature. The Government, in a burst of official relaxation, allowed the citizenry to use binoculars again. If the population were restrained by the scarcity of hard liquor from getting lit up when the lights went up in London, at least they had some sort of fling before the authorities switched them off again through shortage of fuel. On the June day when the world inaugurated the United Nations in San Francisco and so abolished war for ever—for the second occasion in a quarter of a century—both Alec and Desmond found they had qualified as doctors.

Alec quickly found that qualification, like marriage, brought more problems than it settled. His first difficulty was to win a resident post at Smithers Botham. Failing to get a 'house job' in your mother hospital was like being expelled from school, it stuck for life. Besides, he was going to specialize. All the students were going to specialize, their teachers (who were specialists) having freely laced their instruction with their opinion of family doctors as dangerous fumbling ignoramuses. But specialize in what? Psychiatry, Alec decided. It was intellectual, and you never got your hands messy. There was no psychiatric houseman, so as a first step he must land a house physician's appointment. But unfortunately for Alec the jobs had come to be decided solely by Mr Cramphorn, who dominated the selection committee. His methods were simple. He would look through the list of applicants, grunting, and strike out with his gold pencil all coloured students, Jews, those with un-English sounding names, any he had taken a dislike to, and any he had for some reason never heard of. And Mr Cramphorn had taken a fierce dislike to the Trevose family. He thought Graham's treatment of Clare outrageous, and after he had lavished his rabbits on her, too. Desmond, he admitted grudgingly, must be given a job, as the son of a Blackfriars consultant. If that unspoken rule lapsed the whole structure of the hospital might tumble, and there were changes enough in the wind already. But Alec could be sacrificed. In the end, Mr Cramphorn compromised by making Alec the resident anaesthetist, this speciality, Mr Cramphorn believed, being reserved for those unfitted for the practice of medicine at all.

Alec had never administered an anaesthetic in his life, but luckily John Bickley was an indulgent master. He was used to getting the duds. John had been working for Mr Cramphorn and Mr Twelvetrees in the general theatres of Smithers Botham itself since his row with Graham, who often enough had wished him back. But he was not a man to relent on his own rashness. Alec was scared of Mr Cramphorn, but discovered that he treated his anaesthetist exactly as he treated his prewar chauffeur, an underling expected to do his job and keep out of the conversation. Otherwise his new occupation seemed, like the war, ninety per cent boredom and ten per cent panic. He started bringing books into the theatre, reading them hidden in the sterile towels screening the unconscious patient's head. Having a quick mind he could demolish even a Victorian novel in two or three operating sessions. Alec was never sure of the

129

effect of his anaesthetics on his patients, but he felt they were improving his own mind considerably. He was becoming more intellectual and cultured than ever. Desmond meanwhile performed the duties of a house-surgeon, with much correctitude and distinction.

Alec's second problem was his political allegiance. The general election of July 1945 was a nervous experience for the medical profession. Like Henry the Eighth's monks, the doctors quivered, half in indignation and half in fright, as schemes for their official disposal reached their ears. The hospitals were apparently to be grabbed, not only inefficient little institutions maintained by ladies selling paper flags, but those as proud as Blackfriars itself, even though it most regrettably existed at the time only as a pile of rubble with pretty wild flowers growing on it. It would all wreck the 'doctor–patient relationship', everyone declared at Smithers Botham, and though nobody knew exactly what this meant, it was a telling phrase with a ringing note to it, and anyway a substitute for whistling to keep your spirits up.

How should he cast the first vote of his life? Alec wondered. The newspapers seemed poor instruments of political education. The cartoons at least made the issue simple, between bad bald men in top hats and good clean-cut ones in overalls. 'The People' came into it a good deal. Alec rather distrusted The People, who were sadly unintellectual, indeed somewhat dim. Sensitive to the doctors' vote, the local candidates presented themselves on successive nights in the Smithers Botham assembly hall. The Conservative was plump and confident, and based his persuasion on the fact that the Cabinet were a very decent set of chaps (he had been to school with many of them). The Labour man was hollow-chested and nervously respectful, and based his persuasion on the fact that someone was rude to him in a Labour Exchange during the thirties. Mr Cramphorn clapped the first oration to the echo, and walked out of the second.

Alec decided to support Labour, because he learned Desmond was voting Tory. In the end he was too busy in the operating theatre to reach the polls, and the hollow-chested man won handsomely. Mr Cramphorn stayed at home for a week's sulk.

But worse was in store. He appeared in the theatre at the beginning of August white and trembling. 'They sang the *Red Flag*,' he muttered. 'Actually in the House of Commons! Good God! Some woman danced in the benches. It's the end.' But it wasn't. The next day a patient addressed him as 'Mate'. Mate! To Mr Cramphorn, who had given a lifetime to the curing of the poor, who felt the deepest concern for their ills and pains, just like the old Tsars of Russia for their serfs. Social order and sanity were sliding everywhere. They would be swinging from the lamp-posts next. He stayed at home for a month, and his housekeeper sent a message to say he was very poorly.

Alec's next concern was finding his mother about to become a G.I. bride.

Edith Trevose had spent the war in a small Devon seaside town, in a guest-house whose rooms were furnished for a fortnight's summer endurance at the most, but had been occupied since 1939 by elderly middle-class guests from London who complained increasingly about the food, the cooking, the war in general, and each other. Edith had been a typist with a Gray's Inn solicitor, but decided to help a friend run the place as her 'war work'. She was still pretty, and the sun of her affections, which had dawned upon Graham and shone through the noonday of her life on his brother, now glowed upon her son Alec, and was crossed by the first long restful shadows of the menopause. Edith had a split social position in the town. However much she tried to disguise it from herself, in the boarding-house she was taken as a servant. When twice a week she lent a hand in the small local hospital, she was respected by everyone as the widow of a medical missionary and the sister-in-law of Graham Trevose himself. Edith bore the discrepancy cheerfully. She had put up with more disagreeable places in life than the guest-house, and always reflected that the irritations of others, like their illnesses, though painful to witness could hardly kill her.

In the summer of 1943 something happened to change the town's face more alarmingly than the war itself. Strange uniforms, strange vehicles, and strange habits became evident everywhere. The Americans poured from a near-by camp to amuse themselves, having to draw less on their supplies of cash (which were said to be limitless) than on those of their native enthusiasm and optimism. Strange soft-packaged cigarettes, chocolate bars, chewing-gum, and tinned beer circulated everywhere, and the girls' hair-styles improved sensationally. The Americans had glamour, in a land which was short of it outside the overpacked cinemas. All were assumed to come from spacious and labour-saving apartments in Manhattan, though most lived in towns even sleepier than a Devon village, and knew of their hosts only from their official guide-book, which told them not to say 'bloody', that the British could take any amount of aerial bombardment, and were deeply grateful for all the dried egg.

Edith met Hal White at the hospital. He was a doctor, a captain, about her own age, thin, with a large Adam's apple, glasses like Glenn Miller's, and given to long periods of deliberation before opening his mouth about anything. He offered her a packet of Life Savers and asked her to a dance. Edith hesitated. Jennifer, the girl who helped in the kitchen, might be there. Hal explained it was an officers only affair, and she accepted. She loved dancing. It would be really quite fun to be taken out by a man again. And of course he was a doctor, and therefore a gentleman.

The dance was exactly like a thousand others in the kingdom that Saturday night. The local recreation hall was crowded, dirty and ill-kept, with French chalk sprinkled hopefully over a rough floor with painted lines for badminton courts. The decorations were posters urging the merrymakers to dig or save for victory, and that careless talk cost lives. At one end was a trestle table where for half an hour or so they sold gin and lime, and afterwards beer, which everyone hoped would last the evening. Half a dozen G.I.s on the stage were playing with startling professionalism. Hal and Edith danced to *Paper Doll* and *Sentimental Journey*, and she thought him amazingly light on his feet. He said he lived in Yonkers and was a widower. They tried to hokey-cokey, which Edith thought silly, really, but quite fun. Hal explained he had knocked around the world

a good deal, mostly doing medical jobs with construction companies, for a long stretch in Singapore. Edith exclaimed she
knew Singapore well. They cheerfully explored the graveyards of
their memories, exhuming a body or two to see if it were a
mutual friend.

For the last year of the war they saw each other regularly.
Hal brought her a good deal of Spam, *Life* magazine, and some
nylons—her eyes shone as she smoothed the wonderfully sheer
material with her fingers. When he asked her to marry him she
was amazed. Marriage simply hadn't entered into her scheme
of things. Illness and death, yes, but widowhood had become a
settled way of life, to be borne as patiently as residence in the
Malayan jungle or in the Devon guest-house. Yet she realized
that she belonged to the dread class of 'distressed gentlefolk'.
What would she do after the war? She was frightfully poor, she
would have to go typing for solicitors until her fingers became
too infirm for the keyboard. Hal was really very kind. And he
was a doctor. The emotions of her life had been entwined round
doctors, as pliantly as the serpents round Aesculapius' staff.
She would have to live in America, but America was the place
for self-betterment, everyone said so. The ideal of self-betterment had driven her as a girl from her father's butcher's shop in
Ramsgate—to where? After a quarter of a century, to running a
boarding-house. It was a chance. Only one thing could she be
certain of. It would be her last.

That summer, the inhabitants of two Japanese cities were
off-handedly incinerated, and the war was over. A week later
Lease Lend was cut off, equally off-handedly. It occurred only
to Lord Keynes that the country was broke, and the millennium
which so agitated Mr Cramphorn would have to be financed by
a loan of American money. So the country, like Edith, escaped
from the possibility of German mastership to the certainty of
American, with as much excitement and less thought.

Edith, Hal, and Alec met for the first time in the basement
restaurant of the Criterion in Piccadilly. It was a disturbing
gathering. Alec seemed to find Edith's lover only funny. She
had been worried for months at the peculiar excited flippancy

in her son, quite unlike the stolid outlook of his father. She gave him a cheque for a hundred pounds, explaining it was all she could afford, and he must save it to visit her in America, once she was married and transported by the United States Government with eighty thousand other British women. Alec decided to spend it on a car. The medical profession lived at the time in a weird intimacy with the motor trade. Though the petrol ration was small, increased by the new Government so meanly as to arouse the irritation of even the *New Statesman*, doctors, who went on errands of mercy, were allowed more or less as much as they could use, with a bit of fiddling. He'd raise the fare to see his mother when the time came, he decided. He was never able to give a serious thought to the future of anything, particularly when there was fun to be found in the present.

During the rest of the hot summer of 1945 the war began to run down at Smithers Botham as gaily as everywhere else. There still wasn't much to drink, but there was A.F.N. Munich on the radio, the jam ration was said to be going up (incorrectly), and the place was enlivened by the first demobilized medical officers, sent on a six-month course to refit them for gentler practice. Captain Pile was finally demobilized. He went to Olympia for his new suit, and at once returned to Smithers Botham. He had grown to like the country hospital, and the future medical world was filled with half-glimpsed hazards. He had taken the post of medical officer to Smithers Botham as a mental institution, and was charged with preparing its return to normal function whenever Blackfriars could be evicted. As he walked up the long drive from the bus, once again mere Dr Pile, he saw the portico had for a second time been decorated. A Union Jack was spread across the columns, and a painted banner announced, 'Welcome Home Our Heroic Cuthbert'.

## 18

THE FIRST ANNUAL DINNER of the Annex Club at the beginning of 1947 was predictably a noisy affair. It was held at a
restaurant frustrated like all others from doing its best for its
diners, by the Government order that only three courses might
be served, including the soup. The law took itself seriously, an
establishment serving asparagus on a separate plate instead of
accompanying the sliver of meat having already incurred
prosecution. But the millennium had arrived. The coal mines
had been nationalized, the railways and the doctors were next.
The rations were reduced, coupons were needed for bread, and
cigarettes were as hard to come by as ever.

The club was Peter Thomas's idea. Military units seemed
hardly able to await their dispersal before arranging their
reunions, so why not the patients who had passed through the
annex? Besides, some sort of society was needed to help those
who suffered from disability, official meanness, or bad luck.
And it would be tragic for the buoyant comradeship of Smithers
Botham to be lost without trace in the rough waters of the postwar world. The annex itself still existed, almost as busily as
ever, with Tudor Beverley in charge. Graham had left, as he
had promised himself, with the end of the war. His status as a
Blackfriars consultant entitled him to half a dozen beds in the
main wards at Smithers Botham for civilian cases, the arrangement to which Haileybury had tried to condemn him in 1942.
But the time for self-sacrifice was past, Graham thought,
personal and financial. One day the annex would have to close

and Smithers Botham evacuated, he'd be back in the bright new wards of Blackfriars again beside the Thames—though from the permanent look of the hospital's rubble, that day seemed as unlikely to dawn as the one of settled amity across the split face of Europe.

Graham was naturally the club's president. It still gave him a feeling of smugness to see himself described on the printed menu as 'Sir Graham Trevose, K.B.E., D.Sc., F.R.C.S.'. The goodies had been delivered as Val Arlott had promised, and the doctorate of science had been conferred on him at the same time by a provincial university keen on entering into the spirit of the times. He had found himself more proud of the knighthood than he had expected. It was an emblem of something he sought all his life—a recognition that his work was far from trivial, but on a par with that of general surgeons majestically toiling among their sausage-chains of guts. Besides, everyone was terribly nice about it. Haileybury had called specially to congratulate him, almost with tears in his eyes. It was a well-deserved honour, he explained, not only for the surgeon and for the annex, but for the speciality of plastic surgery, to which he was himself about to return. Graham knew that Haileybury, of all his wellwishers, meant every word. He also knew the intense self-discipline which had brought the man to face him, for the first time since their meeting beside the River Itchen. He would know Graham well enough to sense the risk of a cutting rebuff. But Graham told himself the time for wounding was over, and reconciliation was in fashion.

'Thank you,' Graham said solemnly, shaking hands. 'Thank you . . . Eric.'

Haileybury swallowed. 'It is a real pleasure to congratulate you . . . Graham.'

It was the first time they had used each other's Christian names. In a world which could address old Cramphorn as 'Mate', reflected Graham, such relaxations were plainly overdue.

At the dinner, Peter Thomas proposed a toast to 'The Wizz'. Graham replied. Shortly afterwards the patients started singing,

136

something innocuous at first, *Macnamara's Band*, moving on to *Cats on the Rooftops*, an enduring favourite, then the *Ball of Kirriemuir*. Graham knew this always ended in argument, and sometimes in fisticuffs, over such points as the Minister's Wife Who Felt Unweel coming before The Swishing of the Pricks in the Haystacks, or the other way round. When Peter Thomas put a glass of beer on his head to play The Muffin Man, Graham thought it time to withdraw. He leant over to touch John Bickley, two places away. 'I fancy we're a little old for this, old man,' he smiled. 'Shall we see if there's the chance of a taxi?'

The two stood in dinner jackets and overcoats, surveying the ill-lit street from the door of the restaurant without much hope. It was bitterly cold, and snow had paralyzed the country more effectively than the *Luftwaffe*. There was a scarcity of coal, new shoes were on the ration, a warming tot of whisky was a luxury, and the Government had banned even greyhound racing to save electricity on the hares.

'What a bloody night,' muttered Graham. 'I should have brought the car.'

'What are you driving now?' They had spoken little since the incident of Bluey, and since Graham had left the annex hardly met at all.

'I've got a prewar Bentley. A peculiar beast with a fabric body, but it goes like a clock. I bought it from some spiv in the street, who wanted spot cash. God knows where the thing came from, probably stolen for all I know.'

They found a taxi and Graham asked John back for a nightcap. He had a large flat in the Marylebone Road, convenient for his new consulting room in Wimpole Street. John found it furnished stylishly with Graham's stored belongings. There was brandy on the sideboard, a bowl of fruit, even a box of chocolates. Graham seemed to have climbed back on to the lap of luxury.

'I suppose I'm allowed to switch on the electric fire?' Graham removed his overcoat. 'I can never remember what the permitted hours are.'

'Don't they just cut your current off?'

Graham grinned. 'I'm on the same cable as the Welbeck Hospital, so I'm spared.'

'You always did have all the luck.' As Graham poured him a drink, John added, 'It was quite a party tonight.'

'It's good to find the boys enjoying themselves. Though I could see that Tudor Beverley's got a deal of work to do on some of them. But at least it's a club where we can feel glad the membership won't be increasing.'

'It was good of you to ask me along.'

Graham looked surprised. 'But of course you had to be there. We couldn't do without "The Gasman", surely?'

' "The Gasman", if you'll recall, Graham, was requested not to call.'

Graham gave a short laugh. 'The famous Trevose temperament. Do you still hold it against me? I was upset at the time, all sorts of things were pressing on me. After all, they were trying to get rid of *me*, and damn near succeeded.' They took the comfortable armchairs on each side of the fire. The three bars gave a welcome glow. The central heating was off, and the block of flats as inhospitable as an iceberg. 'I know I've been a bastard often enough in my life,' Graham continued. 'As you get older you begin to see yourself properly. It was my temperament which wrecked our partnership. It wrecked my partnership with Tom Raleigh. It wrecked a lot of other relationships in my life. But I couldn't help it. If I'd managed psychologically to emasculate myself, I'd have had no drive to achieve anything at all.'

Graham sipped his drink in silence. The reference to tempestuous partnerships set John wondering about his host's present arrangements for sexual relaxation. He generally had some of a sort, though John had picked up no gossip round the nursing-homes of the West End. He wondered if the fellow were getting past it. By way of a probe, he asked, 'Do you live in this palace all alone?'

Graham nodded. 'It's too big, but I had to take what I could. The squatters were in downstairs, you know.'

'You were lucky to get your hands on it.'

'London's a peculiar place just now. Everyone knows some-one who can obtain the unobtainable. This austerity's a bore, isn't it? I certainly didn't expect it after the war. I thought everything would more or less click back into place again. I must have been mad.'

'You weren't the only one. The Tory party suffered the same insanity.'

'I suppose I'm amusing myself. Though the people you meet are peculiar. Not at all like before the war. I wonder what happened to them all.'

'Haven't they gone to Kenya and Rhodesia and such places?'

'I'd rather put up with things here. I'm not doing badly, you know,' Graham told him defiantly. 'The plastic game's as tough as ever, if not tougher. But I'm well and truly inside the magic circle now.' He smiled. 'The new handle helps, I suppose, "Sir Graham" and all that. The outsiders have a thin time of it, trying to break in. I'm certainly not going to help them. I suffered enough myself, and nobody was inclined to give *me* a leg-up.'

'Aren't you afraid of what Bevan's going to do?'

'Not really. The scheme won't touch us consultants much. We might even be better off—after all, we'll get paid for the work we do free in hospital. The g.p.s will get the dirty end of the stick, and that's too bad. The B.M.A. have spotted that, of course, that's why they're kicking up such a shindy. They're the g.p.s' trade union. The Royal Colleges, who represent people like me, are coming round to Bevan's line of thinking. The letter from the three presidents last month certainly seemed to indicate something like that. You see, Bevan's split the profession. Cunning blighter. I rather admire the man. If I'd gone into politics, which God forbid, I should have modelled myself on him. He knows what he wants, and can be perfectly charming as he invariably gets it. How are *you* doing, John?'

'Very busy. I've Smithers Botham, the Cavendish Clinic, half a dozen hospitals scattered round London. I'd almost forgotten I was on the staff of half of them.'

'I missed you badly at the annex, I don't mind admitting it.'

139

'Nice of you to do so now,' John said drily.

'That Australian we got was all right as a stuffist, but the anaesthetist's the stage-manager of the operating unit. With you, everything went so smoothly.' The vague idea of staging a reconciliation with John, already in Graham's mind before the dinner, now struck him as urgent. After all, he had a real affection for the man, they had been professional brothers-in-arms for the best part of thirty years. 'How's Denise?' he asked.

'She's been a bit off colour, recently. Nothing definite. One of the physicians had a look at her. Trying to run a home these days is enough to get any woman down.'

Graham hesitated, and added, 'If you'd like to get away, I've a villa you could borrow in the south of France. At Roquebrune, up above Monte Carlo.'

John raised his eyebrows. 'How on earth did you get the currency?'

Graham laughed. 'Oh, there are ways and means. I bought it a month ago—very reasonably, once I got hold of the francs. I don't think one should take these restrictions too seriously. After all, there are so many of them, if we observed the letter of all the laws we wouldn't be able to stray from our frontdoors.'

'It's a very kind offer, Graham, but I don't know when we'll have a chance to take you up on it.'

'I've hardly had a chance myself. I'm sending Sheila Raleigh down there next month—you know, Tom Raleigh's widow. She needs a holiday. I've given her the job of secretary to this Annex Club. There's an awful lot of work to do, quite a lot of money in the kitty It's a way for me to make amends. If I have any amends to make.' Graham finished his drink. 'It was sad about Tom. It shook me badly at the time. Too much so, perhaps. I felt somehow I was responsible. But how could I have been? I must have been feeling oversensitive in those days. Anyway, Sheila's getting married again this summer, some fellow out of the Navy. Do you want another drink?'

'No, I must get home, I'm afraid.' John rose. 'I promised Denise I wouldn't arrive back in too alarming a condition.'

'Do you think you'll find a taxi?'

'I'll walk. We're not far away, across the Park.'

'John, I wonder if you'd like to take over my anaesthetic work again?'

John paused, getting into his overcoat. This will prove, Graham thought, if he holds everything against me still.

'It's good of you, Graham, but I'm afraid my time for private work is absolutely booked.'

'Too bad,' murmured Graham.

He *does* hold it against me, Graham told himself. And quite badly. Probably Denise is behind it.

'Perhaps when things become more organized we can team up again?' Graham suggested vaguely.

'Yes, perhaps we can,' said John.

Graham closed the door behind his guest. He stood alone in the middle of the room. Something was disturbing him. He looked round, then sprang towards the mantelpiece and seized the ornamental clock. He looked at it foolishly for a moment, and carried it out to the kitchen. He had let it run down, and the woman who cleaned the flat must have rewound it. He hated clocks. Tick tock, tick tock. Every one a click along the ratchet towards extinction. Such thoughts came upon him often now that he lived alone. He sat down heavily in the armchair, telling himself he was really becoming dreadfully neurotic. Perhaps it was all to do with the symptoms of the male menopause.

## 19

THE PARTY was in Grosvenor Square, in a block of flats occupied mainly by Americans left over from the war, the only class of people in the country who could afford the rent. Lord Cazalay occupied the penthouse which covered most of the top floor. Graham admitted that his brother-in-law seemed to be making a success of his life. Despite the currency restrictions, the travel business appeared to be prospering, and he claimed to have his fingers in all manner of tasty pies. He always treated Graham with the warmest affability. Graham did not deceive himself this was through fraternal love, or remorse for past malevolence. Sir Graham Trevose was a useful name to keep around him. Graham didn't object overmuch. If you wanted such things as whisky, beefsteaks, suit lengths, or villas on the Riviera, you couldn't be squeamish over the company you kept.

'Graham, I'm delighted you could come.' Lord Cazalay pushed his way through the noisy crowd of guests. 'I hope you got over that dinner last night. I read about it in the papers.'

'I left before they started breaking the place up.'

'Very wise. It must be gratifying to know you've got these young men in such good spirits again.'

'I only did my best,' Graham told him modestly. 'Some of them would still give a girl a nasty scare on a dark night.'

'Champagne? I was rather lucky to get this consignment across the Channel. There's someone I'd like you to meet.'

Lord Cazalay led Graham across the room, putting his arm

round his shoulders, to demonstrate either affection or posses-
sion, Graham wasn't sure.

'Fred, this is Sir Graham. I know you'll be glad to meet him.'
Graham found himself facing a short, square man with a
leathery face, smoking a pipe. 'This is Fred Butcher,' Lord
Cazalay introduced him. 'You know, from the War Office.'

Graham recognized one of the Ministers who had been swept
to breathtaking heights by the flood of electoral popularity,
to be left sitting forlornly on his isolated peak as the tide
abruptly turned. He was a rather colourless public figure, a
fair-minded, hard-working, trade union official with a valuable
flair for bedding down lambs with lions. Graham wondered
how he got on with the more peppery generals.

'Glad to meet you, Sir Graham. Heard a lot about you during
the war, of course.'

'Perhaps too much?' Graham asked. 'That's some people's
view.'

'Every word was deserved, I'm sure of that.' He relit his pipe
and added, 'You know a surgeon called Mr Haileybury, I
believe?'

'Extremely well.'

'He got me to speak at a luncheon the other week. About this
burns hospital, and that. He seems a great one for the idea, does
Mr Haileybury.'

'Personally, I think he's got something of a bee in his bonnet
about it.'

'Maybe so,' said the politician guardedly.

Graham had heard of Haileybury's plan only second-hand.
It seemed that Haileybury, once reconciled to the Government's
cossetting the nation's health to a greater extent than providing
clean water and drains, had turned himself into a crusader for
the new scheme. He suddenly woke up to its offering an outlet
for his qualities of administration, sadly frustrated once he put
away his uniform. He was particularly taken with the idea of
establishing a hospital in London for burns and accidents,
arguing that the experience gained during the war should not
be dispersed, but concentrated under one roof and passed to

143

visiting surgeons from countries which had regrettably been spared the opportunity for such practice. The Ministry of Health was sympathetic to Haileybury, but doubtful. They had to find the money to put roofs on the old hospitals before digging the foundations of new ones.

Graham had a dozen questions he would like to have asked the Minister about the fuel crisis. But politicians, like medical men, must learn to keep their counsel, and he found himself talking instead about the restarting of international football. Then Lord Cazalay reappeared and said, 'Fred, I must tear Sir Graham away. There's someone else I'd particularly like him to have a word with.'

As Graham allowed himself to be led across the room, Lord Cazalay asked, 'Isn't Liz coming? I thought you were giving us the pleasure of looking at her?'

'She's meeting me here. The curtain at her show doesn't ring down till after ten.'

'That's splendid news. Graham, this is Arthur King. A very close friend of mine.'

Arthur King struck Graham as resembling a worried ferret. He was a youngish man, certainly not over thirty, with thinning fair hair and sidewhiskers. He wore a smart blue double-breasted suit with over-emphasis on the lapels, a dark striped shirt, and a plain grey tie with a diamond pin stuck in it. His green eyes had an expression of continual anxiety in them, and if he had ever learned to smile he seemed to have forgotten the knack.

'Pleased to meet you,' said Arthur King.

'Of course, you'll know all about Sir Graham's work in the war,' Lord Cazalay said affably.

'Yes, I read about it in the papers.' He inspected Graham anxiously. 'You fixed all them pilots up with new faces, didn't you? Must be a clever feller.'

Graham nodded. To have his work praised by a Minister of the Crown was one thing. Approbation from a man who might have left his fruit-barrow at the door was less welcome. Still, he told himself, society was changing, you had to take

144

people as they came, if you played the snob you got no-where.

'You'll remember, Arthur, that Sir Graham has an interest in our travel business.'

'Smart lad. Going like a bomb, that little company. It's only the beginning, mind. Once these bloody restrictions come off, the market'll be wide open.'

'I hope I'll see something back for my money,' said Graham, for the sake of making conversation. 'It isn't much fun paying it all away in taxes.'

'Oh, taxes,' said Arthur King, contemptuously. 'There's another little idea of ours. Shall we tell him, Charles?'

'Television,' said Lord Cazalay.

'There's not much future in that surely?' Graham looked surprised. 'Nobody will be able to afford the sets.'

'Another ten years and there'll be one in every home,' said Arthur King confidently. 'Just like the toilet.'

Graham's instruction in the mysteries of commerce was interrupted by the arrival of Liz.

Liz was an actress. Not a particularly well-known one—indeed, discovery of her name generally called for a fairly close reading of the programme. She was in one of the postwar revues, with a small part which hardly justified her style of living. She had an enviable knack of getting to know the people who mattered, and an even more valuable one of dropping them before they ceased to. She was a big woman, red-haired, with enormous teeth. Graham supposed she must be well past forty. He had met her a few weeks before, in the dressing-room of an actor whose noble features had illuminated the musical-comedy stage for some decades, and now, with his assistance, seemed likely to continue lightening it for some decades more. Graham had begun to move among theatrical people, even adopting some of their little affectations. It pleased him to see himself as part of their scene, to understand their momentously whispered trivial gossip. He found Liz heavy going, but a man must have a companion, and he was never one to play the monk.

145

'Graham darling, how wonderful.' Liz embraced him warmly, simultaneously managing to take a glass from her host. 'And Arthur, bless you, how nice. Thank you so much for all those lovely nylons. You *are* clever. They're divine.'

'Glad you liked them,' said Arthur briefly.

'Graham, tell me *all* you've been up to,' she invited, though they had parted less than forty-eight hours before.

'I went to a party with a lot of my old patients.'

'Those poor boys! They must look so peculiar, all together.'

'They do, but they've given up thinking about it, which was the object of the exercise.'

'How on earth could they manage to give up thinking about themselves? I should feel dreadful, quite an outcast, if I had the merest scar.'

'They manage it because I always made the effort of having people treat them like normal human beings, not as something out of a circus.'

Liz gave a faint smile. He looked in danger of being serious again. He really was a dreadful bore when he got serious. If he went on mixing with all these awful deformed creatures, he really shouldn't bother everyone by insisting on talking about them in quite repulsive detail.

'Let's go and grab something to eat,' Liz suggested. 'I think they've even got lobster.'

After ten minutes she said to him, 'You *are* grumpy tonight, I must say. What's the matter?'

'Oh, nothing.' An uneasiness had settled on him. These people really were rather dreadful, he told himself. Though why should he complain? There was wine, lobster, and bright company, all hard to come by. 'Shall we go on?' he asked her abruptly. 'To a nightclub or somewhere?'

'But darling! I've only just arrived.'

'I'm feeling restless.'

'Oh, all right, then. You do carry on peculiarly sometimes, darling, don't you?'

'Yes, I know I do. Very peculiarly. All my life. It's a bit late in the day to change my habits, I'm afraid.'

146

'I see you're in your *interesting* mood,' she told him. It was too bad, but she had to put up with it. He seemed very wealthy.

The nightclub, like a dozen others sprouting after the war, was in a basement near Piccadilly. Graham signed an order for a bottle of gin, which was supposed to be sealed and reproduced at the guest's next visit, but somehow never was. There was a rumba band and they danced for a few minutes on the overcrowded floor. 'Let's go home,' said Graham. 'This place is suffocating.'

'Darling, what's wrong with you tonight? You can hardly wait to get at it.'

'You're right. I can't. I feel like it.'

'I don't know!' She laughed. 'You're worse than any of the young ones.'

'The young ones don't need consoling.'

She ruffled the hair in the nape of his neck, which he was allowing to grow rather long. 'What do you need consoling about? You've got everything.'

'I've got nothing. Nothing that counts.'

'Now you *are* being interesting. I can't see anything you lack.'

'A human being, the most precious commodity of all.'

'What about me? Aren't I human?'

'Shall we go?'

'Oh, all right, darling. Though don't rush at me like a bull when we get in, will you?'

When they reached the flat she insisted on taking her time, to put him in his place. 'Can't we have a drink?'

'Yes, of course.'

As he poured out the gin she took a cigarette and remarked, 'That's a pretty picture.'

'Yes, it is pretty. That's its trouble. There's no feeling underneath.'

'Who did it?'

'I did. Before the war.'

'Really?' She looked surprised. 'I didn't know you were an artist. I mean, apart from making people faces. I suppose that's much the same thing, isn't it?'

147

'I *am* an artist. Rather than a surgeon. I am an artist obliged to conform with the discipline of a surgeon's life.'

'That doesn't seem to worry you,' she laughed.

'It does, quite often. For most of my life I've fought against the rigidity and stuffiness of the medical profession. Now I'm not so sure. It's rewarding, being set apart, being someone special. Even if it's only through your own rules, many of which can be extremely silly. I suppose it was the war which changed my mind, though I didn't realize it at the time.'

'Please, darling, don't go on about the war again.'

'I'm sorry. I'm really trying to forget it, but it keeps coming back, more and more.' He sipped his drink and reflected, 'It was really the only worthwhile time in my life, out at that annex place.'

She stubbed out her fresh cigarette. 'Come along, darling, shall we get on with it?' she invited. Anything to stop him talking about the war.

Graham had taken to copulating with the light on. He found it more amusing, and anyway had read somewhere that turning out the light was a suburban habit. Liz, possibly worn out by her exertions on the stage, fell asleep almost immediately afterwards. He lay for a long time looking up at the ceiling. She really was a ghastly female. She was fat, and her breasts fell away to the sides of her chest like a pair of half-filled sandbags. Still, she had a kind heart and she was always available, valuable and infrequent attributes in any female. He would be generous writing her cheque in the morning. He must have been rather difficult to tolerate that evening. His life was all wrong, all completely wrong. But he didn't see much prospect of setting it right, even if he had the remotest idea what the right sort of life for himself should be.

## 20

THE SAME EVENING Desmond Trevose was entertaining his
cousin Alec to dinner at high table in his Cambridge college.

Desmond had spent six months at Smithers Botham as Mr
Twelvetrees' house-surgeon, and a further year as his registrar,
which substituted for service in the thinning ranks of the Army.
He was a good house-surgeon, competent and thoughtful,
skilful enough with his hands as assistant in the theatre. But he
was not really a success.

He was too cold, too brusque with the patients. He had no
sense of human relationships. This was admittedly not a
necessity for the effective, or even successful, medical man.
Many renowned surgeons have been abominably rude. Others
like Mr Cramphorn regarded hospital patients as simple-minded
supplicants, unable to grasp such intellectual matters as the
nature of the disease which irked them, which having a Latin
name could only be discussed, if at all, by educated gentlemen.
But the mood of the patients, like the mood of the nation, was
becoming restless with smug authority. Medicine had advanced
during the war as strikingly as aeronautics, the hospital doctor
found himself turning into an applied scientist, yet the more he
could do for his patients the less they seemed to regard him. It
was baffling, not only for Mr Cramphorn. But the patients were
only daring to express what they had expected from their
medical attendants all along—to be their friend in health, their
ally in sickness, and their companion in death, a relationship

previously accorded only to those among them with a fee in their pockets.

Early in 1947 Desmond applied for a research scholarship at his old college, to study anatomy. It was in the blood. *The Synovial Membranes*, the anatomical thesis by his grandfather the professor, published in the year of Desmond's birth, lay on the desk in his college rooms. The old boy had a few sound ideas, Desmond decided, though the bulk of the book was nonsense. But the synovial membranes, lining the joints of the body, might be worth a second look, and he had decided to spend a year taking it.

He had asked Alec to dinner through no feelings of duty or affection. After living with him for a year in the medical officers' mess at Smithers Botham, Desmond had allowed the lifelong tepidity of his feelings towards his cousin to cool into frosty dislike. But having him up for the night seemed the only way to pin him down. Desmond wanted his money back, and Alec showed reluctance even to discuss such ungentlemanly a subject.

'I hope you won't find that guest room too chilly,' said Desmond, standing before dinner amid the beams of his own sitting-room. 'Did my gyp light a fire? I expect he'll give you a hot-water bottle.'

'Don't I need a gown, or something?'

'Guests at dinner aren't required to wear them,' Desmond told him solemnly. 'What have you got there?'

'Gin.' Alec produced the bottle from inside his jacket. 'A brand I've never heard of, it's probably full of methyl alcohol, enough to turn you blind. Not to worry. I was damn lucky to get it. I thought it would be an acceptable present.'

'I'd rather not risk it, if you don't mind,' said Desmond warily. 'I've got some reasonable college sherry.'

'You won't mind if I drink the stuff?' Alec had brought the bottle only with this intention. Desmond was a mean host. 'Do you remember the trouble we had buying booze at Smithers Botham? That ghastly grocer with his wine counter.' Alec poured half a tumbler of gin, which he started to sip neat. 'It was a kindly Act of God which landed him on us with a strangulated hernia. Afterwards I believe he genuinely tried to do his best for his medical customers. He was dead scared he might find himself in our hands again.'

'Everyone drank far too much at Smithers Botham.'

'You know, I loved the place. A lot of people were browned off with it, but not me. I suppose it was because you could get away with anything. No stuffiness. Do you remember that party when some fellow kept insisting on lighting his own flatus with a match? It was quite sensational. Amused the girls terribly.'

'Aren't you drinking rather a lot yourself, Alec?'

'I expect I'm an alcoholic. My present employment is enough to make me one.' Alec had left Smithers Botham for a hospital in the north of England, where he was anaesthetic registrar. 'It's a ghastly hole. The town's all trains. They seem to go clanking and hooting everywhere, into tunnels, across viaducts, holding up all the traffic at level crossings. The hospital's dreadful. Not a gentleman in the place. All the residents are Irishmen, Indians, Scotsmen, those sort of people. No intellectual conversation. Anyway, drinking seems to do my asthma good.'

Desmond put his hands behind his back and pursed his lips. 'I thought you might have given conventional treatment a chance first.'

'But I did.' Alec finished his gin and poured himself another. Desmond began to feel worried. His cousin had become dreadfully unreliable socially, and it would never do upsetting the dignity of the dons' dining table. 'I was skin-tested, and they told me I was allergic to grasses—crested dog's-tail, sheep's fescue, bird's foot trefoil. Whoever could imagine things with such lovely names doing anyone the slightest harm? It's ridiculous.'

'That's not a very reasonable attitude towards medicine, is it?'

'Well, medicine's only a branch of zoology. We mustn't take ourselves too seriously. But I let them fill me up with grass

151

extracts. They didn't do the slightest good. Did you know I went to a psychiatrist at Smithers Botham?'

'There was a rumour to that effect.' Desmond gave a faint smile. 'Nobody seemed to think it particularly surprising.'

'Of course I kept quiet about it. For a Blackfriars houseman, visiting a psychiatrist would be far more shameful than visiting a prostitute. I went to see old Dency. He said I suffered from *Haltlosigkeit*.' Desmond frowned. 'It means an irresponsible, aimless personality, with no perseverance, no will-power, no concentration, and no particular interests. An optimistic hysteric who lives for the present and refuses to learn from experience. I looked it all up. Possibly he's right. It's apparently due to maternal over-indulgence in early childhood.'

'How is your mother?' Desmond asked.

'She seems happy enough in the States. I suppose it's nice to warm your feet on the small of a man's back again, even at her age. And even with a cold fish like her husband. I always thought Americans noisy and fun-loving, like the ones we used to see lounging about Piccadilly and spitting on the pavement. She's a peculiar woman, my mother. It's odd, the particular severity one judges one's parents with as one grows up. Must be fundamental. Some species eat theirs. Dency looked after *your* mother, didn't he?'

Desmond nodded. He supposed the reminder was vaguely ill-intentioned.

'Do you think he's a pansy?' Alec asked. 'He kept patting me, like the geography master at school.'

'He's got a certain effeminacy of manner,' admitted Desmond awkwardly. Homosexuality was not a subject to be mentioned, even in private.

'Are *you* a pansy, Desmond?'

Desmond went red. 'How dare you ask such a thing?'

'I've often wondered. You're not particularly interested in girls. I don't believe you've ever had one, have you? Even at a Smithers Botham party, where maidenheads popped like the balloons.'

'I can hardly afford to get involved with women,' said

Desmond defensively. 'I'll be here for a year, maybe two, hardly paid at all. Only my keep and an honorarium. I can't expect to sponge on my father at my age.'

'You asked me here to get your money back, didn't you?'

'Yes,' said Desmond.

'You haven't got a hope, old cock.'

Desmond stuck his hands in his pockets and asked angrily, 'Why don't you make some attempt to behave honourably about it? It's a debt. It's on paper. You'd never have qualified at all without it.'

'In good time, all in good time,' said Alec amiably. 'At the moment I've rather a lot of expenses. I'm going to get married.' Desmond stared at him. 'To Felicity, only daughter of Air Marshal Sir Giles Perrins, K.C.B., D.S.O., D.F.C. And bar. Very grand, you see.'

'I don't believe you.'

'Come, Desmond. The only asset I've got is a strange sex appeal. Don't deny me that.'

'I still don't believe you. How on earth would you meet her?'

'At some sort of social to do with my present hospital. She was a W.A.A.F. I asked her and she said yes. Remarkably straightforward. I'm seeing her in Town tomorrow. She's just been demobbed.'

Desmond digested this. 'What can I say? I hope you'll be very happy.'

'Thank you.'

A bell started to ring. Desmond picked up his gown. 'It's time for hall.'

'So you see, Desmond, I shall shortly be in a position to pay you off. I should imagine the dowry will be considerable. They're stinking rich. For the moment, patience.'

As Alec reached for his gin-bottle again, Desmond said testily, 'You haven't time for another.'

'But I must, Desmond, I *must*. I have a pathological fear of meeting strangers. Don't worry, I shan't be sick into the soup, or anything like that.'

Alec was not sick into the soup, but he broke a wine glass, talked continuously and extremely loudly, and told obscene stories. Desmond recognized his invitation as a terrible mistake. He wondered for the first time if his cousin really were a psychopath, a manic-depressive, something like that. He certainly suffered the most alarming swings of mood. At other times he could be solitary, silent, gloomy, and savage. The only course was to get him safely to bed in the college's guest-room. Further discussion about the money must wait until the morning.

But in the morning Alec had gone.

He woke in the dark, had no notion of the time, found his watch was stopped, and felt possessed with the idea of going down to London. The college porter let him out and he started his car. He hadn't even shaved. It was light when he reached Felicity's house in Chelsea. There were few people about. He remembered it was Sunday. He rang the bell. Nothing happened. He stood back from the door and started to shout. A grizzled head appeared at an upstairs window. He recognized Air Marshal Sir Giles Perrins, K.C.B., D.S.O., D.F.C. and bar.

'What the hell do you think you're up to?' demanded the householder.

'I've come to see Felicity.'

'Oh, it's you. Well, clear off. Neither Felicity nor anyone here wants to set eyes on you again.'

'I demand to see my future wife.'

'For God's sake, man! Get away, will you? You know perfectly well my daughter wishes to have nothing whatever to do with you.'

'Felicity agreed to marry me.'

'Please, please be reasonable. You're just causing trouble for yourself and all of us. Felicity never said anything of the kind. You know that as well as I do.'

'You're deliberately keeping her from me.'

'Do go away, there's a good chap. You're disturbing the neighbourhood. It's terribly early.'

'I demand admittance.'

'Oh, clear off, you stupid little bastard.'

'How dare you speak to me like that! I am a healer, I demand the respect to which I am entitled.'

There was a milk-bottle on the step. Alec picked it up and threw it into the closed downstairs window. He thought the crash sounded very satisfactory.

The rest of his morning was confused. There were policemen, the Air Marshal, even Felicity in the background, in her dressing-gown. People kept holding him down. They were persecuting him terribly. They wouldn't listen, however much he tried to explain. There was another man, very worried. He was a doctor, he explained. 'Now calm down, old man, calm down,' he implored. 'Look what a mess you've made of this sitting-room.'

'I didn't make the mess,' Alec protested violently. 'They made it, they're trying to discredit me. It's all a plot. What's that?' he demanded.

'It's only a syringe. I think you'd benefit from a sedative.'

'You're trying to poison me.'

'No, I'm not. You'll recognize the need for it yourself when you recover.'

'Recover? I'm not ill. Everyone's against me. Oh God, everyone's always against me.'

Alec suddenly felt he couldn't be bothered with these unpleasant persons any longer. Drowsiness overcame him. He'd had a tiring few hours, he had to agree. People seemed to be moving him. He let them have their way. He'd let them persecute him. He'd lost the will to resist. He was lying on his back, moving along. In something, a car. Surely not an ambulance, he wasn't in the slightest ill. He was still on his back, in the fresh air again. His surroundings struck him as familiar. The flat dome, the smoke-belching minarets, the magnificent portico. Smithers Botham. They wheeled him to the block which had quartered the Emergency Squad, one of the first sections of the hospital returned to rightful use.

'Hello, Alec.'

He looked up. It was Dr Dency, long fingers playing with the little gold bars of his watch-chain as usual.

'Don't worry, Alec. We'll look after you. You'll be all right here.'

'Home again,' said Alec simply. 'Yes, I always liked this place.'

## 21

'I'M SORRY I'M LATE,' Graham apologized. 'I had to go out
to Smithers Botham. My nephew Alec was admitted there
yesterday.'

'I'm sorry to hear that,' said Haileybury. 'Nothing serious,
I hope?'

'No, not too alarming. He's in the psychiatric block as a
voluntary patient. Dency's looking after him. Alec's landed
himself in a bit of trouble. He's been behaving rather oddly
recently, I must say. I expect they'll get him straightened out.
I gather they've some new drugs coming in for this manic-
depressive business, which should help the poor fellow.'

'Nevertheless, it must be very disturbing for you.'

'It is.' Graham sat down. 'I thought we had enough mental
illness in the family with my wife. God knows where Alec inherited it from. Though his father could be peculiar enough
when he liked. Missionary or not, there were one or two stories
about him I shouldn't care to repeat.'

'No, no, of course not,' said Haileybury hastily.

'Anyway, every family's got one or two mad ones in it, if you
look closely enough. Not that Alec's certifiable, anything like
that. He just needs watching for a while. He's grown into a
peculiar young man all round. And I'm more or less responsible for him, with his mother in America. At least, I promised
her as much. She's a pleasant woman. You've never met her?'

Haileybury gave a faint smile. 'Indeed I have, Graham. You
seem to forget she was our secretary at the plastic hospital near
Ramsgate in 1918.'

Graham laughed. 'I could be forgiven for the lapse, surely? Water has poured over the dam with frightening speed since then. Then you'll also remember I was having a violent love affair with her at the time?'

'I don't think we need go into that now,' said Haileybury amiably.

He's mellowing pleasantly with the years, Graham thought. In those days of far-off passion, he tried to lose me my first chance of a decent job over it. He isn't a bad fellow, really. At least he isn't a hypocrite. As most doctors are obliged to be— half the time for the good of their patients, and the other half for the good of themselves.

'What can I do for you, Eric?' he asked.

They were sitting in Haileybury's club, in the same corner of the morning-room as at the beginning of the war. Haileybury was wearing his usual plain blue suit. Graham could never remember him in anything else. It was early evening, and Haileybury signalled the club waiter to buy Graham a drink for the second time in his life.

'I gather you met Butcher the other evening?' Haileybury asked.

'I bumped into him at a party.'

'I also gather he said something to you about my scheme for a national burns unit?' Graham nodded. 'Would you like to hear more about it? If you don't, if you think it might bore you, if it's a notion you couldn't feel interested in, do please say so. We'll just drop the subject, have a gossip instead. I shan't be in the slightest offended. I've talked about it to so many people, I can't expect all of them to share my enthusiasm.'

'I should be very interested indeed. I suppose I must by now have handled more burns than most people.'

Haileybury nodded slowly. To Graham's surprise he produced a briefcase and laid it on the table. A man like Haileybury would not encumber himself with a showy accessory unless he felt most strongly about its contents. Haileybury extracted some papers.

'These are my ideas reduced to writing. You may like to take

158

them and study them at leisure.' Graham found himself with a thick bundle of closely typed foolscap. 'Since I first talked to Butcher I have raised my sights somewhat. With the Government, the more you ask for the more you get. I see it as a centre devoted to the surgery of accidents in its widest sense. Motor accidents, accidents in the home, industrial accidents. This last, I think, gives me the most confidence of success. It strongly appeals to the trade-union element in the Government. Nobody's really bothered to specialize in the surgery of industry before. To my mind, the need is just as pressing as specializing in the surgery of war.'

'I'm sure you're right.'

'I understand that Bevan himself is very keen on the idea.'

'But when's it all going to materialize?' Graham asked. 'After all, the Government's already committed to taking the profession by the ears and shaking it out of all recognition in the next few months. It's supposed to be building health centres everywhere like luxury cinemas. It's got half the hospitals in the country damaged by air-raids, and the other half falling to bits anyway. When are they going to create your shining new palace? I'm sure the idea will come to something one fine day, Eric, but I'm afraid you and Nye Bevan and I shan't be here to attend the opening ceremony.'

'It already exists,' said Haileybury quietly.

The waiter brought their drinks. As he retired, Haileybury added, 'It exists less than twenty miles from where we are sitting. To be precise, near Iver, in Buckinghamshire. Extremely convenient for London.'

Graham frowned. He couldn't recall such a place. 'Has some genie waved the magic wand?'

'No, but the Americans have. They built a hospital there during the war. It took them, I believe, a matter of some weeks. They are not a people for procrastination. Now the Americans are going home, the building stands there stripped and empty. There seems no obstacle to our taking it over. It is a perfectly adequate structure, single-storey wards, room for five hundred beds. The design of the operating theatres is quite remarkable.

159

There are one or two peculiar features—a soda-fountain, for instance—which can easily be removed. I gather the price will be nominal, particularly if we call it the "Franklin D. Roosevelt Hospital", something of that nature.'

'That sounds a pleasant windfall,' said Graham thoughtfully. 'What would you want me to do? Serve on some committee to raise funds for the equipment?'

'I would want you to head the staff.'

Graham looked up. He had imagined that Haileybury's interest in the hospital came at least partly from the glory of running it himself. 'But what about you?'

Haileybury shrugged his shoulders. 'You would be the better man.'

'Aren't you rather carrying modesty to extremes?' Graham found himself faintly irritated by Haileybury's honesty. It was something of an affront. 'You're the one who's preached for years that plastic surgery was essentially the surgery of repair. As for me, I'm a beauty-doctor, a face-faker.'

'And that, if I may say so, is a rather over-modest view of your work during the war.'

'I thought you imagined my work during the war was grabbing publicity?'

'I did imagine it at the time,' Haileybury told him frankly, 'but I was wrong. I didn't understand the importance of the cosmetic work you were doing. I make all the apologies you feel you deserve. It was difficult, confined to administrative tasks. I was too far from individual patients. I came to appreciate only late in the war how much you did for morale.' He tapped the table with his long forefinger. 'And that is what we need in this new place of mine. Someone to make plain that those mutilated by the hazards of peace can be treated as effectively as those mutilated by the hazards of war.'

'But Eric! This is an enormous job you're asking me to take on. There're all manner of questions for me to decide first.'

'At least the financial question will decide itself. As director, you would draw the appropriate consultant's salary in the new health service. Plus a merit award, doubtless, if that part of the scheme goes through.'

'But what time have I for such responsibilities? Don't forget I've a busy private practice.'

'I regret that private practice would not enter into it. The post would be full-time. You know how strongly the Government feels on such points.'

'Then I'm afraid it's out of the question.'

'Do you know, Graham, it's the second time you have used that expression to me sitting exactly in this spot?'

Graham smiled. 'I'm sorry. I much appreciate the honour you've paid me, but I must look to my own interests. I've landed myself with a hell of a lot of debts, to be paid off somehow before I'm too old to work at all. I'd love to accept, Eric, the idea's got tremendous attraction, it would be like the annex all over again. But I'm afraid it's just not on.'

'Last time, I made the mistake of pressing you for a decision. I shall not repeat it. There is plenty of time—months, perhaps a year, perhaps two. Any moment you feel inclined to discuss the matter further, lift a telephone. Will you promise?'

'Very well,' Graham told him amicably. 'I'll keep it constantly before me. Should I undergo a change of heart you'll hear at once.'

'Excellent. Now let us drop the subject and talk about something else. Very sad, don't you think, Graham, the prospects for the coming county cricket season?'

Graham quickly put the offer out of mind. A salaried post, he decided, would be far more suitable for a man of modest tastes like Haileybury himself. But even Haileybury indulged in a little private practice. He did operations every Saturday morning in a small hospital near the Crystal Palace, which during the war had somehow fallen under the domination of his own in London, King Alfred's, and afterwards never escaped. It had few private beds, the theatres were antiquated, but the nursing was sound and the general atmosphere Haileybury found agreeably modest. John Bickley was a consultant to the hospital and generally gave Haileybury's anaesthetics, though regretting that Haileybury didn't take the same wide view of operating fees as Graham.

The following Saturday, as Haileybury was finishing the repair of a child's cleft palate, he observed to John, 'I saw Trevose the other day.'

'Yes, I ran into him only last week. He seems to be doing as well as ever.'

'He's full of bounce, certainly. With Trevose that generally indicates a stuffed wallet.'

'Did you think him cheerful? I felt he was rather miserable with himself.'

Haileybury inserted the final stitches in the child's mouth. 'He's a man of moods,' he observed drily. 'And that nephew of his has gone off his head.'

John frowned under his surgical cap. 'Alec was my junior assistant. He was something of a queer fish, I must say.'

'That goes for all the Trevose family, doesn't it? They don't make life easy for themselves.'

'Perhaps you're right.' John disconnected the long corrugated rubber tube of his anaesthetic apparatus. 'Alec's mother will be upset. She had high hopes for him. Saw him as a second Horder, I believe.'

'Well, he might achieve it yet. Some of our most eminent breathren have been somewhat unbalanced. It's a matter of survival until they reach the position where nobody dare mention it.'

John removed the throat-pack and the thin, wire-stiffened armoured Magill tube from the child's windpipe. 'I think I'll go back to the ward with this one.'

'All is well, I trust?' asked Haileybury sharply.

'Yes, perfectly. But you can never be sure of anything at all in this game.'

In the children's ward at the end of the corridor he passed his patient to the care of the staff-nurse, and asked, 'Where's Sister?'

'In her office, Dr Bickley.'

John knocked on the door by the ward entrance and went in.

Clare Mills looked up from her desk. 'Hello!' She smiled. 'Quite a stranger.'

'I was bringing back that palate.' He popped a cigarette over his sagging mask and lit it. 'I had a chat with Graham last Saturday night.'

Clare raised her eyebrows. At first she said nothing, but moved some notes on her desk. 'And how is he?'

'He's wearing well. And he seemed to be enjoying life. Or trying to convince himself that he was.'

'I'm glad he's all right.'

'Do you ever hear from him?'

'Oh, no! I would never have expected that. Not with Graham.'

'He didn't mention you at all,' John volunteered.

'I wouldn't have expected that, either. Once anyone's left his orbit he likes to cut them out completely. To forget about them, as though they'd never existed.'

'Even you, who tried to save him from himself?'

'I wasn't conscious of doing so at the time, but I suppose that's true.'

'It's all part of his selfishness, I suppose. Rejecting even those who've helped him, once they're no more use.'

'I don't think so. Not entirely. We can understand his trying to spare himself the pain of sad memories. He inflicts enough on himself. Anyway, he doesn't know where I am,' she added more briskly. 'He doesn't even know if I'm still in the country.'

'Do you want to see him again?'

She looked at him hard for a moment and said, 'What's the point?'

John nodded understandingly and asked, 'Have you any plans—for getting married, that sort of thing? Anyone in mind? I hope you don't mind my asking, Clare. I've come to feel something of an uncle to you.'

She smiled again. 'A very useful uncle. You found me this job.'

'I felt I wanted to do something for you. If you remember, we were both suffering from the Trevose temperament rather severely at the time.'

163

'Perhaps it was all something to do with war-weariness.'

'You haven't answered my question.'

'No, I haven't anyone in mind. I don't suppose I shall. I've got my work.'

'At which you're extremely efficient.'

'Thank you. Everyone regards me as a dedicated and completely sexless ward sister. There're plenty of them about. The backbone of any hospital. The whole system would fall to bits without such women. When I was in training, I often wondered exactly what created them. Now I know.'

'That sounds a gloomy prognosis for yourself.'

'Perhaps someone will turn up. You never know. Otherwise I shall sister on, until I'm pensioned off and go to live in a seaside boarding-house.'

'But don't you bear any resentment? Towards Graham?'

'How can one bear any resentment towards a maladjusted child?'

'I daresay you're right,' John told her.

## 22

THE GOVERNMENT was out of luck. The worst snowfall of the century was followed by the worst floods that could be remembered at all. The cascade began in the middle of March 1947, the rivers spilt disastrously across the countryside, swamping the roads and railways, drowning the sheep, ruining the potato crop and countless carpets. Two years after victory the people who had given blood, toil, tears, and sweat were left standing in queues holding damp ration-books.

The postwar disgruntlement which affected everyone began to depress Graham. He was starting to confess himself bored and disgusted with his brother-in-law and his cronies. The girl Liz was really a shocking creature, though he felt disinclined to ditch her with no replacement in sight. Perhaps there never would be, he reflected. He was becoming a shade elderly to play the rake. He would have liked to stay at the villa after Sheila Raleigh came home, he craved for luxury and sunshine, but he had too much private work in London. There seemed to be a dammed-up demand for plastic surgery, as for other prewar luxuries like chocolates and cars, and plastic surgery was readily obtainable for your money. And at least, he reflected, he passed most of his time in hospitals and nursing homes, where it was warm and there was plenty of hot water.

He was still living alone, and trying to reconcile himself to it. To make his evenings more bearable he started to write a textbook on the surgery of burns. He had never written much before, though he felt that if he could paint he was equipped with the right sort of mental muscles for self-expression. He turned out a trunkful of notes from the annex, sorted them into bundles, and started work with his portable typewriter. Progress was slow. As he read his scribbled pages, he found himself drawn back to the atmosphere of the bungalow where he had jotted most of them down. He found the composition becoming dominated by Clare. He remembered exactly what she was saying or doing when he had drawn up some particular account of a patient or an operation. It disturbed him. He had thought about her often enough since they separated, but he told himself she was in the past, finished and done with, like Edith. He determined to put her resolutely out of his mind. It was the only way. Anyway, if he didn't, the book would never be finished.

He was working alone one evening towards the end of March when the telephone rang. It was Lord Cazalay.

'I say, Graham, are you still at home? We were expecting you tonight.'

'I'm sorry, but I couldn't make it.' Another one of his damn parties. 'Didn't you get the message? I asked the Clinic to phone you.'

'Some signal got through to me, but I didn't take it seriously.' Lord Cazalay sounded offended. 'You remember you particularly promised to come.'

'I've got an urgent case coming in, I'm afraid. You'll have to excuse me.'

This pretext being unanswerable, Lord Cazalay added, 'I wonder if I could have a word with you fairly soon? It's a matter of some importance.'

Graham gave a grunt. He probably wants more money out of me, he thought. Money is the only matter of importance that he knows. 'I'm dreadfully booked up this week, Charles, professionally.'

'Surely you can spare a moment? It's rather pressing. How about lunch tomorrow at my club?'

'It's a miserable confession, but my lunch is always a sandwich between cases.'

'Can't I call tomorrow evening? About seven?'

'All right, I'll make a point of being here,' Graham told him, giving in.

'I'm much obliged. By the way, you'll make sure we're undisturbed, I take it? It's extremely confidential.'

'I'm nearly always on my own,' Graham assured him.

In the next morning's paper he saw that Fred Butcher had resigned from the Government. He wondered why. He had seemed from brief acquaintance a likeable, down-to-earth sort of fellow. He couldn't be bothered to read the story running down the column. Politics was a bore, and the newspapers only made up fairy-stories. When someone mentioned the incident in the theatre of the Cavendish Clinic during Graham's first case, he said, 'Yes, I met the chap the other day. Seemed a very solid citizen.'

'*Did* you?' asked his young assistant, looking up.

'What's the matter?' Graham was surprised at the tone. 'Is he in disgrace, or something? I supposed he'd resigned on some lofty point of political principle.'

'Reading between the lines, he's in the cart. Something very peculiar about Army contracts. A number of old Army wireless sets seem to have gone sadly astray.'

'Who on earth would want an old Army wireless set?'

'People want anything these days. In Germany you could refurnish your house with a few hundred cigarettes.'

'I suppose so,' said Graham sombrely. 'Everyone seems to be on the make. There's a spiv in all of us.'

Lord Cazalay arrived promptly at seven. With him was the ferret-faced Arthur. Graham invited them in cordially. If they had some proposition for him, he had already decided to reject it. But at least he could politely offer them a whisky. After all, it had come via Lord Cazalay.

For a while Lord Cazalay talked about the obstacles to making money in the postwar world, a subject he seemed inclined to leave with more impatience than usual. Arthur sat sipping whisky nervously and said nothing. After a few minutes Lord Cazalay declared, 'Graham, I've found you a new patient.' He inclined his head. 'Arthur here.'

Graham looked at the ferrety man with mild interest. 'What's the trouble?' he asked.

'I'd like you to fix my face up, Sir Graham.'

'But you haven't any scars or blemishes that I can see.'

'I'd just like you to change it a bit. Like you did to the pilots during the war.'

Lord Cazalay gave a harsh laugh. 'Plenty of room for improvement, eh, Graham?'

Graham put his finger-tips together and gave the proffered features a more careful inspection. It wasn't a bad face. The nose was too pointed and the jaw underslung, but not to the point of unsightliness. But he appreciated, even if he still never understood, the psychological forces urging patients towards him. A crooked nose or a dropping eyelid, passing more or less unnoticed by the world, could incite any amount of self-torture. He remembered a youth during the war with a leg withered from polio. All the frustrations of his life were ascribed to his leg. He implored one of the general surgeons to chop it off, to cast it from his life altogether, replace it with one of the splendid artificial ones they were designing for the wounded. The surgeon obliged. Six months later the young man committed suicide. We must all find something to blame, Graham thought, even if it's a bit of ourselves.

'Of course, you realize that a cosmetic operation, like any operation, carries a risk?' Graham explained, as he did to every patient. Arthur nodded. 'Nor is it free from pain and bother. Some can be distinctly uncomfortable for weeks afterwards. And even I can't guarantee a perfectly successful result.'

'The bill will be rather painful too, I fancy,' said Lord Cazalay, laughing again.

'I wouldn't conceal that, either,' said Graham.

'You'd be looked after, Sir Graham,' Arthur assured him solemnly. 'Rely on me for that.'

'As this is turning into a consultation, I'll have to ask you to leave us, Charles,' Graham explained to his brother-in-law. 'It's rather irregular to conduct one with an audience.'

Arthur looked at Graham imploringly and asked, 'Can't he stay? He's a friend.'

'Oh, very well, if you wish,' Graham conceded testily. 'In what particular way do you want your appearance changed?'

'I just want it changed. I'm not fussy.'

Graham frowned. 'But what's the object? What is it that distresses you about your looks?'

'I want it changed for business reasons.'

Graham looked at Lord Cazalay. 'What's going on?'

'Graham, do you have to ask so many questions?'

Graham paused. 'I'm sorry, Mr King, but I'm afraid I can't take you as my patient.'

Lord Cazalay glared angrily. 'Look here, Graham, you're being ridiculous.'

'I apologize if it strikes you that way. But I couldn't possibly operate on a patient without satisfying myself over the reasons. Some of them are pretty obscure, admittedly, but at least they hold water. I'm inclined to think there's something behind all this. I'd prefer not to ask about it. There're plenty of other plastic surgeons in London. You can always try your luck elsewhere.'

Lord Cazalay brushed his moustache, 'I'm sorry you're being so unco-operative. Perhaps you'll think again.'

'Why don't we tell him the truth?' suggested Arthur, as if struck by a novel thought. As Lord Cazalay made no reply, he went on, 'Look, Sir Graham—I'm in a bit of trouble.'

'We're all in a bit of trouble,' muttered Lord Cazalay.

'You saw in the papers this morning about Fred Butcher?' Arthur continued. 'It's the beginning of something. People have been nosing about where they shouldn't, making trouble. Mind, I've always acted in good faith, always. But you've got to cut a few corners these days. I'll have to lie low for a bit. I thought if you changed my face it would all be a bit easier to avoid the publicity.'

Graham sat staring at him. 'You mean, you're a crook and you want me to alter your appearance to escape your just deserts?' As neither visitor said anything, he continued, 'Well,

169

I shan't play the outraged citizen. I've had a few requests of a similar nature in my time. I'll only tell you the whole idea is reprehensible, and ask you to leave at once.'

'I'll make it well worth your while, honest I will,' Arthur repeated hopefully.

Graham got up. 'You could never do that, Mr King.'

'Just a moment,' Lord Cazalay interrupted. 'We're none of us shining with innocence. You seem to have forgotten the few favours I've done you. That foreign currency for your villa. It would look pretty nasty if it came into court, wouldn't it? They'd hand out a stiff sentence for a fiddle on that scale. You'd go to jail, wouldn't you? And your medical authorities would have a few words to say about the matter, too. They'd hardly let you go on practising after that.'

'You mean you're blackmailing me?' demanded Graham.

'Blackmail? I don't know what that means. Business is run on a system of favours done and granted. Persuasion is necessary from time to time.'

'Get out.'

'I'm not going to let you take this high-and-mighty line,' Lord Cazalay continued more confidently. 'For your own good, Graham. You won't do yourself any harm, tidying up Arthur. You get dozens of people coming to have their faces altered, you said so yourself. You aren't to know he's in any trouble. Not yet. In a week or two it'll be a different matter. You're going to do this, my boy. I'm not given to idle threats. You've known my family long enough to realize that we get what we want. Either you do something for Arthur, or the details of your little currency transactions end up on the desk of the Director of Public Prosecutions.'

'Get out,' Graham repeated.

'No, I shan't get out. Sit down and think it over. I'll give you five minutes.'

GRAHAM WAS STARTLED how old Denise looked. Then he
remembered she had been ill. As she opened the front door she
stared at him with surprise, quickly trying to find a smile.

'Could I see John?' Graham asked at once. 'The Clinic told
me he'd gone home.'

'Yes, of course, Graham. Come in. How are you keeping?'

'Oh, pretty well.'

'The weather's ghastly, isn't it?'

'Yes, ghastly.'

'And all this dreadful austerity we're supposed to put up
with.'

'Yes, yes,' said Graham.

He came into the cold hall of the Bickleys' flat overlooking
Regent's Park. It was barely an hour since his confrontation
with Lord Cazalay.

John was in the sitting-room, reading the evening paper and
tickling the dog. He stood up as Graham entered, saying
amiably enough, 'An unexpected pleasure. Or have you come
for a contribution towards the damage the boys did to that
restaurant?'

'I won't stay a moment.' Still in his overcoat, Graham looked
pointedly at Denise.

'Would you like a cup of coffee or something?' she asked with
great reluctance.

'Please. That would be very kind.' As the door shut he turned to John and said, 'I wonder if you'd stuff a case for me? Tomorrow morning.'

John knocked his pipe on the fireplace. 'I expect I could squeeze it in, if it's early enough. Has everyone else let you down?'

'It's a special case.' Graham hesitated. 'It calls for a great deal of discretion. I'm going to do it at that little nursing-home place out at Ealing.'

'Graham!' John laughed. 'Don't tell me you're branching into the abortion racket?' Seeing Graham's troubled expression, he added seriously, 'But what is it? Some actress with a secret scar? Stella Garrod all over again?'

'Oh, it's a much nastier business than the Stella Garrod affair. I've got myself in a bit of a mess.'

John raised his eyebrows. Hardly the first time. At Graham's age, he really should start to learn. Perhaps Clare was right about the maladjusted child.

'A woman, you mean?'

'No, not this time.'

Graham explained about Arthur King.

'I see,' said John calmly when he had finished. 'So you're going to do the case?'

'I've no alternative, have I? I was a fool having anything to do with that Cazalay bastard. He tried to bring me down once before. This time he's going to make a proper job of it.'

'But if you do it, and the fact comes out in the papers, it's going to look pretty nasty for you.'

'Perhaps nothing will come out.'

'These things generally do.'

Graham looked more uneasy, and said, 'It isn't the first time, you know. Before the war I did a couple of patients like this. I had my doubts about them, but didn't delve very deeply. I just blinded myself to the fact they were a pair of crooks. I was disgusted at myself afterwards. I don't want to repeat the experience, quite apart from risking my neck. But if I don't . . . why the hell did I buy that villa, anyway? I've never had a chance to use it.'

'I don't think I can really give the anaesthetic for you, Graham.'

'No, I didn't expect you would. It was selfish of me to ask. I wanted the moral support, I think, that's all. I'll see what I can do under local. Probably I can manage more than I expect. We get spoiled, with good general anaesthetics always available from experts like you. Some of our more unfortunate brethren manage to run a flourishing practice in cosmetic work under locals. The ones who get themselves struck off for advertising.'

'Won't you take my advice and not touch this case, Graham?'

'You mean to substitute the certainty of trouble with the law for the possibility?'

'It's two sorts of trouble. The operation would spoil everything you gained for yourself during the war.'

'What did I gain? A knighthood. For services to publicity.'

'You know that's not true.'

'Not completely so, perhaps. But it's near enough to the mark.'

'I was speaking to Clare about you two or three weeks ago,' John remarked unexpectedly.

Graham looked at him sharply. 'I thought she'd disappeared off the face of the earth?'

'She's at the Kenworth. Children's ward sister. I do a list there once a week.'

Graham made a wry expression. 'How is she?'

'Very well. She likes her job.' John paused and added, 'Do you want to see her again?'

'She'd hardly want to set eyes on *me*,' Graham told him impatiently.

'I'm certain she would.'

'No, that's ridiculous. Not after the way I treated her.'

'Is it ridiculous? You'd know. You've had more experience of women than me.'

Graham stuck his hands in his trouser pockets and started pacing the room. 'Everything's wrong, isn't it? You see things differently as you go through life, and often enough you realize all the time you've been seeing them wrong. When I was young

173

I could view the way ahead, and I tramped up it not caring overmuch how I muddied my boots. Things didn't go all that smoothly—Maria, all that fuss. But I got where I wanted. In the war, I didn't really want anything for myself and I was happy. Now I'm trying to worship my old gods, but they don't represent anything any more. They're like native idols discovered in some jungle. Incomprehensible, frightening to look at, make you wonder at the simplicity of the people who venerated them. I'd got no proper sense of values. The war imposed one on me.'

'Graham, you're making yourself sound a horrible type,' smiled John.

'Well, I am. Though let's hope it's not because I can't help it, but because I try to be.'

'Because you think it's smart?'

Graham shrugged. 'I can't even contemplate meeting Clare again. Not at this particular crisis in my life.'

'She might be glad to help you. She did during several others.'

'I suppose she loved me.'

'You loved her, surely?'

'Deep down, I told myself I didn't. It was the same with every woman I've got mixed up with. I never wanted to give myself to them completely. At the age when you can face these things, it's too late to rectify them.'

Denise appeared with the coffee.

'Graham wanted to discuss a case he's doing tomorrow, darling,' John explained.

'I'm not doing it,' said Graham briefly. 'I've decided it's inoperable.'

He'd forgotten about Denise and her coffee. He then had to sit down and make conversation of some sort while he drank it, and she always made dreadful coffee, anyway.

## 24

HAILEYBURY HAD HARDLY SHAVED when Graham arrived the next morning at his house in Richmond. His sister, who had seen six years' service in the A.T.S., had returned to offer the same dutiful devotion to her brother as to her King. She showed Graham in to the cold sitting-room, which was filled with models of railway engines. Graham sat in his overcoat, looking at them in puzzlement. He supposed Haileybury had constructed them all with his own hands. A strange secret for a man to have.

'I'm sorry to keep you waiting, Graham.' Haileybury appeared in his usual blue suit.

'And I'm sorry to have telephoned for an appointment so early. But I have some news. I have decided to accept your kind offer of a job.'

Haileybury inclined his head silently. 'That is good news indeed. It is all I will say, but I think you will understand how I feel. The new project is very near to my heart.'

'On one condition.'

'I'm sure any reasonable condition can easily be met.'

'I don't know if this one can. The condition is that I stay out of jail.' Haileybury looked at him blankly, wondering if he were joking. 'I've been involved in some currency deals. About five thousand pounds' worth of French francs. If it comes to light, I've had it. I've reason to expect it might.'

Haileybury put the tips of his fingers together and blew on them. The noise still irritated Graham.

'I see.'

'It's all mixed up with Cazalay and your unfortunate friend Fred Butcher. You know a fine rumpus is blowing up?'

'I see,' Haileybury repeated.

'Of course, the very fact I've misbehaved might be enough for you to withdraw your offer. I'd quite understand that.'

'Could you explain the details?'

'I gave Cazalay a cheque for five thousand pounds and he gave me the francs. He wants me to do a job on one of his little crooks to stop the police recognizing him. I won't. It's as simple as that. So Cazalay will cook my goose.'

'But what on earth were you doing with all this foreign money?'

'Oh, I haven't it hidden in a biscuit-tin, bricked up in the chimney, anything like that. I never actually handled it. Cazalay bought me a house in France.'

'I see,' said Haileybury again.

Graham rose. 'That's the situation, Eric. If I don't land in abject disgrace over the next few weeks I presume you'll take me on?'

Haileybury made an accommodating gesture. 'I'm only sorry you should find yourself in such a predicament.'

'It isn't my first,' Graham told him. 'But, whichever way it goes, it will be my last.'

He couldn't face operating or seeing patients. He rang Smithers Botham and a couple of nursing-homes, putting his day's work off, excusing himself with illness. He walked the shabby streets of London, hardly noticing where his feet took him. He found himself in Piccadilly, not far from Half Moon Street, and turned towards the Cazalay family's old town house. A hole in the ground. As he started walking northwards the rain began to fall. It was the same route he had taken thirty years before, tramping home through a thunderstorm to his father's home in Hampstead after he had first met Maria. On that walk he had decided three things—to become a plastic surgeon, to grow rich, and, more immediately, to ditch his fiancée Edith. He had done all three, and ended up with nothing but the prospect of prison. He plodded on. It wasn't so easy to walk these days. Well, your arteries and joints had to grow stiff some time, it was inevitable. At least you were saved the effort of struggling against it, as he'd had to struggle against tuberculosis in his youth.

He decided to make for the house in Hampstead. It was still standing, but horribly dilapidated. It had been turned into flats before the war, now there seemed to be a dozen families living in it, with washing forgotten and soaking in the front garden. The professor would hardly have countenanced that, Graham told himself. He wondered what his father would have to say of his misdeeds, personal and professional. Perhaps the old boy would have the chance to give him a celestial wigging soon. He had rather let down the family. Even the piss-prophet didn't get himself locked up.

He looked at his watch, and was surprised to find it almost six in the evening. He made for Hampstead Tube station, where he bought an evening paper. The storm had broken. The police were looking for Arthur and for Lord Cazalay, neither of whom could be found. Graham wondered if Cazalay had gone to Venezuela, too. But the stop press revealed he had gone no farther than Newhaven, where he was assisting the police with their enquiries. Graham stuffed the paper in his overcoat pocket. He would have to face the music, and the grisly concert had begun.

In the hallway of his block of flats a woman approached him.

'Graham! I'm sorry to sit on your doorstep. But I've been trying to get you all day. There's something terribly important you really ought to know.'

Graham recognized Sheila Raleigh. She must have just returned from France. 'I must apologize,' he told her absently. 'I've had rather a lot of things occupying me. It's about the Annex Club, I suppose?'

'No, it isn't.' She looked round. 'Could we have a moment alone?'

'Yes, of course.'

They said nothing until he let her into his flat. He felt she had chosen a damn inconsiderate moment to call. 'I hope you're liking the job?'

'Yes, it's wonderful. I can't thank you enough. Particularly after I said such bitter things to you once.'

'I deserved them.'

'No, you didn't. But you can understand how I felt at the time? I had to blame someone. It all seemed so pointless otherwise.'

Impatient to get rid of her, Graham asked, 'What can I do for you now.'

'It's about your house, Graham. In France.' She sat down, frowning. 'There's something fishy about it. There was a man who came to look at it, just before I left yesterday. A Frenchman, a very nasty piece of work. He arrived in a Citroën with two others, who looked like thugs. Apparently . . . well, apparently you don't own the place at all. Lord Cazalay does. He's been "selling" it to a dozen different people. Oh, Graham, I'm so sorry! It must be awful to have lost all that money.'

## 25

FOR A WEEK Graham read the morning and evening papers
with eagerness and apprehension. But the Press stayed infuriatingly bare of facts, reassuring or deadly. Lord Cazalay
and ferrety-faced Arthur were remanded in custody by the
Bow Street magistrate on some comparatively trivial charge, a
detective-superintendent implying from the witness box that
all hell was in store for them once it could be properly docu-
mented. The disgraced Fred Butcher was announced by his
distraught secretary as having entered an unnamed nursing-
home for 'nerves'. He had sent his passport to Scotland Yard,
though purely as a matter of courtesy.

The Tory party, squashed for a couple of years under Mr
Attlee's majority, fell like bluebottles on the festering wound in
the pure-white body of socialism. They even stripped the
friable wrappings from the mummified first Lord Cazalay,
recalling with glee that his disgrace had occurred under the
sway of Ramsay MacDonald. There was a dreadful fuss in the
House of Commons. The Speaker twice suspended the sitting,
leaving the chamber like a despairing headmaster shaming his
boys with a display of dignity. Two more Ministers resigned
(but kept their passports). Then the Government neatly announced an investigatory tribunal to be established, under a
judge of unassailable wisdom and impartiality. The matter was
henceforward *sub judice*, and could not with propriety be raised
in public at all. The House simmered down, the legislators

turning their vigilance to the raising of the school-leaving age to fifteen.

After ten days of uncertainty, paralysing all his activities and most of his thoughts outside his professional ones, Graham ran into John Bickley in the Cavendish Clinic. He had just finished his last case of the afternoon, loosening a Dupuytren's contracture in the palm of a stockbroker (the deformity interfered badly with his shooting). As he pushed open the door of the surgeons' room to change, he found the anaesthetist in his long green theatre gown, packing away rubber masks, tubing, swabs, syringes, and other tools of oblivion into a square black-leather bag.

'That was the best advice anyone's given me in my life,' Graham said at once.

John looked up. 'About not operating on that spiv fellow?' He gave a smile. 'You know, I hadn't the slightest expectation that you'd take it.'

'If I had, I'd be well and truly up the creek by now, wouldn't I? With all this fuss, all these political people getting interested, trying to outdo each other scratching up the dirt. The ridiculous aspect of the whole affair is that I'd nothing to worry about from Cazalay. Nothing at all. He simply swindled me out of my money. He didn't even buy those pernicious francs in the first place.'

'How much did you lose?'

'Five thousand quid.'

John's eyebrows shot up.

'Yes, I'm a mug,' Graham admitted. 'Cazalay might as well have sold me a gold brick or the Eiffel Tower—didn't some bright Frenchman flog it to the Germans for scrap during the war?' He undid a length of bandage round his waist, and slipped the white linen operating trousers from his spindly legs. 'But perhaps it was a reasonable fee to pay for the shock treatment. I've learnt my lesson. Henceforward Trevose sticks to the straight and narrow path.'

'Oh, come, Graham! You're making yourself sound like an old lag, not an ornament to one of our Orders of Chivalry.'

Graham threw his trousers into the corner with an impatient gesture. 'You know what I mean. Well, you ought to. You don't imagine I'm unaware of your going about referring to me as "Flash Harry"?' John laughed. 'By the way, I'm giving up my private practice,' Graham added.

The anaesthetist paused in packing away his apparatus and stared at him. 'You're not serious?'

'I'm perfectly serious. I'm abandoning the private racket for a full-time job. On the new unit Haileybury's always talking about. I'm to be its first Director.'

'But Graham—your whole life's been built round your private work. Everyone in London is green with envy at your reputation. You already get patients sent to you from all over the country. Once things get really back to normal you'll be getting them from all over the bloody world. Surely you can't throw all that away?'

'My life wasn't built round private work during the war, and that was the only time I was happy.' He pulled on his grey suit in silence. As John snapped the two catches of his leather case, Graham continued, 'Perhaps the Government are right to set themselves against fee-paying medicine. It's immoral really, if you look at it carefully. It didn't matter so much even thirty years ago, when the doctor could generally do damn all whether you paid him or not. Besides, I want to think. Perhaps to write. Rushing round nursing homes chasing guineas, you haven't a chance to do either. Perhaps I've an academic streak in me somewhere—don't forget my father was a professor. He left a massive volume on the synovial membranes as his tombstone, which is more than I shall ever achieve.'

'I still can't take you seriously, Graham.'

'Then wait and see. You won't even have to wait long. The appointment's being announced by the Ministry at the beginning of next month. I'll have to resign from Blackfriars, of course, which will be a wrench, though mainly a sentimental one. There doesn't seem the slightest prospect of the place being rebuilt in my own lifetime. And the staff there will all be working for the Government anyway, whether they like it or not.

I'm giving up my flat—I've got to economize and I want something smaller, nearer the site, to organize things.' Graham's face suddenly lit up. 'It'll be like those early days at the annex, all over again. Except this time everyone will be on *my* side. I'll only have to snap my fingers for equipment to arrive by the lorryload.'

John stood looking at him, his bony long-fingered hands resting on the top of his case. 'It must have been a sacrifice. Or at least a horribly difficult decision.'

'Not really. Like most of the big steps in my life, I didn't think twice about it.' As John slipped the green gown from his shirt, Graham added as off-handedly as possible, 'You know, I really would rather like to see Clare again.'

'That's the best news you've given me today.'

Graham felt this sounded vaguely condescending, but asked, 'Do you think she'd respond to some sort of social invitation? To dinner, a show, something like that?'

'Why don't you come and find out? I'm just off to the Kenworth to do a case. I know for a fact she's on duty. Are you free?'

Graham hesitated. Then his natural impulsiveness made him say, 'All right. You can give me a lift.' As John picked up his instrument-case he added, 'After all, I've nothing to lose, have I? If I admit to you now that I treated Clare quite disgustingly, it's something which I have only just come to admit to myself.'

'Quite so,' said John.

It suddenly struck him how much Graham was starting to sound like Haileybury.

It was fortunate for the reputation of Sister Mills at the Kenworth Hospital that she had charge of a children's ward. Unlike the adult patients, who had little to do except listen to *Workers' Playtime* through the headphones and intensely observe the personal behaviour of the staff, the youngsters saw nothing remarkable—only some welcome entertainment—in a wide-eyed little man bursting among them, a startled cry from Sister, a whispered conversation, glances between bewildered nurses, a brisk retreat to Sister's office, a slamming of the door. Graham reflected afterwards he could as well have telephoned, but his unexpected appearance was much more dramatic and much more satisfying. In the office, they were far too confused and embarrassed to say very much, nor even to approach within arm's length of each other. Graham told her he must see her, it was desperate—couldn't he even take her to dinner? She demurred, trying to adjust her mind to the situation. But he was never a man to lose the advantage of a woman's hesitation.

'All right,' Clare agreed doubtfully. 'All right, Graham. For old times' sake.'

'That's wonderful! We'll have so much to talk about. It's almost three whole years since we—' He wondered how to put it. 'Went our separate ways.'

She couldn't prevent herself asking, 'Did you miss me?'

'Like an amputated limb. You know how the patients get pain in them, don't you? "A phantom limb." It hurts worse than ever, even if it isn't there.'

She gave a nervous smile and said, 'You mustn't forget the limb's always amputated for the patient's own good.'

There was a pause. Neither of them felt entirely sure where the conversation was leading. Both were relieved for it to be frustrated by a knock on the door and the news that a child due for release, overcome by excitement, had vomited copiously over the newly cleaned floor.

Two evenings later they met. Graham had chosen a restaurant in Soho, whispered among a small and knowing circle as providing with its generous portions not only butter but crisp, white, mysteriously unrationed bread. By then both he and Clare had found time to adjust themselves, and were perfectly charming to each other. They sat in the corner of the small, rose-lighted room, chatting gaily of pointedly inconsequential generalities. Graham had really no precise idea what he was going to propose to her, and hoped he could rely on her delicacy to raise nothing that would make him feel too uncomfortable. He picked up the wine-list and suggested champagne, adding half-humorously, 'This place is terribly black market.'

'Oh, everyone these days knows someone who can get them

183

something.' Clare smiled. 'Our theatre porter finds us the most lovely nylons—"They dropped off a lorry" is the story. It must have been an extremely large pantechnicon.'

'I'm growing rather tired of all that, you know. I've had some sort of moral conversion. And, like most converts, I was scared into it.' He picked up the evening paper, beside them on the table. Lord Cazalay and Arthur had been charged that morning with a number of offences from bribery of Government officials to possessing unauthorized sweet coupons. To Graham's relief, there was still no mention of currency transactions. 'You've read all about this, I suppose?'

'Is there anyone who hasn't?'

'But I think I can entertain you with some unpublished details.'

Over dinner he gave a frank account of his life since she had walked out of Cosy Cot, with the exception of Liz. In his penitent mood he was half-inclined to throw her in too, but consoled himself that Clare would certainly suspect he had been mixed up with a woman or two, and through natural female pride and vanity imagine them goddesses. If she became increasingly serious and sympathetic, Graham had been smugly confident of as much. His moral weaknesses had always been of as much concern to her as his physical ones, he reflected, and she accepted both with the same resignation. She hadn't changed, he told himself. Though if she had changed towards *him* was a separate question. When he finished the tale she held his hand under the table, and said, 'Poor Graham! You did get yourself in a mess, didn't you?'

'I didn't have you to keep me out of it.'

He started to talk about his new job, a conversation which drifted naturally back to the annex and Smithers Botham. Her eyes began to sparkle, she gripped his hand tighter than ever, and he felt a sudden glow of relief. It was going to be all right. She had forgiven him, they could pick up neatly where they had left off, except this time he really would marry her, just as soon as the little formality could be arranged. He was starting to believe she would go that very night with him to the flat, when

184

she said, 'Graham, it's been simply lovely meeting you. We must have another reunion one day, mustn't we? Perhaps when all this black-market and rationing nonsense is over.'

He looked blank. 'But Clare! Aren't you coming back to me?'

'Don't be silly, Graham.'

'But this time, I mean . . . we'd be married, it would be different.'

'It wouldn't be different in the slightest. As I told you once before, it wouldn't work.'

'You're being ridiculous.' He sounded quite cross. 'Everything was abnormal in those days '

'Yes, there was a war on.'

'I mean everything about *me*. I was selfish then, foolish, chasing all the wrong things. I've changed. I know I've changed. I've got my sense of values straight. I don't give a damn for the fripperies of life any more.'

'You sound like Sir Stafford Cripps,' she told him.

By the time he reached home Graham was furious. It was beyond him why Clare had refused to fall gratefully into his arms. All this effort to turn himself into a decent human being, he reflected petulantly, would be absolutely wasted if nobody was going to take it seriously. He poured himself a whisky and sat in the armchair. For the first time there stole upon him the black realization that he had lost Clare for good. A solitary life stretched ahead, as bleakly as the concrete corridors at Smithers Botham. And at fifty-one you needed someone beside you, much more desperately than at twenty-one. But there was nobody who cared a damn about him. Only his son Desmond. At least, he presumed so. The young man had more or less given up speaking to him.

The next morning Graham had a letter from Haileybury, confirming his new appointment and inviting him to lunch with some political figures who were enthusiastic over the new hospital. Mr Bevan himself, he added, might possibly be joining them for the coffee. Graham wrote resigning his post as consultant surgeon to Blackfriars. He would devote himself wholly to his new interest. He would have the best part of fifteen years

185

in the place before he retired, and he would leave it as a splendid monument to himself. He would meanwhile live alone and put up with it. After all, he was a widower, not some crabby never-loved bachelor like old Crampers. He wondered vaguely if Crampers were still alive. He doubted it. The Welfare State seemed to have been the death of him.

## 26

THE POLITICIANS' LUNCH was held in the House of Commons,
a fair proportion of which, like a fair proportion of the capital
itself, lay in apparently permanent ruins. Graham was interested to see for the first time the inside of the place, though
confessing as he was escorted rapidly through the corridors and
stairways a feeling of disappointment. The marble floors, the
vulgar murals, the pillared corners and vaulted ceilings, the
solemn dress-suited attendants, reminded him of somewhere—
yes, it was the casino at Monte Carlo. He supposed that both
structures had been raised about the same time, and had much
in common in their function.

The party gathered in a smallish upstairs room with mullioned
leaded windows and an over-abundance of carved pale oak,
overlooking the river. Graham at once realized the importance
of the affair. Of the thirty-odd men in the room, about half he
recognized as top medical people, including Haileybury.
Clearly, the Government had taken the new hospital to its
heart.

Never a martyr to the self-inflicted tortures of modesty,
Graham was flattered to notice the stir his arrival made among
the politicos. They would have heard enough of him during the
war, he supposed. Or perhaps, he reflected wryly, they were
aware of his having married the daughter of the first Lord
Cazalay, and his kinship to the rogue at the seat of their present
troubles. Graham was coming to detach himself from the man
in Brixton prison with more assurance every day. He decided

his brother-in-law had enough on his hands without dragging him into the mess—though with a man like that you never could tell. But if anything about himself was exposed by the promised radical surgery of the tribunal, he fancied even the memory of the present feast would induce in his hosts an attack of acute dyspepsia.

Graham found himself sitting next to a young Member of Parliament with junior rank in the Government, though he was vague what, and felt it would be discourteous to reveal such ignorance. Graham was far too self-centred to have much interest in politics, a quality which, combined with his exhibitionism, might have made him a successful politician. He had troubled neither to vote in the recent election, nor even to hear Churchill's broadcast speeches during the war. Like most medical people, he saw mankind less as noble sufferers in adversity than as sadly muddle-headed ignoramuses, to be saved from themselves by well-educated ladies and gentlemen as kindly as possible. With a lazy if reasonable over-simplification, Graham wrote off the Tories as appealing to the populace's natural greed, and the Socialists to its natural envy. If the Government were now trying to organize everyone's life from the cradle to the grave he felt it probably a sound idea, most inhabitants of a growingly complicated world apparently being incapable of even crossing the road with impunity. Long ago, in the days of the first Lord Cazalay, he had grasped that politicians ran to their own rules, as detached from those of everyday life as the rules of some game of cards. You had to let them get up to whatever they wished, running your life as best you could and allowing for their existence like the bacteria contaminating every article you touched.

The young M.P. revealed himself over the soup as a strong enthusiast for the coming National Health Service.

'My father,' he explained forcefully to Graham, 'suffered from bad eyes. He couldn't afford to attend a doctor, or an optician, or anyone qualified for the job. Do you know what he was obliged to do? Go to one of the cheap sixpenny stores, where they had a card affair, with those different-sized letters on it. Right on the counter, among all the tubes of toothpaste. He'd pick up lenses and try them till he found the right ones. Thousands of sufferers from bad eyesight had to do exactly the same. Those cheap stores were providing a valuable social service on behalf of their shareholders, if they but knew it. But it's disgraceful, isn't it, Sir Graham? In future, every citizen will be entitled to a properly fitted pair of spectacles as a right. Just as he's entitled to clean water or the protection of the law.'

'It'll probably be equally expensive,' Graham demurred mildly.

The politician's gesture brushed this aside impatiently. 'Naturally, there'll be a pent-up demand, but the whole point of a proper health service is that it gets progressively cheaper. When people are given the proper treatment they've been denied through poverty—not to mention given better working conditions, better houses, and a higher standard of living from decent wages—the need for medicines and doctors will simply diminish. We'll all live healthier and longer. Eh, Sir Graham?' He grinned. 'As a medical man, mustn't you agree?'

'But if we all live longer we'll simply suffer more intractable ailments and need even more doctors.'

'Sir Graham! You're belittling your profession. What about the inevitable great advances in curative medicine?'

'And the inevitable increases in expensive drugs? Penicillin's a dreadful price as it is.' Graham felt uneasy entering in an argument with a professional debater, but to his relief the waiter interrupted by serving the main course. 'What on earth's this?' he exclaimed in surprise.

'Whale steak,' the M.P. told him proudly. 'We're importing tons of it to eke out the meat ration. I assure you it's absolutely delicious.'

Then the young man began talking equally energetically about India, a subject which bored Graham even more than cricket.

It was clear that Haileybury was enjoying the occasion immensely. He rose to make a short if wholly unmemorable speech, and as they prepared to break up Graham noticed with amusement he was noticeably flushed with official port.

'Graham, old fellow, if you're going my way perhaps we can stroll together?' Haileybury suggested with an unknown heartiness.

'I'm not going anywhere in particular. Shall we take a turn round St James's Park? We've plenty to talk about.'

As they walked round the lake, the chilly spring air restored Haileybury to his usual oppressive sobriety. They talked animatedly for half an hour about the first steps for bringing the new unit into being, until Graham broke off unexpectedly, 'You know, Eric, this new task you've saddled me with has saved my life. Literally, I mean. I've never thought of suicide —and I know a surprising number of one's acquaintances have at least once, quite seriously. But I wouldn't have been too sure of myself, not at this stage of my life, without some fresh interest.'

'You're being fanciful again,' Haileybury told him with a thin smile.

'I suppose you're entitled to think so. You know me better than almost anybody. But I mean it. Without something big to tackle, some worthwhile achievement to make, I'd get depressed. Dreadfully depressed. It seems to get worse with age. And when a patient's depressed, you know well enough, they've a different personality, there's no knowing what they might do. It's as dangerous as walking along the edge of a cliff.'

Haileybury nodded slowly as they walked. 'What makes you imagine I haven't suffered myself?'

Graham looked at him sharply. He had imagined Haileybury's personality breasting the tides of life with the unexciting stability of a coal-barge on the Thames. It struck him that although Haileybury had grown to understand a good deal of his own inner workings, he knew absolutely nothing of Haileybury's.

'I hope the intolerable amount of work you are about to undertake will put such unpleasant notions from your mind,' Haileybury added.

'I'm safe as long as I'm occupied every minute of the day. I hate living alone.' Graham hesitated, but decided to go on. Haileybury, of all people, had become his only confessor. 'I'd hoped to cure that particular deficiency, but I'm afraid it's not to be.'

'You're thinking of taking a companion?'

'I notice you avoid the word "wife", and I can't blame you for that either.' Graham sounded a shade weary. 'You know I lived with a girl during the war? She was my ward sister from the annex. We've met up again. I want to marry her. I can't live without her. That's a stupid expression, much overused, but as I explained a moment ago it might have been quite literally true. But she doesn't want to take the same risk with me twice, and I can hardly object to her point of view.'

'Who might this lady be? Would I have met her?'

'I should imagine so. She's the children's ward sister at the Kenworth.'

Haileybury stopped dead. 'Sister Mills? But what an amazing coincidence!'

'It isn't at all. John Bickley got her the job after I kicked her out in 1944.'

'I see,' said Haileybury. He put his fingers together and blew on them.

'I do wish you wouldn't do that,' Graham burst out. 'It's irritated me for years.'

Haileybury hastily thrust his hands in his pockets. 'I'm sorry there's a difficulty between you,' he sympathized.

'She can't understand that I don't *want* to go back to my old ways—because of the war, or old age,' Graham ended gloomily, 'or perhaps just disgust with myself in general.'

'I suppose to some extent the seven ages of man are all strangers to each other,' Haileybury observed.

'Just look at those ducks,' said Graham, pointing across the lake. 'They must run up a tremendous oxygen debt, keeping their beaks under water as long as that.'

He didn't care to reveal more of himself to Haileybury. He had said too much as it was. He had written Clare a long and thoughtful letter, uncloyed with passion. There had been no reply. It seemed best to forget about her, as deliberately as he had once forgotten about Edith. As the two surgeons resumed their walk, Graham began with growing disquiet to hope that Haileybury would forget about her too. Haileybury had been his enemy once, and in this shifting and faithless world who knew when he might be again?

## 27

BUT HAILEYBURY did not forget about Clare at all.

He had heard some rumour during the war of Graham living 'in sin' at Smithers Botham, but had vaguely imagined his consort some painted and skittish female of the type portrayed on his rare visits to the cinema by Dorothy Lamour (Hailey-bury suffered a guilty affection for the comedies starring Bing Crosby and Bob Hope). That she was the quiet and efficient Sister Mills, whom he had encountered almost weekly for a year, seemed inconceivable. But Haileybury decided he had never been able to comprehend the powerful mysteries of sexual attraction, no more than he could grasp those of the atomic physics you were beginning to read so much about in the newspapers. He had never felt drawn to one woman rather than another in his life. He felt annoyed that John Bickley had kept Sister Mills' relationship from him—but he supposed it wasn't a matter you wanted revealed in such a gossip-ridden place as a hospital. He anxiously tried to recall if he had made any particularly uncharitable remarks about Graham in her presence.

Haileybury thought about it all the week-end. He kept shaking his head and chuckling faintly to himself, much alarming his sister. It certainly took him back. The only other of Graham's women he had met was that girl Edith, secretary on his plastic surgery unit in 1918. He had taken a distinctly dim view of *that* connection, Haileybury remembered. But that was long ago; now they were growing into old dogs and learning not to bark and bite so much. He began to wonder if he might say something on Graham's behalf to Sister Mills. An outrageous idea, of course. But Haileybury was a fair man and felt the lady was perhaps being unjust. As for the injustice he had himself done Graham in 1942, he felt it more keenly than Graham now did himself.

Sister Mills might make the man a good wife, Haileybury speculated. Graham had sobered down, there was no doubt about that. For him to have thrown away his profitable private practice would before the war have been as inconceivable as his entering a monastery. But no, Haileybury finally decided, he had no right to intervene. It was a personal matter for the pair of them. Besides, he was still not entirely certain how much in these strange postwar years he had come to like or even to tolerate Graham.

On the Monday, Haileybury was visiting the Kenworth Hospital to see his patients. He had two cases of cleft palate recovering in the children's ward, which he usually visited ceremonially escorted by his house-surgeon. But this young man, whose services he shared with the throat department, was occupied in the theatre with the emergency of a postoperative bleeding tonsil. Haileybury found himself alone with Sister Mills in a small room off the ward known as the nursery, which contained a slide, a rocking horse, and various toys, all of which some half-dozen small children were enjoying with an amazing amount of noise.

'I believe you know Graham Trevose?' Haileybury asked her suddenly, above the din.

'Yes, that's quite correct,' Clare told him calmly. 'I was one of his ward sisters during the war.'

'How very strange.' Haileybury looked uneasy. 'I have enjoyed his acquaintance for years, you know.'

'Yes, he used to talk a lot about you. Particularly when there was that fuss in 1942.'

Clare noticed Haileybury had the grace to turn pink.

'I think we have made all that up between us, Sister.'

'I hope so, Mr Haileybury. He was very upset at the time. Almost out of his mind.'

Haileybury made no reply. He had long ago ceased caring what Graham said to him, but the cloaked rebuke from Sister Mills was surprisingly wounding. A shocking illogical thought crept upon him—perhaps it was he who had behaved so badly over the years of their acquaintance rather than Graham?

'I hope I have undone any damage by arranging to some extent his appointment to our fine new accident hospital. You must have seen the place mentioned in the papers, surely?'

'I don't think anything could compensate him for those few terrible weeks. He had built up the annex at Smithers Botham, and it was to be taken away from him.' She paused, and added, 'It was like a mother losing a child.'

Haileybury didn't know what to say. So he put his finger-tips together and blew on them.

'I saw Graham just before the week-end,' he admitted. 'Naturally, with the new project we shall be thrown on each other's company a good deal.' He hesitated and added, 'I understand he wishes to marry you, Sister?'

He could not remember uttering anything making him feel more uncomfortable in his life.

'That is correct, Mr Haileybury.'

Clare leant down to pick up a crying child who had tripped over a pile of wooden bricks.

'Forgive me—this is really nothing to do with me—but I gather you are not agreeable?'

'That too, is correct, Mr Haileybury. I am not agreeable.'

Haileybury hesitated again. He decided that having got this far he would charge bravely on. In 1942 he may not have been motivated by spite, as Graham suggested, but he had found the delicate negotiations leading to the man's dismissal from the annex not wholly unpleasurable. Yes, he must make amends, it was his duty. The new job was not enough. After all, Graham could have earned that easily on his own merits. It was only a matter of his stooping to take it.

'I'm sorry to hear that,' he said, quite sternly. 'I hope you appreciate the extent of his emotional disturbance? I have known him for years—since before you were born—and *I* can appreciate it very keenly myself. Quite frankly, he talked to me of suicide. Oh, I know it's a common enough threat in such circumstances. From a boy of twenty, perhaps. But not from a mature man. And a man of the world, like Graham.' He saw she looked alarmed, and went on, 'Perhaps I can see your point of view. He would never conceal from society that he was lavish in his affections. But he's a better man. It was a process which probably started during the war, when he had no alternative but to follow his natural instinct and devote himself to others. I fancy his life in the world of fashion merely expressed his taste for self-indulgence, pursued with the energy which he devotes to everything.'

There was a pause, filled with the screaming of children.

'Perhaps so,' was all Clare said.

Haileybury shrugged his shoulders. He felt no need to say more. He had done the duty. He made a peculiar jerky bow and sidled away. He sincerely hoped the girl would take up with Graham again and marry him. After *that* conversation, it would be outrageously embarrassing always meeting her in the hospital.

Clare went to her small office and sat at her desk. It was all dreadfully confusing. Of course, she still loved Graham. Of course, she would happily marry him. Had she been five years younger she wouldn't have hesitated. But the lesson of Cosy Cot was not one she was anxious to learn over again—unless that funny old stick Haileybury was right, and Graham had really shed his old habits. When they had lived together she had seen mostly Graham's best side, and that was certainly something worth taking a risk for. On the other hand, with Graham you could never tell how he was going to behave about anything, even the way he liked his shirts ironed.

There was a knock. A cheerful curly-headed young man in a white coat, the thoracic surgeon's houseman, put his head inside. 'All right if we have a look at that patent ductus, Sister?'

'Yes, of course, Mr Cooper.' Clare got up. The surgeons

196

were daringly starting to operate in the area of the heart itself, and had tied off an abnormal blood-vessel in a little girl suffering this congenital defect. She gathered up the notes. 'The patient's doing very well, I'm glad to say.'

'That's splendid. Then we'll have another one for you to nurse next month.'

'I'm afraid I shan't be here by then, Mr Cooper. I'm leaving to get married.' Clare stood looking at him, still wondering why she had said it.

Graham found a wedding in middle life a surprisingly agreeable experience. Though after all, he told himself, unlike most bridegrooms he wasn't marrying an almost total stranger.

Graham's first marriage had been one of the social landmarks of 1920. Maria had worn a train twelve feet long, there had been a shoal of expensively outfitted bridesmaids, all of whose names and faces he had long ago forgotten, and the first Lord Cazalay had driven her up in a brand-new Rolls Royce. The young John Bickley had been his best man, and the second Lord Cazalay, now calculating his chances in a remand cell, had become embarrassingly drunk. The reception had been in some official building, though Graham had gathered the bride's father would have preferred Buckingham Palace could he have arranged it. As Graham had expected, nobody had taken much notice of himself. He had later come to appreciate this was true of even the humblest marriages, which he supposed were largely occasions for the parents to entertain their friends and show off without risk of later backbiting.

His own wedding was the first Graham had attended since the miserable afternoon at the marriage of Peter Thomas—who Graham was delighted to find from the newspapers seemed to be making a fortune with some sort of cross-country air service. There were to be only four onlookers at the registry office. Clare's mother and father appeared from Bristol, to Graham's relief too flattered by their daughter's unexpectedly turning herself into Lady Trevose to utter anything but the platitudes of the occasion. He asked John Bickley to repeat his rôle of best man. Denise had to be invited as well, of course, but to Graham's intense joy was too ill on the day to go out.

Afterwards, Graham stood them all lunch in a hotel, where they had champagne and *snoek piquante*. There was a wedding-cake, with an iced covering made, in the way of the times, from detachable white cardboard. There were no speeches, though Graham's new father-in-law had by then so fallen under the influence of his charm and his title that he had to be restrained from making one. They caught the train for a week-end's honeymoon at Bognor Regis. Everything was punctiliously correct. The rushed two weeks since Clare had accepted him were too occupied with her work in hospital and her visits to Bristol to give them more than a moment or two together over lunch in Claridge's. Graham mounted to their seaside bedroom reflecting with amusement that he was facing his bride like the most moral of newly wedded husbands—if one overlooked a year or two during the war. He got into bed making jokes about consummations and such other horribly dignified words festooning the sexual relationship. This time he put out the light, feeling he wanted to be as respectable about everything as possible. Then suddenly he broke into tears.

Clare held him tight in the darkness. 'Darling, what is it?' Weeping was something she had never known in him before. 'What is it? What's upsetting you?'

'I don't know, I don't know,' Graham told her. 'For once I just can't express myself any other way, that's all.'

Her hand under the bedclothes stroked his penis, that organ of superb anatomical ingenuity.

'I thought I'd lost you for good, Clare—I really did. I could have taken it a few years ago, but not now. Not any longer.'

She said nothing for a minute, then confessed, 'We have a fairy godfather. Someone who came and changed my mind.'

'Oh? And who might that be?'

'Mr Haileybury,' she told him cheerfully.

Graham sat bolt upright. 'Haileybury? My God! That pie-faced fossil Haileybury?'

'He told me you could be relied upon to be a good boy in

future,' she added teasingly. 'And of course, nobody could possibly doubt the good word of Mr Haileybury.'

'Good God!' muttered Graham.

But the news was too much. For almost the first time in his life when in bed with a woman, Graham was put off his stroke.

28

AT THE BEGINNING OF JUNE in the hot and thundery summer
of 1947, it was starting to sink into the British public that of all
the 'shortages' bedevilling the country, which ran from electri-
city-generating stations to milk chocolate, a lack of United
States dollars was the most serious, intractable, and baffling.
After all, General Marshall was proposing to give dollars away
by the shipload to European countries who had spent the war
defeating one another—even to Germany, or the bits that the
Russians had left of it. And we were the victors. We had fought
the war from the first shot, we had won it (admittedly with a
little American assistance), we had paid our whack of it. It was
most frustrating. Why, the Government were even contemplating an unbelievable economy—of denying the twenty
million weekly cinemagoers their accustomed Hollywood films.

Graham then had a letter from Edith, demurely congratu-
lating him on his marriage. He supposed she had learnt of it
from some regular bundle of English newspapers dispatched to
soften her exile. But most of the half-dozen pages in her large
round hand concerned her son Alec. She was dreadfully worried
about him. He had written early in the year explaining he was
in hospital with some mild psychological disturbance. She just
couldn't understand it. Alec had been a highly strung child, of
course, and was still inclined to be excitable, but he was perfectly normal, and very clever, really. There was certainly no
madness on *their* side of the family (Graham felt slightly irritated at the barb, but supposed it unintentional). Edith hadn't
heard from Alec since. She has no idea if he were still under
treatment, or where he was. She hesitated troubling Graham,

who must be terribly busy, but she was becoming desperate. It seemed such an awful pity that all Alec's splendid education should go to waste.

Graham tossed the letter on to the desk in his Marylebone flat. Edith was always a great admirer of education, he reflected. Even as a girl she placed it among the noblest of human qualities, when it was only another pair of hands, to be used for good or evil, but mostly for feeding yourself.

But he supposed he had better do something about Alec.

He knew the young man had been discharged from Smithers Botham, taking some new drug which Dr Dency assured Graham would have a tranquillizing effect, rather than a soporific one like the barbiturates. Graham telephoned the psychiatrist's consulting room, to learn that Dr Dency had left for a six-months' lectureship in the Union of South Africa, where he was doubtless enjoying steaks and as many eggs as he cared to eat for his breakfast. He telephoned Smithers Botham, but could get no sense from anybody. The next afternoon he was himself delivering a lecture at Addenbrook's Hospital at Cambridge, and had arranged to dine in hall afterwards with his son. Perhaps Desmond might be able to help, Graham wondered. He had more reason for keeping track of Alec than anyone.

'How did the lecture go?' asked Desmond, welcoming his father amiably enough with a glass of sherry in his rooms.

'I don't really know. It was my standard one. I've delivered it so often it comes out automatically. It's a useful opportunity for me to think about other matters.'

Desmond gave a faint smile. Now that he's started wearing his hair long, thought Graham, he really does look tremendously like Maria.

'How's Clare?' Desmond asked.

'She's splendid! You didn't particularly want to attend the wedding, I suppose?'

'I'd have come if you'd asked me.'

'Then perhaps I saved you some embarrassment by omitting to. By the way, you don't happen to know where Alec's got to, I suppose? His mother's worried stiff about him.'

Desmond looked surprised. 'I was going to ask you the same thing. I heard some sort of rumour that he was doing anaesthetic locums round London.'

'Then perhaps John Bickley might have a clue,' Graham suggested hopefully.

'I'm not going to let him get away with it, you know,' said Desmond more severely. 'The money's mine, and he's showing absolutely no inclination to pay it back whatever. It's just as if he'd put his hand in my pocket and stolen it.'

'My dear Desmond!' Graham leant back in his armchair. 'One of the things you should now be learning in life is the right moment to cut your losses. With either bad debts, bad women, or bad operating techniques. Enjoy your mistakes, but don't lose sleep over them.'

'*I* didn't want to pay for his bloody upbringing! It was you who took it on.'

'I agree, but anyway the unpleasant experience will do you good.' Graham sipped the sherry, which was really rather good. It was stupid to worry about grabbing money all the time, he told himself. One of the more depressing of the herd instincts. A wonder he had fallen for the idea for so long. Since marrying Clare he was becoming quite righteous.

'If I'm going to start making self-improving donations to charity I certainly wouldn't begin with Alec,' Desmond declared crossly.

'You've got paranoia about him, haven't you? That's a waste of time, too. Old Haileybury and I were daggers drawn for years, and it didn't get us very far. Only recently I've realized that everyone was killing themselves laughing behind our backs. I'd forget Alec, if I were you.' As Desmond continued looking disagreeable, Graham added, 'All right, all right, once I've got my affairs straight I'll make up the sum to you. Does that make you feel better? Count your blessings. You're set for a brilliant academic career; while Alec will never come to anything.'

Desmond seemed to consider this proposition for some moments, then announced, 'You know I've decided to prepare a new edition of grandfather's book? There's a tremendous amount of work involved, but I think it will be worth while.'

'That's excellent news.' Graham felt deeply gratified. ' "Trevose on the synovial membranes". I remember the old boy writing it, donkey's years ago, when I'd escaped with my life from that sanatorium. He'd be pleased to think the family were keeping it going. There's a weight of medical tradition on your shoulders, you know, Desmond. It gets heavier every generation, like our debts.'

'Perhaps that's why I decided on the task,' said Desmond solemnly. 'It's something for posterity. It doesn't seem I shall father another generation of Trevoses. Our branch of the family will die out.'

'Oh, I don't know,' Graham told him cheerfully. 'You've forgotten about Clare and myself.'

'Good God,' murmured Desmond, looking thoroughly alarmed.

Graham decided to take Desmond's guess about Alec's whereabouts as fact, and wrote Edith a consoling letter saying her son was making his way in the newly flourishing specialty of anaesthetics. He supposed he could have made more energetic enquiries, but he was tremendously busy with plans and committees for the new hospital. For the third time in his life he was starting a new unit from scratch—first at Blackfriars in the twenties, backed by Val Arlott, secondly at Smithers Botham, discouraged by everybody, and now in the abandoned American building with the full resources of the Welfare State at his elbow. It was the most exciting, if the most exhausting, of all. He could hardly be expected to play Alec's nursemaid at the same time. Anyway, the man was in his middle twenties, a qualified doctor, and should be able to look after himself. Edith wrote again rather pathetically. Graham finished her long letter with a deep sigh. The woman really was rather a nuisance. She'd never missed a chance to make use of him. Never since he'd deflowered her in a seaside summerhouse during the warmer months of 1918.

Graham let young Alec drop from his mind. Then one after-

203

noon in November he was hurrying along Shaftesbury Avenue from a lunch appointment in Soho, and saw the name ALEC TREVOSE facing him from a placard outside a theatre. Graham stopped, frowning. He felt for his newly prescribed glasses, the announcement not being in particularly large type. The name was among three others claiming authorship of a revue, which Graham vaguely remembered as wringing amiable notices from the critics (he had turned his back on the theatre of late). Lower down, there was Alec Trevose again, in even smaller letters, among the cast. Well, it was not an uncommon name, Graham reflected, and sounded well enough for any player to sport. There was no immediate way of telling if the actor-dramatist might be his own nephew. The simplest course seemed to buy a couple of tickets for the show, which he obtained for the following evening, with the greatest difficulty.

A glance at Clare's programme as they took their seats told Graham it was Alec right enough. The sketch he had written and in which he was about to display himself was entitled simply *At The Doctor's*. The pair of them sat through the foregoing scenes, which struck Graham as exactly like every other revue he had seen, with mounting impatience and foreboding. Then Alec finally appeared. He acted a patient, subjected to an ingenious variety of indignities and discomforts by a dozen white-coated doctors. The audience bellowed. Once recovering from the shock of his nephew's entrance, Graham had to admit it was well put together and surprisingly funny, perhaps because every line that Alec had written and every situation he had depicted occurred often enough in a real hospital. He turned his head, to see Clare dabbing away tears of laughter with her handkerchief. He wondered what Edith would have thought.

After the final curtain Graham said without enthusiasm, 'We'd better go round and have a word with him, I suppose?'

'Yes, I'd love to,' agreed Clare eagerly. 'I've never been behind the scenes before.'

Graham gave his name to the stage-door keeper, who directed them down a flight of stone stairs leading to a narrow, green-painted, ill-lit passage, smelling strongly of disinfectant.

The dressing-rooms that Graham had visited during his theatrical phase had been spacious flower-filled apartments, but Alec's seemed hardly bigger than a railway compartment, with a wooden stand in the middle for the mirrors fringed with electric bulbs, at which three other young men were busy wiping away their make-up.

'Why, it's Uncle Graham!' Alec leapt up, a scrap of filthy towelling in his hand. 'But what a lovely surprise! And Auntie Clare. I say, I should have congratulated you or something, shouldn't I? I'm dreadfully sorry. Life's been an absolute rush, I've had hardly a moment to think of my nearest and dearest.'

'Perhaps it is we who should congratulate you?' remarked Graham rather drily, shaking hands.

'Did you enjoy the show?' asked Alec, with a pressing eagerness he shared with even the greatest actors.

'I'd hoped we clapped loudly enough to make that an unnecessary question.'

Alec lit a cigarette. 'I expect it shattered you a bit? Seeing me from out front?'

'It's admittedly an unexpected talent brought to light.'

'It all started in Smithers Botham. Dency thought it would help if I tried some form of self-expression. He knows someone in the management here, and sent the sketch along. At first I was only supposed to help out with the technical details— you know, wearing your stethoscope the right way round, putting on gloves the regulation way, that sort of thing. After I'd been fooling about at rehearsals one of the cast went sick. So they gave me a chance. Success story.'

One of the other young men, none of whom Alec had introduced, picked up his jacket and with a call of 'Good-night, darlings,' left them. Graham noticed with amusement Clare looked shocked. He himself had come to learn the endearing expression was merely the equivalent of the Communists' 'Comrade' in an ever-shifting and commendably classless society.

'A success story so far,' Graham agreed, nodding.

'Now, Uncle, you're being damping. But I've half another

205

show written, I'm getting work on broadcasting—I've even got an agent. Oh, I know it isn't a solid job like medicine, but you can't imagine how much better I've been feeling since I tried my hand at it. And this poisonous underground atmosphere has absolutely cured my asthma. The pollens can't get at you.'

A girl, who seemed to Graham to be wearing only her under-clothes, put her head round the dressing-room door, said, 'Oh, sorry,' and disappeared again.

'I was a misfit in medicine,' Alec continued cheerfully, wiping off the remains of his grease-paint. 'God knows why I started it in the first place. Mother, I suppose. Weight of family tradition. Or perhaps you think I've let the side down?' he asked, genuinely concerned.

'Not entirely. I was something of a misfit myself.'

'Well, I'm not the first doctor to make an exhibition of my-self in public. The great Charles Wyndham was qualified. He ended up a grand actor-manager, with a knighthood and a theatre called after him.'

'I don't think Wyndham ever played in revue,' Graham observed. With the vague feeling that Alec was probably starving in some attic, he added an invitation to supper. But his nephew declined graciously, explaining he was already engaged to sup with some important director who thought highly of his work. Graham imagined the girl in the underclothes his more likely companion, but was glad enough to accept the refusal.

'You really ought to send some sort of word to your mother,' he finally admonished him. 'She's written saying how disturbed she is about you.'

'Dear mother!' Alec started putting on his shirt. 'She always did fuss so. Yes, I really must send her a line.'

'Or perhaps you'd prefer me to write?' Graham saw Alec in his present mood as a doubtful correspondent.

Alec turned with a bright smile. 'Just do that little thing for me, will you, Uncle?'

In the taxi going home, Graham said, 'God knows what will come of Alec's wild ideas. It *is* a bit of a let-down for the family, however broadminded you try to seem about it. A hell of a lot of people took enormous trouble teaching him medicine. Now he throws it all away to become a professional buffoon.'

'Haven't you said often enough, darling, you can't suppress a true artist? Even if he can only chalk sunsets on the pavements? You never let them suppress you.'

'Perhaps so,' he admitted. 'Perhaps Alec and I are the same thing, really.'

He took her hand and stared gloomily out of the cab window. It would all be intolerably difficult to describe to Edith. But his thoughts as usual turned back to the new hospital, and he said, 'Remind me I've got to go to the Board of Trade tomorrow afternoon. Something about importing American equipment. I'm seeing the new Minister—fellow called Harold Wilson. One of Attlee's bright boys.'

Clare said, 'Tomorrow I'm going to listen to the wedding on the radio.'

'Wedding? What wedding?'

'Oh, Graham! Princess Elizabeth's wedding, of course.'

'I'm sorry, it was out of my mind for the moment.' After another long silence he said, 'It's odd to think that one day we shall have a Queen on the throne again. Though I shan't be alive to see it. I just remember when the last Queen died. At least, I imagine I do. I have a mental picture of my mother telling me the news in father's old study in Hampstead. I could only have been seven years old at the time. It was just before my mother died herself of T.B., and I remember that well enough. "Queen Elizabeth" has a fine ring about it, hasn't it?' He began to sound more cheerful as the problem of Alec settled into its true insignificance. 'The country's having a pretty thin time of it at the moment, but perhaps a new Elizabethan age will dawn upon us. Oh, we'll end up top dogs again, sooner or later, like we were before the war.'

That so many fellow-countrymen imagined the same as Graham Trevose at the time was the great mid-twentieth-century British tragedy. Or perhaps comedy. They are only two ways of looking at the same thing.

## 29

WHEN THEIR TRIDENT landed at Heathrow there was a reporter and a photographer waiting. Graham had lost nothing of his attraction for the Press.

'How kind of you to come along,' he smiled. He had also lost nothing of his touch with newspapermen.

'Good evening, Sir Graham. I hope you had a good trip?'

'Splendid, thank you, splendid. Aeroplanes make everything so convenient these days. I still haven't quite got used to them. All that messing about one used to do with trains and boats was quite exhausting. Yes, Rome was wonderful. In September I think the light is just right. In summer the sun's too strong, and the shadows are the most intriguing part of any building—or of any human face.'

'I gather you made a quite sensational speech to the Plastic Surgery Congress, Sir Graham?'

He chuckled. 'Hardly sensational. My days for making sensations are past. But I put over a few of my old ideas, which still hold good. The basic principles have been rather swamped by the enormous advances in surgical technique and technology. But to my mind, it's as important to grasp them as firmly in 1968 as it was in 1948, when I took over the Directorship of the National Accident hospital. In fact, these basic principles haven't changed since 1940, when I was proud of being in a position to put them to good use.' He always referred to 1940 in front of the Press.

'I hope you've managed to get some holiday in Italy at the same time, Lady Trevose?' the reporter asked Clare.

'Yes, we had an absolutely wonderful fortnight in Positano.'

'Despite the continuing currency restrictions?' grinned the reporter.

'We are extremely modest abroad,' Graham told the man, quite sharply.

It was nine o'clock before they emerged from the Customs into the bright and confusing concourse. 'It's strange how this place always looks entirely different depending on whether you're going or coming,' Graham observed. 'It's the difference between hope and anticlimax, I suppose. A common enough sequence, in my own experience.'

'You've nothing to complain about this trip, darling.'

'Perhaps a little. They didn't take my speech seriously at the Congress, you know. Not entirely.'

'But they were absolutely charming,' Clare protested. 'Particularly the Russians.'

'Yes, but they think I'm old hat. Perhaps they're right. I'm a realist. Anyway, I livened them up. We'll see how the Americans take to me in Baltimore next spring.'

Graham looked round hopefully for the chauffeur booked to drive them into London. He felt that at his age the shunning of airport buses was a luxury worth indulging in. He was spry, and as thin as ever. He let his wispy hair grow overlong, and strands of it poked under his hat. He wore glasses all the time, large and round, making his eyes look more owlish than ever. He had grown rather untidy in his clothes, presenting an amiably donnish look to the world. Clare thought fondly he resembled an elderly elf.

The car had hardly reached the M4 before Graham fell asleep. Clare picked up the tartan rug provided by the hire firm and carefully laid it over him. This was less to prevent any malevolent chill taking advantage of his unguardedness—her nursing training enabled her to take a strictly scientific view of Graham's management—but an indulgence on her part, an expression of the steadfast tenderness she had shown towards him in their twenty-one years of marriage. She settled back in her corner, looking at the street lights, trying to correlate them with the necklaces she had admired from the air. She had grown fatter, but kept her pale good looks, and, with assistance, her fair hair. Graham tended to drop off to sleep rather often these days, she reflected. Perhaps he shouldn't gad about the world so much. But seventy-three, though a respectable age, was hardly over the threshold of senility. If she remembered, Churchill was rather older when he became Prime Minister through the persuasion of the ballot-box rather than the approaching muzzles of the German guns.

They had a small flat in Chelsea, and an unimposing house in the country on the way to Oxford, past the National Accident Hospital. Graham had worked there almost a dozen years, until his retirement in 1959. They had been the happiest of his life, happier even than at the annex. It was mainly because nothing had happened to him. He sometimes wondered if it were the security of a settled job, or the fires of his personality dimming to a comfortable glow, or simply Clare keeping a firm hand on him. He had busied himself with his work, developed a relish for committees, lectured enthusiastically, and drew veneration from the world as effortlessly as a well-established oak draws moisture from the soil. He enjoyed the respect, though it amused him. It was not so much the poacher turning gamekeeper, as the swashbuckling pirate becoming Admiral of the Fleet. Perhaps he possessed the same luck as his seafaring Cornish ancestors, he wondered, who had never turned from a chance of smuggling and generally ended clothed with gold lace and dignity.

There was a pile of letters inside the door.

'I can't face that lot at this hour of the night,' Graham said, as Clare started gathering them. 'I'll have a go at them in the morning. Anything from Dick?'

Their nineteen-year-old son was on holiday in Spain, with, Graham suspected, the girl he had met at the university. Well, it would be a bit of fun, he wished he'd had the chance to do the same at Dick's age, but then trips to Spain were only for the rich and venturesome. And the sunshine would do the girl good, he thought. She had struck him as a dismally anaemic young woman.

'There's a letter he seems to have sent from Malaga.'

'Read it to me, darling, will you?' Graham sat in the arm-chair. 'I'm rather tired, and his handwriting's dreadful.'

'And there's something from Blackfriars.' She tore open a large envelope. 'They've made it at last,' she exclaimed. 'They're actually going to open the new Arlott Wing by Christmas. Of course, they want you to perform the ceremony.'

Graham laughed. The rebuilding of Blackfriars beside the Thames had long ago become a harmless joke. When the war had ended, the staff imagined they would quit Smithers Botham in a year or two, but the volume of hospital work so increased with the National Health Service, and the volume of hospital building so diminished with the national bankruptcy, the country was several times on the brink of another war before they finally parted company. 'I think we've beaten St Thomas's to it, haven't we?' he asked. 'Or is it more or less a dead heat?' He opened and closed his hands. 'Perhaps they might ask me to perform an inaugural operation on some unlucky fellow? It's an amusing thought. I wouldn't mind having a knife in my hands again. After all, John Bickley's still giving anaesthetics for private cases all over London. Though perhaps he only does it to get away from Denise.'

John had worked for Graham again. Graham's private practice had in fact continued almost as busily as ever, through an interesting fraction written into the Health Service known as 'nine-elevenths'. The consultants were paid for the nine-elevenths of their time spent in the Service, the other two-elevenths being free to extract money from those members of the public feeling disinclined to accept its benefits. And two-elevenths of a consultant's time, with evenings, early mornings, and week-ends, was a handsome period for profits. Without this concession, the consultants would have dug in their toes and there would have been no Health Service at all. But Nye Bevan was an even more penetrating realist than Graham.

Clare read their son's letter, which said a lot about the sunshine, wine, beaches, and bullfights, but nothing about girls. The omission confirmed Graham's suspicion. He got up to pour himself a drink, and said, 'I suppose he'll get married pretty soon?'

'I don't know. He's no one in mind.'

'But they all seem to get married these days as soon as they're legally entitled to. Perhaps they look upon it in the same light as learning to drive a car. Once the obstacle to any enjoyment's removed, you indulge yourself automatically.'

'He'll wait until he's qualified, surely?'

'In my day, even in Desmond's day, that seemed to be the rule. But of course we lived on our parents or our wits. Now they live on everyone else's parents. Doubtless it's all a good idea.'

'He'll wait till he finds the right girl. He's terribly sensible.'

Graham smiled. 'I had to wait a very long time till I found the right girl. Even then I didn't realize it, did I?' She said nothing. He seldom brought up their times at Cosy Cot. She felt he liked to imagine the episode had never happened, that he had met her for the first time when he had entered, extremely dramatically, her children's ward one wet March morning in 1947. It was a forbidden topic, just like Maria's divorce.

Graham sipped his whisky. 'Do you know, Clare, I'm beginning to think that life resembles something I haven't experienced for donkey's years—it's like Saturday night in an old-fashioned public house.' As she looked puzzled, he gave a grin and said, 'It gets better towards closing-time.'

When they went to bed he lay reading for half-an-hour. He snapped the book shut and said, ' "Birth, and copulation, and death. That's all the facts when you come to brass tacks:" Strange how those lines of Eliot's keep coming back to me. I must have read them years ago, when I first started at the annex. But it's right, isn't it? Everything else is the trimmings. It's the most useful thing you can learn from medicine. How to sort the two out. What's the time?'

'Half-past midnight.'

Graham turned over. 'For God's sake remind me in the morning I'm due to see a fellow at the Royal College of Surgeons. He wants to touch me for some charity, I imagine.'

He turned out the light. At twenty to four he woke, switched on the light, gasped at the pain exploding from his throat into his left arm, and died.

## 30

CLARE HAD RATHER HOPED for something at the Abbey, but whoever invisibly decides such delicate questions demurred. Official memories are long and not subject to the mellowing of human ones. A knighthood for Graham Trevose had been acceptable, in times when a man's merit mattered more than the man himself. But a memorial service at the Abbey . . . the doctor, though distinguished, was far from impeccable. Someone in some small quiet office remembered there was really a bad scandal—he had lived openly with a mistress during the war.

In the end, the final pageant was held in St Pancras Church, a frequent choice for such affairs in memory of medical men, possibly because of its nearness to the red-brick ramparts of the British Medical Association in Bloomsbury. It was a befittingly miserable day in late September, with cold wet winds from the north blowing down the railway lines to the termini which dominate that depressing area of London. Haileybury stumped along, a thick overcoat over his blue suit, wondering if it were going to trigger off his bronchitis again. It was becoming increasingly burdensome to run the laps of the years. It occurred to him to list mentally his own infirmities. Apart from the chest, there was presbyopia, ptosis, arthritis of the left hip, a bilateral hallux valgus, a small inguinal hernia he ought to have something done about, and of course the piles. But a man was as old as his arteries, as the physicians kept saying when everything else was falling to bits. He supposed if his number didn't come up in the cancer lottery a good surgeon and antibiotics would keep him going a while. At least that morning he was alive, while Trevose was dead. To Haileybury's mind, death restored the formality of surnames.

'Excuse me, Sir Eric—'

Haileybury paused on the pavement outside the church, staring blankly at a young man in a raincoat.

'I'm from the *Daily Press*,' said the young man.

Graham deceased had the news value of Graham alive. The London evening placards had announced FAMOUS SURGEON DEAD, and middle-aged men in crowded trains heard the echo of Churchill's funeral drums. Sir Graham Trevose was part of the legend. And if young pilots in Spitfires and Hurricanes had shot out of the sky only half the enemy aeroplanes they thought they did, the legend could shine when required as brightly as ever. It seemed about the only thing the country had got out of the war.

'Do you think,' the young man continued, 'that Sir Graham deserved his distinction as "The Wizard" of plastic surgery?'

'I don't know. How could I know?' Haileybury started edging away. 'Wasn't the term invented by you people in Fleet Street?'

'I understand you had certain differences with Sir Graham?'

'I was never aware of any,' Haileybury muttered.

'Do you think it morally wrong, using surgery to construct new noses and such things for people who can afford it?'

Haileybury sniffed. 'I have never given the matter any thought.'

'Perhaps, Sir Eric, you have a comment on Sir Graham's great work in the war—'

But Haileybury had escaped into the sanctuary of a holy place, like a medieval criminal.

The church was crowded and warm and smelt of damp overcoats, reminding Haileybury of the out-patients' clinic. He was shown to a pew at the front. He decided his arthritis put even a perfunctory kneel on the hassock out of the question. At least the service would be short and businesslike. Services for dead doctors generally were. Medical men live in far too close intimacy with death to regard its arrival as other than an unexpected stroke of treachery. And at his age, Haileybury reflected, such functions become occasions less of pain than foreboding. He adjusted his glasses and reached for the folded sheet of printed paper set before him. Experience told him they would have *O God, Our Help In Ages Past*. He found he was right. He felt pleased with his little guess, it brightened his morning considerably.

He folded his arms and stared along the pews. The widow, of course. Rum sort of business, really all over and done with now. Her son. The first son, now an academic, he believed. He'd forgotten what line. These days they made professors in all sorts of peculiar little subjects. Woman doubtless his wife. Been trouble there in the past, too, he seemed to remember. Trust the Trevose family to make fools of themselves when a female came into it. Other man the nephew, Alec. Always seeing him on the television. Looked damned prosperous. Needed a haircut. The other people around him were elderly men of washed-out military appearance, and of course the surgical big wigs. The biggest wig was giving the address. Wouldn't say anything about Trevose, really, of course. At least, Haileybury reflected, he sincerely hoped not.

Odd chap, Trevose. Neurotic, of course, but he supposed all medical men were to some degree. You must be, to pick such a strange occupation. As slippery as a snake, unreliable, abominably self-centred. Fond of fame, money, and women. The first two failings didn't matter much, but the last did. Women were human beings. Trevose always seemed to forget that little fact. Of course, it all changed in the last twenty years of his life. I always rather liked Trevose, Haileybury decided, even when I didn't care to admit it to myself. He livened things up. Didn't take life too solemnly. I rather wish I'd had the courage to be more like him myself.

Haileybury looked behind him. Full of Trevose's patients. It suddenly struck him these men had hardly aged. Over twenty-five years ago they had been dragged from blazing aeroplanes, shattered tanks, and ships' scalding engine rooms; now the skin collected in bits from all over their bodies had frozen on their faces in unwrinkled youth. He supposed it was some compensation for having your features ravaged by a shell-splinter at twenty, if you were immune from the ravages of time at forty-five. He searched for some more delicate examples of Trevose's reconstructive art. But all the worldly and often charming men and women who had besought Trevose at considerable discomfort and expense to make them new faces seemed disinclined to show them in public.

A fitting epitaph, Haileybury thought, dragging himself to his feet as they began.

*The career of Graham Trevose up to the outbreak of the Second World War is the subject of Richard Gordon's novel:*

## THE FACEMAKER

'Mr Gordon publicly outgrows his hospital farces and becomes the novelist his fans have always seen in him. The hero is a brash, randy, skilful plastic surgeon, whose high-spirited fight for social and financial success is mingled with a fight to establish the new speciality against professional conservatism. Set in the age of Gillies and McIndoe, the novel dramatizes a period of medical and social history.'

R. G. G. PRICE in *Punch*

'Just as Simenon tends to be unfairly dismissed as merely the creator of Maigret, Richard Gordon may find it hard to live down the success of the "Doctor" stories. But his latest book, *The Facemaker*, should firmly establish his reputation as a serious novelist, for it is highly enjoyable and amusing without the benefit of slapstick.

The book tells the story of the rise of Graham Trevose from idle obscurity as a young doctor in 1918 to rather tawdry fame as a plastic surgeon in 1940. At the same time—though this is clearly not the author's prime intention—the charlatanry of part of the medical profession is exposed with knowledge and wit.'

ROBERT BALDICK in *The Daily Telegraph*

'Mr Gordon depicts Graham Trevose as a more than average sensual man driving his way upwards with some ruthlessness. There are several vivid minor characters, lots of sex, and much not too gruesome operating detail. I wish some more solemn novelists had half Mr Gordon's professional skill.'

JULIAN SYMONS in *The Sunday Times*